Julia was so graceful and slender that he guessed she would be a delight to dance with. Even more of a delight to hold and kiss...

Just then he realized she'd found the blackberries for herself because she turned to call back. "Look, Mr. Smith! Here's a fine patch of blackberries. Gorgeous ones."

She was already gathering them avidly, so he joined her as she started to fill her little basket. "They are delicious," she breathed as he drew nearer. "Try one."

Her expression brimmed with delight. Her lips were stained dark red, and when she licked them and gave a little sigh of pleasure, his pulse thumped. He said quietly, "My name is Ben. Please call me Ben."

Then he reached out and brushed away a bit of blackberry that clung to the corner of her mouth. He could have sworn a slight tremor ran through her as his finger touched her skin, then she gazed up at him and whispered, "Ben."

His hand still hovered. He felt an overwhelming urge to haul her against his body and kiss her senseless. She would never, he hoped, guess at the willpower it took him to step away. He said, in a voice that was harsher than he intended, "It's time, I think, for you to go home."

Time too for him to come to his senses.

LUCY ASHFORD

Lord Lambourne's Forbidden Debutante

HARLEQUIN
HISTORICAL

HARLEQUIN®
HISTORICAL™

ISBN-13: 978-1-335-59590-4

Lord Lambourne's Forbidden Debutante

Copyright © 2023 by Lucy Ashford

For questions and comments about the quality of this book, please contact us at CustomerService@Harlequin.com.

Harlequin Enterprises ULC
22 Adelaide St. West, 41st Floor
Toronto, Ontario M5H 4E3, Canada
www.Harlequin.com

Printed in U.S.A.

Lucy Ashford studied English and history at Nottingham University, and the Regency era is her favorite period. She lives with her husband in an old stone cottage in the Derbyshire Peak District, close to beautiful Chatsworth House, and she loves to walk in the surrounding hills while letting her imagination go to work on her latest story.

Books by Lucy Ashford

Harlequin Historical

The Major and the Pickpocket
The Return of Lord Conistone
The Captain's Courtesan
"Twelfth Night Proposal"
in *Snowbound Wedding Wishes*
The Outrageous Belle Marchmain
The Rake's Bargain
The Captain and His Innocent
The Master of Calverley Hall
Unbuttoning Miss Matilda
The Widow's Scandalous Affair
The Viscount's New Housekeeper
Challenging the Brooding Earl
Lord Lambourne's Forbidden Debutante

For Alan.
Thanks for your help, as ever.

Chapter One

London, September 1817

As the clock in the corner of the drawing room struck ten, Lady Julia Annabel Emilia Carstairs counted off the chimes on her fingers. The clock was very old and its chimes stuttered with age. But she was only eighteen and so she had no such excuse for the way her pulse was jumping all over the place.

Her father cleared his throat, which was something he always did when he was about to issue a rebuke. 'I hear from your mother, Julia,' the Earl of Carstairs pronounced, 'that there was an unfortunate incident this evening at Lord and Lady Bamford's party.' He stood with his back to the fireplace, looking every bit as tall and stately as you would expect of an eminent aristocrat. Next to him stood Julia's brother, Charles, who was gazing at her even more disapprovingly than her father.

Oh, dear.

Julia, who was sitting on the velvet sofa beside her mother, swallowed down the sudden lump in her throat.

She loved her family, truly she did—her father, her mother and her two sisters, Penelope and Lizzie, who would doubtless be upstairs waiting to sympathise with her over her latest misdemeanour. She even loved her twenty-five-year-old brother Charles, when he wasn't being a pompous ass.

Everyone was waiting for her to speak. Even her father's Labradors, Rex and Mollie, were gazing at her slightly sadly as they lay in their usual places on the hearth rug. 'I did my very best to behave at the party,' Julia said at last. 'Only, you see, I didn't really know anyone except Mama. So I was sitting in a corner, on my own.'

As usual, she silently added.

'And then, I heard Lord Bamford's son say something rude about me.'

'What, exactly, did he say?' demanded the Earl.

Julia had begun fiddling with some of the stupid bows and ribbons that adorned her yellow muslin dress. She hated it. She hated going to these 'little *soirées*', which her mother insisted she attend in order to prepare herself for her presentation to London's elite as a debutante next May. That truly would be a day of doom.

She met her father's stern gaze and said with a slight shrug, 'Tristram Bamford told his friends that I resembled a stick insect wrapped up in a frilly yellow curtain.'

Her father's frown deepened. Her brother Charles muttered an oath. Her mother moaned softly, not for the first time that night.

Charles said at last, 'I must say, Mama, that Julia's dress is a little over the top, you know.'

Her mother, who was dressed in a startling shade

of pink and who very much prided herself on her taste in fashion, visibly bristled. 'Nonsense, Charles! Julia looked perfectly delightful tonight—Lady Bamford herself said so. Besides, our dear Pen wore a gown that was almost identical when she attended Lord and Lady Bamford's autumn party last year and she surpassed everyone there with her loveliness. No wonder she succeeded in winning the heart of a viscount's son!'

'Mama,' pointed out Julia patiently, 'my sister Pen is everything a girl should be. She's blonde and beautiful. Men fall over themselves at the sight of her. But look at me! My hair is dark and straight, despite all your efforts to make it curl. I'm too thin for most men's tastes. Worst of all, I like taking long walks by myself and reading books about far-off countries. I don't like parties and I particularly dislike being insulted!'

The silence that followed was broken by her father. 'Which is doubtless why,' he said, 'you spoke as you did to Lord Bamford's son. I gather from your mother that you were not polite.'

Julia lifted her chin to meet her father's clear gaze. 'I told him he was an ignorant boor and looked like a toad. Which I'm sorry about,' she added swiftly, 'because actually I *like* toads, very much. They are exceptionally intelligent creatures.'

'And then,' put in her father softly, 'you threw a glass of champagne over him?'

'It was only a very small glass. I'm sure it will wash out of his shirt!' She looked round at them defiantly. 'After that, I went to collect my cloak and I walked home.'

'On your own?' exclaimed Charles incredulously.

'On my own, Charles, yes. After all, Lord and Lady Bamford's house is only a couple of hundred yards from ours and there were plenty of respectable people around. Besides, who is going to try to molest a stick insect dressed in a frilly yellow curtain?'

She gestured at her horrid dress and tried to laugh, but honestly, she felt more like crying. Rex the Labrador lifted his head to gaze at her mournfully, then padded over to lie by her feet. Swallowing down the lump in her throat, she reached to stroke one of his silky ears.

'Julia. You're mad,' Charles said with a sigh.

Her father, bless him, looked at her brother rather sharply. 'Charles, I don't like the way you're speaking to your sister. Don't forget, she deserves our loyalty in spite of this unfortunate incident.' He sighed, too, and turned to Julia. 'My dear, you must try to understand that we want the very best for you. We really want you to be happy, as Pen is.'

'But I'm not my sister!' cried Julia, almost in despair. 'I've told Mama over and over that I hate parties and shopping for clothes. And I hate gossiping with other girls about eligible men and how they plan to ensnare them—it is truly sad!'

At which her handsome brother, the heir to the earldom and target of female wiles from every quarter, smirked a little. Which annoyed her even more.

'Yes,' she declared, 'it's all very well for you to laugh, Charles, because you're a man. You can do as you please, spend your money as you please. Why, even after you're married, you can carry on having mistresses—'

'Julia! For pity's sake!' Her mother's cheeks were as pink as her dress and she was fanning herself in agitation. 'You shock me! You are eighteen and old enough to show the manners of a lady. You could have had your Season last year with dear Pen had you not broken your ankle riding your horse at a gallop in Richmond Park. And now—*now*, the scandal of tonight's episode will be all around town by tomorrow. You need a wise husband to teach you to control your behaviour!'

'I'm sorry, Mother,' said Julia rather desperately. 'But I don't want a husband to teach me anything. In fact, I'm not sure I want a husband at all and I doubt very much anyone would want me, even though I'm the daughter of an earl. I just want things to be as they used to be!'

Her father looked grave but kind. 'What do you mean, Julia? What used to make you happy?'

She felt the tears welling up and blinked them back furiously. 'I loved it,' she said in a small voice, 'when we lived most of the year at our house in Richmond. I loved it when Pen and Lizzie and I could go out and play all day in that big garden, or ride our ponies in the park. I don't like being here in the middle of town. I don't like the crowds and the noise and the way people talk all the time about money and marriage. I don't want to have a Season at all.' She gazed up at her father almost desperately. 'I'm sorry. But I really don't feel I can go through with it.'

Her mother was reaching for her smelling salts. Even Charles appeared a little shaken. 'Look, Ju,' he said, 'I'm sorry you have such a bad opinion of men. But I assure you, you'll find there are a lot of decent fellows who would make you a kind husband. In fact, if you like, I'll look out for a few.'

'No! I do not want to be married off! I would quite honestly rather be a—a spinster!'

'Steady on,' said Charles. 'You're not *that* bad-looking, you know.'

'Charles,' pronounced her father, 'you are not helping matters in the least.'

'No.' Charles looked a little bashful. 'I apologise.'

The Earl looked almost sorrowfully at his daughter. 'I'm afraid that your mother is correct, Julia. There will be a good deal of talk by tomorrow about tonight's unfortunate exchange with young Bamford. I think it may be as well if you stop attending these pre-Season parties, just for a while.'

Julia flinched. A scandal—that was what she'd become—and her dreaded Season hadn't even begun. 'I'm sorry, Father,' she said in a low voice. 'Really, I am.'

He shook his head. 'It's by no means the end of the world, but I do have an idea. I think that perhaps we ought to let you have a brief respite from London society.'

Julia's eyes opened wide. 'You mean—I can go to our house in Richmond?'

'No,' her father quickly said, 'not to Richmond, since neither your mother nor I could leave London to stay there with you. But I've been wondering. I believe you'll remember my elderly cousin in Somerset, Lady Harris?'

'Aunt Harris, my godmother? Of course I remember her! We used to visit her for at least two weeks every summer. It was fun.'

Her mother frowned. 'The journey there was a nightmare.'

The Earl just smiled. 'You never were fond of travel, my dear, were you? But the children always found it a great adventure and you must admit you did enjoy the odd day trip to Bath whenever we were there.'

Julia listened to all this eagerly. Lady Harris, aged around sixty or so, had a splendid old house that was surrounded by wild woodland, like something from a storybook. Lady Harris was also outspoken, self-opinionated and distinctly odd, but Julia and her sisters used to love her company, not least because she was the only person they knew who dared to tease their mother about her rigid sense of propriety.

'The last time I saw my aunt,' Julia said, 'was when she came to London for our grandmother's funeral two years ago.'

'Yes,' said the Earl, 'and she vowed she would never come to London again.'

Julia hid a smile. Lady Harris had always declared that she hated London and at the moment Julia was in complete agreement. She looked up at her father. 'I like Lady Harris,' she said, 'very much. But why have you mentioned her, Papa?'

'We correspond regularly,' he replied. 'She always asks after you, Julia, and I was wondering if perhaps you might like to go and stay with her for a while.'

Julia's mother almost leaped from the sofa. 'My dear husband!' she cried. 'Lady Harris may be your cousin, but she is surely no fit companion for Julia! She is eccentric. She shuns society.'

'My cousin is much cleverer than most people give her credit for,' said the Earl firmly, 'and she does have considerable experience of life. She's nobody's fool, believe me.'

Charles was looking as amazed as his mother. 'But

Somerset! Are you truly serious, Father, about sending Julia so far away?'

'It would be for a few weeks only, Charles. That would allow ample time for any gossip about Julia and Tristram's unfortunate altercation to be replaced by something far more exciting. As further reassurance, we will of course send one of our most reliable maids to stay with our daughter during her visit—though I imagine even Julia would be able to get up to little enough mischief in such a quiet spot.' He smiled down at her as he spoke.

Her mother still looked upset. 'Oh, Julia,' she cried. 'I do declare that after staying there, you will surely come to appreciate what is on offer in London!'

Julia wasn't at all certain about that. In fact, as her father explained his plan, she'd begun to feel a ray of hope. Yes, her godmother lived in a remote place, on her own, but she was *happy*—she'd told Julia so after the funeral two years ago. 'Take no notice,' her aunt had said, 'of those who say you must be put on the marriage mart like a prize cow. You do what you want, my girl. You live the life you want!'

The life Julia wanted was certainly not the life of a debutante. 'Papa,' Julia said, a little hesitantly this time. 'How do you know that my aunt will agree to have me?'

'I will write to her first thing tomorrow,' answered her father, 'and I would be amazed if she did not wish for your company. She once called you a girl after her own heart. So...' he looked around '...are we agreed on this?'

Charles shrugged. 'If you say so, Father. Though I

think my friends will be laying bets as to how soon Julia
will be pleading to come back to London!'

Julia saw her father give his son and heir the kind
of look that was guaranteed to put anyone firmly in
his place. 'Charles,' he pronounced, 'I hope very much
that your last comment was made in jest. If any of your
so-called friends should lay bets on the futures of my
daughters, I trust you will show your disapproval instantly.'

Charles flushed slightly. 'Yes, Father,' he said stiffly.

'Julia,' said the Earl, in a far milder tone, 'you may
leave us now. Perhaps we can discuss my plan for you
in more detail tomorrow morning.'

Julia rose and went to quickly hug him. 'Thank you,
Father,' she whispered. 'I'm truly sorry I've caused a
stupid scandal. And thank you for thinking of Lady
Harris. I should love to go and stay with her!'

Her father smiled and touched her cheek affection-
ately. 'Off you go to bed, then, my dear. Sleep well.'

Julia dutifully kissed her mother goodnight, then
dashed off before anything more could be said. Though
as she climbed the grand staircase to her bedchamber,
she guessed yet more questions awaited her—and she
was right, because she found her two sisters sitting on
her bed.

'Julia!' cried Pen, who was twenty years old and due
to be married soon. 'What has *happened*?'

Then Lizzie, who at fourteen was the baby of the family, burst out, 'We heard Mama crying and Papa speaking sternly. Was it because of the Bamfords' party? Was
it just awful?'

'Appalling,' said Julia, as she tugged off her yellow

satin shoes and sank into a nearby armchair. 'Though I survived it until I heard that horrid Tristram Bamford say that I looked like a stick insect with frills, so I threw some champagne over him.'

'You didn't!'

'I did. Though honestly, who can blame him for laughing at me?' She pointed at her now very crumpled frock. 'I hate this silly dress! Hate it!'

'Is that what you were all arguing about downstairs just now?' Pen asked with sympathy.

'Oh, the truth of it is, I'm an embarrassment to them and no doubt Tristram will tell everyone around town what I said. But Father was superb. He stayed calm when Mama was on the verge of hysterics and told me he had an idea. He suggested that I could go and stay for a while with Lady Harris in the country.'

'No!'

'Yes. He did.' Julia still couldn't quite believe it herself.

'But that's amazing.' Lizzie clapped her hands in glee. 'We used to love it, didn't we, whenever we went to visit her in that big old house of hers. She was such fun. She drove Mama wild because she encouraged us to roam in the woods and have adventures!'

'She is rather mischievous,' agreed Julia. 'But Papa likes her and so do I.'

'I wish I could come, too,' said Lizzie. 'But what does Charles think?'

'Naturally, our brother was as horrified as Mama. But he disapproves of anything I want to do—and I've decided I really, really want to stay with Aunt Harris and to put my Season off for as long as possible. Especially as I'm quite sure it's going to be a disaster.'

'Nonsense,' said Pen briskly. 'You'll have plenty of men falling for you if you only give yourself a chance! But Lizzie and I shall miss you dreadfully while you're away. Besides, won't you be lonely? I've heard that Lady Harris hardly sees a soul.'

'Being lonely would be an improvement on being insulted at parties.' Julia shuddered.

Suddenly their mother's piercing voice rose from the bottom of the grand staircase. 'Lizzie. Lizzie, darling, are you with your sisters? Your maid is looking for you. It really is time you were in bed!'

Lizzie jumped up. 'Oh, no. I'd better go. But first, can the three of us have our usual hug?' She held out her arms and the sisters embraced. 'There,' declared Lizzie happily, 'that's better. We'll stick by each other to the end, isn't that right?' She popped a kiss on Julia's cheek. 'Dear Julia, some day you will find a man who is truly amazing. I just know you will!'

After Lizzie had scurried off, Pen sat down again slowly. 'I suppose I ought to go as well. But, Julia, I just want to tell you something.'

Julia grinned. 'Secrets? Oh, good.'

Pen blushed a little. Then she said, 'Yes, it is a secret—sort of. You see, I've discovered that…well, it's rather marvellous being in love.'

'I can see that.' Julia pretended to scrutinise her. 'Pen, you positively glow with it.'

Her sister blushed even more. 'Do I?'

'Most definitely. You have a mysterious smile every time you mention Jeremy's name.' Jeremy, who was the son and heir of Viscount Dersingham, was going to marry Pen in less than two months. He was exceedingly pleasant and anyone could see that he adored his bride-to-be.

'Oh, Julia!' Pen sighed. 'I really can't help being happy. You see…' and she lowered her voice to a whisper '…whenever darling Jeremy kisses me, it makes me just long for our wedding night!'

Julia sat on the bed beside her. 'Pen, darling, I'm sure you'll be terrible happy with him. You deserve to be, you're so lovely and kind. But I'm neither and I do not want to marry the kind of man who finds himself an heiress, then goes off and grabs a mistress to have fun with, as soon as his wife has had a baby or two— Oh!' Julia clapped her hand to her mouth at the look on her sister's face. 'I'm so sorry, what a dreadful thing to say. Everyone can see that Jeremy adores you and I'm sure he'd never take some silly mistress, ever!'

Pen nodded. 'I know he won't. But I'm also quite positive that Father will never make you marry someone you detest—so please, don't give up before you've even started looking!' She glanced at the marble clock on Julia's dressing table and stood up. 'I really must go, too. No doubt one of the maids has been waiting in my room for ages to help me out of my gown. Shall I help you with yours before I go?'

'No, I'll ring for a maid myself. Though I'd rather tear this dress off piece by piece!' Julia tried to laugh as she, too, rose to her feet.

Pen studied the yellow gown sympathetically. 'When it's time for you to make your debut, I shall insist to Mama that she take you to the most fashionable dressmaker in town and I shall come with you both. There'll be no yellow, no frills—but you will look gorgeous, I promise! Goodnight, Julia dear. Sweet dreams.'

With that Pen, after blowing her sister a kiss, flew off down the passageway to her own room.

Julia went to close her bedroom door, but halted when she caught sight of herself in her mirror. Gorgeous? Never. She didn't have the feminine curves her sister had. She didn't have the angelic blue eyes either; instead, her eyes were a strange shade of pale greeny-grey—'rather like the sea on a cold day in midwinter,' an anxious man trying hard to be polite to her had once said. Distinctly unappealing, in other words.

Otherwise, Julia supposed there was nothing exactly *wrong* with her face—in fact, a noted London artist had once wanted to paint her, because of her delicate cheek-bones, he'd enthused. But even he had confessed that her hair was all wrong for a portrait, because it simply refused to curl.

Mama always insisted on her having it wound tightly in rags for hours before Julia was due to attend any social event. 'Then,' her mother would promise, 'one of the maids will put it up in ringlets for you, just like Pen's!' But the attempt was futile because during the evening the curls would gradually flop, making Julia look like an over-warm spaniel with its ears drooping in the heat.

She shut her bedroom door and sat rather despondently on the bed. A moment later though, she jumped up again—because she'd just remembered that she'd left something rather embarrassing downstairs in the hallway.

She had put her beaded silk purse on the table there, the one she'd taken to Lord and Lady Bamford's horrid party, and in it was her tiny diary. Well, it was more of a private notebook really, because there wasn't room for all the engagements her mother dragged her to. But the worst thing was that she used it to keep a list of young men to avoid like the plague. She called it her *Guide to the Gentlemen of London* and it wasn't a flattering list, because beside each man's name she'd scrawled his deficiencies.

Sir Frederick Timms. Breathes garlic everywhere.
Lord Percival Sumner. Always lets his clammy hands stray to your bottom when he dances with you.
Viscount Clive Delaney. Walks like a waddling walrus.

And so on. Good grief. If her mother were to read it, she would faint.

Hurriedly Julia descended the broad staircase and sighed with relief to see that her reticule was still there. She was about to grab it when she realised her father and Charles were still talking in the drawing room— and they were talking about her. Sidling close to the not quite shut door, she listened carefully.

'There's another thing, Father, about this plan of yours,' Charles was saying, 'to send Julia to Lady Harris. You do realise, don't you, who might be staying close by?'

There was a brief silence, in which Julia was convinced they would hear her heart thudding. At last came her father's terse reply. 'There's not much chance of him being there, Charles, since the last I heard, the fellow had no intention of leaving Vienna any time soon. So you needn't worry about him.'

Julia listened intently. Who did they know in Vienna? Why were her father and Charles worried about him? They talked on in lowered voices, though at one point her father spoke more clearly.

'I suppose,' he said, 'that like the ladies, you and I ought to retire. But there's one last thing, Charles.'

'Which is?'

'I fear there will be talk around town about Julia's behaviour tonight. So you'll do what you can to quell any malicious gossip about your sister, won't you?'

'Of course. But she really must learn to use some tact!'

'She's Julia,' said her father. 'We all love her dearly, but she's different, Charles. She wants to feel she has choices in her life. Obviously she must learn to restrain her impulsiveness, but we must all do everything we can to support her, do you understand?'

Before she could hear what her brother had to say to that, Julia, clutching her reticule, fled back up to her room.

Different. In other words, she was an oddity who would probably end up a spinster—and all she could say to *that* was that spinsterhood was a far better fate than being married to someone like Tristram Bamford. Yes, she'd written about him in her notebook, too, only the other week.

His eau-de-cologne reminds me of mothballs.

She remembered a little despairingly what Lizzie had

said to her. *'Dear Julia, some day you will find a man who is truly amazing. I just know you will!'*

Not at Lady Harris's. Julia almost laughed at the thought. Not in the wilds of Somerset.

Absolutely no chance.

Chapter Two

Two weeks later, Benedict Lambourne was chopping down some overgrown ash saplings on a wooded hillside in rural Somerset.

The saplings had sprung up around an old summer pavilion that was in sad need of repair. Slates had fallen from its roof and the stone walls were crumbling. The ash saplings had claimed his attention because soon their roots would be clawing their way into the building's foundations, so since dawn he'd been swinging his axe like a labourer, clad in an old linen shirt, corduroy breeches and scruffy leather boots.

It would, he reflected, be hard for any passer-by to believe that for several years he'd been working as a diplomat for the British government in Austria. Hard to believe also that he was the Fifth Baron Lambourne, the new owner of the historic Somerset mansion in whose lands this pavilion stood. His father, the Fourth Baron, had died three months ago, but by the time the news reached Ben he was lying in a hospital bed in Vienna with a badly broken leg.

His father's lawyer, Thomas Rudby, had travelled from London to visit Ben there, bringing countless documents for him to read and sign.

'Your Somerset estate, Lord Lambourne,' Rudby had warned, 'is not in a good way. You'll be giving up your post here, I imagine?'

Ben had nodded wearily. He was still fighting the pain from his injury and the nausea from the medicines he'd been given. 'Of course,' he said. 'But the doctors have warned me it could be weeks before I can travel.'

'With you permission, my lord,' said Rudby, 'a cousin of your father's has offered to organise the funeral and it will be a quiet affair, as your father stipulated in his recent will. As for Lambourne Hall, you probably realise it requires a considerable amount of renovation and might not be suitable for you if you are still…' he glanced at the bandages and splints encasing Ben's leg '…encumbered by your physical condition. Perhaps London would be more appropriate?'

Ben had shaken his head. As things stood, he had no desire to live in London. Instead, when he was finally well enough to travel, he'd come home to Lambourne Hall, accompanied only by his valet, Peter Gillespie, who'd been with him for years. No one else knew he was here, except Rudby.

Ben was twenty-five years old. He was lame and God knew when he'd be able to walk properly. He didn't even know if there was enough money in the estate to make the Hall fit for living in again. But he wanted to be here and nowhere else, for he knew that he should have been here during the last year of his father's life.

He should have realised the extent of his father's troubles and supported him in his adversity—

'Yoo-hoo!'

What on *earth*? He almost dropped the axe he was holding because he'd heard footsteps, followed by a most distinctive voice.

Carefully he laid the axe down, realising what—or rather who—was heading his way. It had to be Lady Harris, his one and only neighbour, whose land bordered his.

'Now, it's no use pretending,' the piercing female voice went on, 'that you're not there. Or ducking behind those trees, since you've chopped most of them down.'

Ben straightened himself up as a tiny, grey-haired lady dressed in a voluminous purple cape came along the path to where he stood. 'Lady Harris,' he said. 'And a good day to you, too. It's been a long time since we saw one another. How are you this morning?'

'A good deal better than you, I imagine,' she replied, 'because you must have had weeks of travelling and that leg of yours can't have healed up yet. Yes, I heard you broke it in some far-flung country. Whatever were you up to?'

'I was thrown from my horse in Austria,' he said. 'A sudden thunderstorm spooked the animal.'

She nodded. 'It was a bad break, too, wasn't it? No wonder you had to miss your father's funeral. But I knew you were back at Lambourne Hall, because I spotted some smoke coming from one of the chimneys up there last night.'

Ben liked Lady Harris, he really did. She was, he guessed, around sixty years old; he also knew she'd lived at Linden House, down in the valley, for almost all of her life. 'Lady Harris,' he said, 'I don't want anyone to know that I'm here. Not yet.'

'Any particular reason, young man?'

'Yes, plenty. There are things I want to do. Matters I need to sort out.'

She nodded. 'Matters concerning your father? Here's a word of advice, then. Your father was a good man, but he had his problems and it's no good ruining your own future by dwelling on them.'

'I want,' Ben said quietly, 'to restore the estate for him. I also want to clear his name.'

'And you're going to do that all by yourself? Here, at the back of beyond?' She pursed her mouth. 'Wouldn't it be easier doing all that from London? You have a property there, don't you?'

'I do, but it's rented out at present. Anyway, I wanted to come to Lambourne—and, Lady Harris, I must emphasise that I don't want anyone to know yet that I'm here.'

'But you're Lord Lambourne! People will be curious. You'll be seen when you go out and about—bound to be!'

'My manservant will get in any provisions I need. No one will recognise him—besides, I only need my privacy for a short while.'

'So you're up to something, are you?'

He shook his head, smiling. 'Very little, but I'm not really in the mood for company. So will you do me a great favour? Will you tell no one that I'm here?'

She put her head on one side, bright as a little bird. 'So you won't even come down and play chess with me, like you used to whenever you came home?'

Chess. Yes, he used to enjoy those games with her.

She was good. He smiled and said, 'Why? Are you lonely down there, Lady Harris?'

'Lonely? Ha, no chance of that! Don't forget I have my servants, who drive me to distraction as usual. Besides, I'll have a guest soon.'

He'd noticed she was looking mysterious and a moment later she was pulling a folded sheet of paper from her pocket.

'A guest?' he said.

'Indeed. I got this letter last week, from a cousin of mine in London—which, by the way, is a place I can't abide.'

'You've told me so before, I believe.' Ben grinned. 'What does this letter say?'

'My cousin says—' and she peered at the paper closely '—that he hopes I'm well and all that kind of nonsense. Of course I am! Then he asks if he may send his eighteen-year-old daughter to visit me, as soon as possible.'

'I see,' said Ben. But in fact it seemed to him a mighty strange decision to send a girl of that age out to Somerset, in the care of the eccentric Lady Harris.

'You'll be wondering why, young man.'

'I was, rather.'

'Well, as it happens, I know the girl pretty well. She's my goddaughter and I've always liked her. Why? Because she refuses to act all sweet and obedient like girls her age are supposed to. And I would guess—mind, this is only a guess—that she's been in a bit of bother, so maybe her parents think a spell of isolation is in order.'

Ben was curious. 'So you don't mind having her to stay with you?'

'Of course not. In fact, I'll look forward to seeing her again.'

'Good for you.' Ben nodded his approval. 'But why are you telling me all this?'

'Because I wouldn't be surprised if she's still just a little bit wild. Likely to go roaming, you know? And though there's not much to harm her in these parts, I thought that since you were around, it's possible you might run into her. From what you say, I imagine there's little chance of you rushing off on foreign adventures for quite a while.'

'Little chance indeed,' he acknowledged rather quietly. 'You may be sure of that.'

Lady Harris wagged her finger. 'Don't let this business over your father embitter you, young man, will you? It's the last thing he would want for you, believe me. Now, this girl could be arriving any day, so you'll know who she is if you come across her.'

'I very much hope I won't. Lady Harris, let me repeat— I do not want the news that I'm here to spread around so you won't tell this girl about me, will you?'

'Don't worry, she won't be interested in *you*. Have you looked at yourself in the mirror lately? It must be days since you shaved. As for your clothes, words fail me.'

She chuckled and Ben had to grin, too. His valet Gillespie, generally known as Gilly, had begun to despair of dressing his master like the lord he was supposed to be.

'Do you know something?' Gilly had told him only this morning. 'Unless you get that hair of yours cut soon, people will think you're some kind of mad poet, wandering the countryside for inspiration.'

A poet? Yes, that was quite likely, thought Ben, especially since he had a lame leg into the bargain—just like Lord Byron. Then he realised Lady Harris's expression had changed.

'Your father was very fond of this place, wasn't he?' She was gazing up at the pavilion now.

'I think it reminded him of my mother,' Ben replied quietly. 'He often told me that she used to adore coming here.'

'Then I'll let you carry on, young man.' She nodded, her usual brisk self. 'Help me over this pile of rubble, will you? And I'll be on my way.'

He guided her over an obstacle of fallen stones and watched as she set off along the path that led past a small lake, then down through the woods to her house in the valley. But suddenly she stopped and called out to him, 'I forgot to tell you the girl's name, didn't I? It's Julia.'

After that she carried on, until she was out of sight.

What, Ben wondered, had this Julia got up to in London? Trouble with a man was the usual problem. Perhaps sending the girl to her godmother's was a punishment for some mild flirtation? He pondered a moment, recalling his own encounters with well-born young females in London and Vienna. Quite frankly, he couldn't imagine a single one surviving more than a week here in the wilds without screaming to be sent home and he guessed this Julia might find even a week too long.

His leg had begun to ache again, so he picked up his axe and began to swing it at yet another stray sapling. Action. That was the remedy for most problems—and he certainly had plenty to keep him busy here, in all kinds of ways.

Chapter Three

'Lady Julia? My lady? Do you realise that we're almost there?' Betty leaned across to tap Julia's arm.

The gentle rocking of the Earl's luxurious travelling carriage had almost lulled Julia to sleep, but she woke with a start at the sound of her maid's voice and quickly looked out of the window. There, in the distance, was the steeple of the little church rising above Lambourne village—which meant they were less than a mile from her aunt's house.

'You'll regret this, Julia,' her brother Charles had warned her three days ago as the family gathered outside their Mayfair home to bid her farewell.

'Nonsense!' she'd replied. Then she'd hugged her two sisters, who'd both looked a little tearful. 'I'm going to have a grand adventure,' she'd whispered to them, 'and I'll write often, I promise I will!'

The journey itself had been uneventful. Toby, her father's chief coachman, was a silent fellow, but he had dealt excellently with any awkward inn owners or ostlers who weren't immediately ready to change the horses on the way. But it was in Betty's nature to talk constantly, even in the bedchambers she and Julia shared each night in the different inns. The worst of it was that she was going to stay at Lady Harris's, as Julia's maid.

'Yes. We're almost there,' Betty was saying as the carriage rolled onwards. 'Though why you wanted to leave London and go to the back of beyond, my lady, I shall never understand. All these fields and blessed trees—give me town life any time!'

Julia said nothing. She was gazing out of the window again, because now she could see the old stone bridge over the stream where she and her sisters used to paddle when they were little. Lady Harris had always encouraged them in their adventures, which had annoyed their mother extremely.

She smiled at the memory. Being with her aunt was going to be a treat, but oh, if only her maid would stop talking!

'Of course,' Betty said, 'I don't mind staying with you in Somerset, my lady, not in the least. But there's many who wouldn't like it, no, not at all— Oh, my saints!' Her voice suddenly became a squeak. 'What on earth is happening?'

For the carriage had suddenly lurched to a juddering halt and Toby could be heard cursing vociferously. Julia opened the window and called, 'Toby. Is something wrong?'

The horses were stamping and snorting. Toby had already jumped down from his seat and was trying to soothe them. 'It's a wheel come loose, my lady,' he called back. 'Might take me a while to fix it. I could walk to your aunt's house to get help—it's only half a mile—but I can't leave these horses. You see how frightened they are?'

Julia was already climbing out. 'I can go,' she said. 'I can fetch help.'

Betty was beside her now. 'You must not even think of it, my lady!' she exclaimed. 'Tramping through those woods, who knows what might happen? And besides—'

She broke off.

All three of them had seen a man up in the woods, who stood looking in their direction. Toby cupped his hands round his mouth and bellowed, 'Hey. You up there, fellow. Come and give us a hand here!'

At first, Julia thought the man was going to ignore them and move on. But then, slowly, he began descending the hill towards them. 'Oh, my,' breathed Betty as he drew nearer. 'Will you look at *that*?'

Julia, as it happened, was already looking.

He was around her brother's age, she guessed. He had thick brown hair that clearly hadn't been trimmed for some time and an unshaven jaw. He wore a loose linen shirt and breeches and walked with a noticeable limp. After scanning the scene, he said, 'I gather you have a problem?'

He was well spoken, but he didn't smile or offer to introduce himself and to Julia it was clear he would much rather not have been summoned like this. But Toby was already beckoning him bossily over to the side of the carriage.

'You see this rear wheel? That, my man, is the problem. The bolt's come loose. Now, you look a strong enough fellow, so if you put your weight just here—' he tapped the side of the carriage '—to keep it steady, then I can tighten up the bolt again. Then we'll be all right and tight.'

The man nodded and was about to put his shoulder to the carriage when Julia stepped forward. 'Toby,' she said, 'it's really very heavy. Perhaps we shouldn't be asking him to do this!'

The man looked at her steadily. His eyes were a rich brown and she noticed that they darkened as she spoke. Had she insulted his pride? Was he angry with her?

But he merely said to her, 'It's no problem at all. I assure you.' Then he proceeded to apply himself to the task Toby had set him.

Julia watched in silence, fascinated by the way the muscles of his arms and shoulders bunched beneath his shirt as he took the weight while Toby worked on the wheel. Betty was more vocal in her appreciation of the handsome stranger. 'Will you look at him?' she kept murmuring. 'Will you just look at that fine man?'

It was all over very swiftly. Soon the wheel was secure and Toby straightened himself with a nod of satisfaction. 'Thank you, my man,' he said loftily to the stranger. 'We're obliged to you, I'm sure.' He turned to Julia and Betty. 'Ladies. Shall we be on our way?'

But Julia didn't move. She wanted to do something to thank him; she felt she *had* to do something to thank him, so she reached for her purse and called out to the man before he left. 'Please. Let me offer you some money for your trouble!'

He turned to look at her, then said, 'There is no need at all, I assure you. I bid you good day.' Then he set off, walking up into the woods again, and Julia felt mortified. She knew she'd offended him with her offer of money and she was more sorry than she could say.

Soon the carriage was on its way once more and Julia tried to concentrate on the pleasures in store. No parties to attend! No pompous idiots to insult her! But somehow all she could think of was that man.

Her spirits, though, began to rise as they emerged from the woods and Linden House came into view. Built by a noted maritime explorer from Bristol, it was a rambling building that its owner had filled with reminders of his love of the sea. There were stained-glass windows portraying his various vessels, there were stone lintels carved with the dates of his most notable voyages and even the weathervane fixed to the highest roof was in the shape of a ship.

This was truly one of the most fascinating places Julia knew and its surroundings were exquisite, too. Now that autumn was here, her aunt's extensive gardens were filled with the purple and pink hues of Michaelmas daisies, while the leaves of the beech woods on the surrounding hills shone like polished bronze in the sun.

So much to explore again. It was just like old times—and indeed, there was Lady Harris standing outside her front door, looking as she always did, tiny but bold and bright in her startlingly colourful attire. As soon as Julia had emerged from the carriage her aunt strode briskly up to greet her.

'Well, my dear,' pronounced Lady Harris, 'it's about time they let you escape from that ghastly city.'

'Aunt, it's lovely to be here with you again.' Julia took her aunt's hands and smiled, though then she couldn't help but burst out, 'Did you know you have twigs in your hair?'

'Have I? That's because I've been chasing the pig boys. You'll remember what a pest they are.'

'You mean the boys from Lambourne village? Do they still bring their pigs to your oak wood for acorns?'

'They do indeed, but I'm not having it. Cheeky young things!'

Julia hid her smile. From what she remembered, it was a fine game for all, because Lady Harris enjoyed chasing the boys just as much as they enjoyed teasing her.

She realised her aunt was glancing with narrowed eyes at Betty, who was haranguing Toby over the unloading of the luggage. 'Is she your maid?' said Lady Harris. 'Is she staying?'

'She is, Aunt.'

'Hmmph. Well, let's go inside and you can get your bearings. Welcome to Linden House, my dear. It's very good to see you.'

'You, too, Aunt,' said Julia warmly. 'Oh, you, too!'

An hour later, Julia stood on the front terrace, watching Toby prepare his team of horses for the first stage of the long journey home. She'd left Betty upstairs in her bedchamber and the maid had speedily expressed her feelings as she set about unpacking Julia's clothes. 'If I were you, my lady,' she'd pronounced, 'I'd not be staying here for one night, let alone a matter of weeks. Feel free to change your mind, because Toby can always take us back to London with him!'

Back to odious noblemen like Tristram Bamford?

Julia shook her head, appalled. 'No,' she declared firmly. 'I will be fine here, Betty. Absolutely fine.'

With an audible sigh Betty went on with her work, rattling drawers and glancing with dismay at the model ship in full sail that sat on a table by the window. Julia loved the ship, which she remembered from when she was a child, but Betty shook her head. 'It does nothing but gather dust,' she said. 'As for all the boat paintings hanging everywhere, they make me feel all at sea myself.'

Ships, Julia wanted to say. *They are ships, not boats.*

She refrained, however, and decided to go downstairs, for Toby and the coach were surely almost ready to depart and she wanted to bid him farewell. As she walked through the house she passed two young maids—sisters, she guessed—who curtsied to her shyly. She smiled at them and hurried outside to Toby.

'Thank you for bringing me here safely,' she said. 'I hope you have a swift journey home.' Then she stood and watched the departing carriage until it was out of sight. *'Freedom,'* she murmured softly.

'Freedom indeed,' said her aunt, who had suddenly appeared at her side and must have heard. 'Which is exactly what you need. Now, where's that maid of yours?'

'She's still unpacking my things upstairs, Aunt.'

'Thank God she's out of the way, for a while at least. Does the blessed woman ever stop talking?'

'No,' said Julia and laughed aloud. 'Oh, Aunt. It's lovely to be here with you again!'

'Of course it is. Now, you've already seen your bedchamber, but I'll show you the rest of the house, shall

I? Just in case you've forgotten your way around. Most people do.'

Linden House was indeed a puzzling old building, for one room opened into another, then another, and if you weren't careful you could get completely, delightfully lost. Julia, though, remembered it well, for she and her sisters had taken great delight in the way that if you went through one door, it could lead to a twisting staircase or if you opened the next, you might find the library or the music room. Everywhere there was evidence of the house's first owner and his travels, in the form of lamps shaped like giant seashells and draperies embroidered with images of exotic birds.

'Nothing has changed since you were last here,' said Lady Harris as they finally reached the hallway once more. 'Though my staff can be most irritating. I have my work cut out keeping them in order.'

Julia smiled. Lady Harris always grumbled about the variety of servants who had passed through her doors. 'Do you still have Miss Twigg?' Miss Twigg was unforgettable: she had been her aunt's companion and housekeeper for many years.

'Yes. I put up with her and she puts up with me, somehow. My last butler left long ago, but since I've so few visitors, I don't really care. A couple of lads come from Lambourne village two or three days a week to tidy around outside, then there are the two girls who come every day to do the washing and cleaning. They'll be in the kitchen. Grace! Dottie!' she called in her piercing voice. 'Come and meet Lady Julia!'

The two maids she'd seen earlier, both wearing huge

white aprons and white caps, hurried from the kitchen and curtsied. 'Welcome, my lady,' they chorused.

Julia smiled. 'Thank you.' They looked friendly. They looked fun.

'Twigg tries to push them around,' said Lady Harris to Julia. She turned back to the maids. 'But you put up with her. Don't you, you flighty pair?'

'Yes, Lady Harris!' they spoke in cheerful unison again.

'Off you go, then.' Lady Harris turned to Julia. 'They take very little notice of Twigg in fact. Can't say I blame them. And of course, there's Sowerby—you remember him, I'm sure.'

'He's your handyman, isn't he? And he was your groom, but do you still keep horses, Aunt?'

'I still have Nell. Do you remember her?'

'I do.' Julia hesitated. 'But looking after Nell is hardly a full-time job, is it? And surely Mr Sowerby is—'

'Getting rather ancient? Yes, he is.' She led Julia outside and along the side of the house, where some hens clucked at their approach. 'He and Twigg are forever arguing, but they do enjoy their battles. Talking of battles, I often find Sowerby skulking in the barn here and playing at soldiers.'

'I remember!' exclaimed Julia. 'He used to make tiny figures from copper wire, then put them on painted boards and pretend they were at war.'

'Exactly. He still does.' Lady Harris walked towards the barn and bellowed, 'Sowerby. Are you in there?'

A rather elderly man emerged. 'My lady?'

'Sowerby,' said Lady Harris very loudly, 'you remember Lady Julia, don't you? She's staying with us for a while—yes, staying—so don't go boring her to death with your endless soldierly talk, do you hear?'

'I'm sure I'd never be bored,' Julia said quickly.

'It's a pleasure to have you here again, my lady.' Sowerby bowed. 'You'll doubtless remember that your aunt is one of the best people one could meet.'

'Stuff and nonsense,' declared Lady Harris. 'Now, you get back to your battles, Sowerby.' She waved him away, then led Julia to the stables. 'Here's Nell—she's still going strong. There's an ancient gig round the back which Sowerby sometimes drives down to the village on errands for me and that gives her some exercise.'

As Julia stroked Nell's velvety nose, Lady Harris inspected the large old watch she kept on a chain at her waist. 'Now,' she said, 'it's just gone two o'clock. Are you hungry?'

'No,' said Julia honestly. 'I had a huge breakfast this morning, at the last inn.'

Lady Harris nodded. 'Then we'll have afternoon tea at four, shall we? Twigg's made some chocolate cake. But before your chatterbox of a maid finds you again, I'd like to know exactly why you've been packed off here. Well?'

Julia hesitated, not knowing how much her father had told her aunt in his letter. 'I'm afraid I was rude to a man at a party, Aunt.'

'Did he deserve it?'

'Oh, yes.' Julia was emphatic. 'Most definitely.'

'Then good for you.' Lady Harris grinned.

Julia had to smile back, but then her spirits sank anew. 'Yes, but it's my Season coming up soon and I shall have to behave myself! Though I detest the prospect of being paraded before ogling suitors and so far I've not met one I can abide.'

'Hmm.' Lady Harris pulled a thoughtful face. 'There are ways to put men off, you know. Maybe I can give you a few hints that will send them scuttling for the door.'

'Can you? Really?'

'Of course. Express your own opinions and if you know they're wrong about something, then tell them so. Make them aware, too, that you're full of oddities, like going off and roaming the countryside whenever the fancy takes you. Which reminds me—I think you should go off and take a long walk.'

Julia's eyes opened wide. 'Now? By myself?'

'Why not? You've been travelling in that blessed coach for days and it's a lovely afternoon, so make the most of it. Oh, and there's something useful you can do. I need you to gather some burdock leaves, for my rheumatism.'

'I didn't know you had rheumatism!' Julia was surprised, since her aunt seemed to her to be extremely sprightly.

But Lady Harris groaned a little and put one hand to her hip. 'Sometimes it's really bad. So I make a concoction with burdock, but I've nearly run out.' She pointed towards the woods. 'There's often some growing by the lake up there. It's close to the pavilion—do you remember it?'

'The old stone pavilion? I've seen it from a distance. But—is it yours?'

'Oh, nobody cares what belongs to anyone around here. There are no walls, no fences. Besides, you know what I always say. Property is theft!'

Julia couldn't help but remember her aunt's aversion to the pig boys on her land. But Lady Harris had already changed tack because she'd caught sight of Miss Twigg, who was hanging out some washing in the side yard.

'Twigg! Twigg, you remember Lady Julia, don't you? She's escaped from London for a while—isn't she the lucky one? Now tell me, Twigg, where on earth have you put that book I was reading about herbal medicines? Really,' she muttered in an aside to Julia, 'can't the woman leave anything where it was?'

Off Lady Harris set to harangue her housekeeper and Julia glanced down at herself. As soon as they arrived, she had changed out of her travelling habit into a pink, long-sleeved cotton dress and light shoes, but she definitely needed some more suitable footwear if she was going exploring. She went upstairs cautiously.

There was no sign of Betty, but the maid had been allotted a small bedchamber next to hers and from there Julia heard the sound of snoring. She peeped in through the half-open door to see Betty lying fast asleep on the bed.

Quickly she changed into a pair of laced walking shoes, slipped on a simple blue jacket, then pushed her diary and a pencil into a pocket, just in case she was inspired to write something. The path through the woods beckoned. Freedom beckoned.

How absolutely wonderful.

Chapter Four

Ben had finished his tree work and was up on the pavilion roof, fitting in a new corner-stone to replace one that had crumbled with age. He knew that Gilly would tear a strip off him if he saw him. 'Are you mad?' Gilly would say. 'Scrambling about up there with no help?'

He'd certainly been mad to let himself be seen by that coach driver earlier, especially as he'd guessed immediately that the girl in the coach was Lady Harris's new guest. With luck, he'd never see her again. She had fine clothes and haughty manners, and no doubt she'd remain indoors at Linden House, doing a little watercolour painting or gossipy letter-writing to alleviate her boredom.

He doubted she would even mention their meeting to her aunt. She had assumed he was a labourer and such men were quickly forgotten by the likes of her.

After climbing carefully back down the ladder, Ben stood and looked up at his work. He'd noted already that his white linen shirt was speckled with lichen from the stones he'd been heaving around earlier, as were his boots and breeches. When he got back to the Hall Gilly would issue a stern rebuke, but then he would grin and say, 'I can see you've been having a fine time of it, my lord!'

Which he certainly had. There was still plenty to be done, but the pavilion was just starting to look something like his childhood retreat of old, the place he used to pretend was a castle or whatever took his fancy long, long ago.

Brushing the lichen from himself as if trying to banish old memories, he put the chisels away in his toolbox and set off towards the lake to rinse his hands and face. But all of a sudden he stopped—because something had caught his eye. There had definitely been a flash of movement down by the water's edge and he would swear he'd seen something that was pink. Pink? What on earth…?

All was still now, but he didn't move a muscle.

There it was again, that burst of colour. Some birch trees partly blocked his view, so he moved silently between them until the lake's edge was only yards away. That was when he saw her—a girl with long dark hair, sitting on a slab of rock down by the water and writing something in a small notebook she'd rested on her knees. Her pink dress and white petticoat were pulled up well above her ankles, while her stockings, shoes and jacket lay discarded some yards away. She was dabbling her bare feet in the shallows and he could hear her humming softly as she wrote.

It was the girl from the coach. Lady Harris's young relative, Julia. Damn it all, what was she doing up here, on his land? Obviously his best tactic was to promptly retreat and leave her to it, but he was too late because somehow she'd sensed his arrival and was looking around. On seeing him, she jumped to her feet with a gasp. Already she was tugging her skirt down, although Ben had been offered a very fine view indeed of her slender yet shapely calves.

She looked confused. She blurted out, 'How long have you been there?'

He frowned, wondering if maybe she feared he'd been staring at her for ages from the undergrowth. He raised his hands in a gesture of both protest and apology. 'I've only just arrived,' he said. 'I was working up there on the pavilion, then I headed down here to wash the dust off my hands. I didn't mean to frighten you.'

'No. You didn't, not really.' He saw her draw a deep breath. 'As it happens, meeting you like this gives me the chance to thank you properly for helping my coachman this morning. It was very good of you. I fear that Toby imposed upon you.'

When he saw her glance at his leg, he felt a familiar spasm of anger, which he swiftly quelled. But he hated receiving anyone's pity.

He said rather coolly, 'It was no trouble, I assure you. I might be lame, but I'm still capable of most physical tasks.'

'Yes,' she said. 'Obviously. And I'm sorry that I offered you money; it was thoughtless of me. But you see, I'm from London, and there—well, there such things are expected.'

'You're a long way from London now.'

'Indeed.' Her tone softened. 'I've come here to stay with my aunt, Lady Harris. She lives at Linden House, just down in the valley—and she's not my aunt, exactly, but a cousin of my father's.' Suddenly a little smile brought life to her face. 'When people talk of my aunt,' she added, 'they use the expression "Once met, never forgotten".' She gazed up at him. 'My name is Julia. And I would be most obliged if you could tell me who you are, Mr…?'

She was actually quite pleasant, thought Ben. Rather pretty, too—her figure was slim, her features delicate. And he knew exactly what he should do. He should tell her right now that he was Lord Lambourne, owner of these woods, many acres of farmland, the mansion nearby and a large house in London.

But he didn't. He needed a few weeks of complete privacy here and he could only pray that Lady Harris would never mention him to anyone, especially this girl. So he said at last, 'My name is Smith. Ben Smith.'

'I see. And who is your employer, Mr Smith?'

Damn, that was a tricky one, but she was bound to discover who owned this land sooner or later. 'Why, Lord Lambourne, of course.' He spread out his arms to indicate the woodland. 'All this is his.'

He saw fresh dismay ripple through her. 'So I'm trespassing?'

'He won't care,' said Ben quickly. 'Trust me.'

She shook her head. 'Nevertheless,' she said firmly, 'I would be much obliged, Mr Smith, if you would say nothing to either my aunt or your employer about finding me here like this.'

He said softly, 'Did you really think that I would?'

That veiled rebuke made her look thoroughly miserable. 'No,' she whispered. 'Of course not. And I truly did not mean to insult you.' She was casting glances now at her discarded items of clothing nearby, but no doubt she was horrified at the thought of having to dress herself with him in the vicinity.

'Mr Smith?' she said at last.

'Yes?'

'Would you mind… I mean, I wonder if you would leave me now, so that I can, er, put on my things before I return to Lady Harris's house?' She gave an awkward laugh. 'Oh, dear. This is so very different from my life in London, you wouldn't believe it.'

'I suppose you have servants there,' he said. 'Maids everywhere, rushing to do your bidding.'

'Well, yes.' She hesitated. 'Though I love it here, I really do. But you see, I decided I needed a rest from town life. Dear me, there are so many parties to attend in London, and trips to the theatre, and outings with friends—' She took a delicate step forward and slipped. 'Oh, bother,' she muttered.

'I'm afraid,' said Ben, 'that you have mud on your feet and on the hem of your dress.'

She blushed madly. Her attempt at sophistication had vanished and she gazed up at him almost pleadingly. 'I wonder, would you grant me a little privacy, Mr Smith?'

He would rather have liked to watch her pulling on those silk stockings, but her discomfiture was almost painful. 'I'm going,' he said. 'But if you're cleaning yourself up, watch out for the frogs. There are dozens of them around here.'

He'd said it in downright mischief, expecting her to scream or shudder at least—but instead she just nodded and said, 'I like frogs.'

That was very much not what he was expecting. Feeling

almost as though he'd been put in his place, he nodded his farewell and began to head back up towards the pavilion.

As Julia watched him walk away, she realised her heart was pounding. She'd been alone with a strange man half a mile from her aunt's house—and he had seen her bare legs. Perhaps he didn't see them, she desperately tried to tell herself. Perhaps he wasn't looking…

Of course he was looking. He must have noticed everything, just as she'd noticed a good deal about him.

Betty's admiration of him had been ridiculous, for he was clearly just a workman. His thick brown hair was untrimmed, he hadn't shaved for a while and his clothes were grimy from his labours. But he intrigued her, more than she cared to admit. She'd noticed again how he limped, though he did his best to hide it. He spoke far too well for a labourer and his manners were… well, his manners were lacking in the sense that she felt he was gently teasing her. But she did not feel in any way unsafe with him.

She sighed. Clearly he was not impressed by her, but few men were. She began pulling on her stockings, knowing she would have to keep completely quiet about this encounter, because if her parents were to hear of it, she would be hauled back to London immediately. But unfortunately there was yet more trouble to come, because just as she was lacing up her shoes, she was forced to utter a moan of exasperation.

Mr Smith, who hadn't gone far, was still within hearing distance for he turned round and called, 'Is something the matter?'

'Yes,' said Julia miserably, rising to her feet and facing him. 'I've completely forgotten that my aunt sent me up here on an errand.'

He returned to where she sat and she saw him frown. 'What did she ask you to do?'

Julia rose to her feet. 'She said there was a patch of burdock growing near the lake. She asked me to pick some leaves—oh!' She put her hands to her cheeks and gazed up at him, now thoroughly confused. 'But surely she realised that the lake was on Lord Lambourne's land?'

A corner of his mouth lifted in amusement. 'I believe she doesn't approve of fences or boundary walls. She likes to declare that property is theft, so, as far as she's concerned, there's nothing wrong with trespassing.'

'Except,' she murmured, 'in the case of the pig boys.'

'I beg your pardon?'

'The pig boys,' she explained. 'She doesn't like them bringing their pigs on to her land. But you're right—it wouldn't occur to her that I was doing wrong. Though even so…'

'I'll tell you what,' said the man. 'I happen to know where the burdock grows. I'll fetch some for you. I won't be long.' He picked up her little basket and off he went.

Slowly Julia fastened her boots and pulled on her blue jacket, feeling more confused than ever. He seemed to know a fair amount about her aunt and maybe that wasn't so very odd if he'd been working here a while. Probably her aunt had come across him in her wanderings. Yes, that must be it. Her aunt would talk to anyone.

By the time she had buttoned her jacket and brushed down her skirt, the man was returning with a basket full of leaves.

'Here you are,' he said.

She took her basket carefully, suddenly feeling shy again. 'Thank you. And I really am truly sorry if I insulted you earlier by offering you money for your help, Mr Smith.'

'Think nothing of it.' He smiled and, though it was only a brief smile, it did something rather odd to her, because all of a sudden she felt breathless and a little dizzy.

There was just something rather disturbing about Mr Smith, with his over-long hair and his brown eyes that always seemed to be teasing her. For some reason he made her senses swim quite confusingly.

He was also clearly waiting for her to go. She blurted out, 'I hope you don't mind me asking, but how did you injure your leg?'

His expression grew instantly cooler. 'I broke it months ago, in a fall from a horse. It's taking a while to heal, that's all.'

'I'm sorry. That must have been a blow for you.'

'It was, but life goes on.' He looked around. 'It really is time for me to get on while the light lasts and I'm sure your aunt will be expecting you back.'

'Of course. But what kind of work are you doing here, exactly?'

'Do you see that pavilion behind the trees? Well, I'm repairing it.'

'Are you a stonemason, then?'

'Julia,' her mother was always saying, *'young ladies of good birth do not ask questions, especially of men. Young ladies should be mysterious and aloof.'*

She saw him hesitate, but then he nodded. 'Yes,' he said, 'I am a stonemason. Among other things.'

'And of course, you can't wait to get back to your work.' She gave a little laugh. 'How very different this is from London life and how utterly refreshing! Thank you for helping me find the burdock, Mr Smith.'

'It's no trouble,' he said politely. 'No trouble at all.'

She did her best to walk off down the path with dignity, like the well-brought-up young lady she was supposed to be. But unfortunately she'd not got far before she tripped over a shoelace that had come undone.

She didn't quite fall flat on her face, but it was a near thing. Muttering under her breath, she knelt to retie the lace, absolutely refusing to look back in case the man was still watching her. Her cheeks, she was sure, were crimson with embarrassment.

After that, she walked very carefully and, she hoped, very calmly. But as she approached her aunt's property she stopped abruptly. Her afternoon of disasters wasn't yet over, for she had forgotten her blessed notebook. She'd been writing in it as she sat by the edge of the lake, so she must have left it there—and of course at the back of it was her *Guide to the Gentlemen of London*.

What if Mr Smith were to find it? To read it, even? She burned with mortification. It was too late now to return for it, but she resolved to sneak up there tomorrow, somehow. She could only pray it would still be there.

Ben watched until her pink dress quite disappeared from view.

Dear God, that meeting had been unfortunate, to put it mildly. Besides, he was puzzled. He'd already guessed the girl had come to stay here because she'd got herself into a little bit of trouble in London and her parents had decided to send her away until the tattle died down. But why had Lady Harris told her to come up here for burdock? Didn't she realise they might meet?

He needed time alone. He needed space and privacy. He knew London society would welcome him back even if he was on crutches—his title ensured that. But before he returned to the life expected of a peer of the realm, he had to fulfil his obligations both to the estate and to his dead father's memory.

The Hall had been the home of the Lambournes for generations, but Ben was an only child whose mother had died when he was six. His life had followed the expected pattern; he went to Eton, then Oxford, and when Ben was offered a diplomatic post abroad, his father had supported him wholeheartedly. Often Ben had not come home for months on end, so he'd known nothing about the fact that around a year and a half ago his father, who was passionate about his fine stables here at Lambourne, had sold a promising young gelding to a friend of his, a fellow aristocrat.

The horse's name was Silver Cloud. Ben had seen the beautiful dapple-grey thoroughbred only once and his memories were vague; however, there were many paintings of his father's horses hanging still in the main hall and the one of Silver Cloud took pride of place. But the gelding had proved to have a serious flaw; Ben's father had been accused of making a fraudulent sale and the feud that followed had blighted the remainder of his life.

Ben's father had isolated himself here in Somerset, renting out his London house while Lambourne Hall sank into decline. Now most of its rooms were closed off, while the furniture—what was left of it—was covered in dust sheets. The whole magnificent building spoke of neglect and dereliction. If during his infrequent visits Ben had noticed a similar decline in his father's well-being, he'd done nothing about it.

He knew, though, that his father would never have sold a damaged horse, so how had this happened? Why hadn't his father realised that Ben would have abandoned everything to help him in his time of crisis?

But he hadn't known anything about the horse sale. He hadn't even been in the country. Nevertheless, he was going to clear his father's name now, whatever it took, and to achieve that he wanted no visitors, no distractions. He felt confident he would see no more of Lady Harris's young guest, for she believed him to be a stonemason and girls of her kind were not even supposed to look at men of trade, let alone talk with them.

It was time to go, so he picked up his heavy tool box, intending to head back to the Hall. But as he cast one last glance at the lake, something caught his eye, right down by the edge of the lake where the girl had been sitting. He headed down there and picked it up. It was a small notebook—a diary, he guessed. Hers.

He shook his head in sheer exasperation. Damn. What should he do with it? He could just leave it here, but the night-time dews were heavy and it would be ruined by the damp. Maybe he could tell Gilly to deliver it to Lady Harris's house in the morning? Certainly the last thing he wanted was for the girl to call here again.

While he pondered the matter he flipped idly through the notebook, but found nothing of interest until his glance strayed to the final pages. *Guide to the Gentlemen of London*, he read.

His eyes widened.

Sir Frederick Timms. Breathes garlic everywhere.
Viscount Clive Delaney. Walks like a waddling
walrus...

Stifling a chuckle, he pushed the book in his pocket.
He knew Delaney and she was absolutely right. It appeared there was rather more to this girl than he'd realised.

On returning to Lambourne Hall he headed straight
for the large kitchen, which was one of the few rooms
in this building that was usable. Gilly looked up from
the pan of stew he was cooking for their supper. 'I take
it you've been busy, my lord?'

Ben poured himself some ale from the jug on the
table. 'I met someone,' he said. 'A girl. She's staying
with Lady Harris.'

'Is she, now? And there was I, my lord, thinking
you'd said you were giving yourself a rest from the fairer
sex—from everyone, in fact—while you were here.'

Ben shook his head. 'She has no idea who I am. And
actually—' he thought of the diary '—she appears dis-
enchanted with all men, me included.' He sat at the table
and swallowed a welcome draught of ale.

'She's staying with that old lady, is she?' Gilly
plonked down both plates of food and drew up a chair
for himself. 'Then good luck to her.'

'I rather like Lady Harris,' said Ben thoughtfully.

'Ha! You're starved of proper company, that's your
trouble. You should go back to London and live in com-

fort. There'd be good doctors, too, to help that leg of yours to heal. You'd also have the women queuing up— they all love a wounded hero, especially if he's got a title. Maybe this place should be locked up and left to the spiders and the mice.' Gilly suddenly reached up to shove aside a particularly lively spider dangling on a thread just over his head.

They ate for a while in silence. Then Gilly cleared his throat and said, 'The girl you mentioned.'

'Yes?'

'What are you going to do, my lord, if she finds out from Lady Harris who you are? She'll be up here again and again, because she won't be able to resist a prize like you!'

'I don't think for a minute,' said Ben, 'that Lady Harris will break her word to me and tell her who I am.'

Gilly was still curious. 'Is the girl very plain?'

Ben shrugged. 'No. No, I suppose she's not.'

Gilly interpreted that instantly and chuckled. 'Pretty, is she? Then I'm telling you, my lord, beware.'

'She thinks I'm a stonemason, Gilly!'

'Maybe. But she'll have noted a thing or two, like the way you speak, and no doubt she'll want to find out more. You'll have another visit from her soon, I reckon.'

Ben shook his head. 'This fine weather won't last for ever and she's not going to come marching up to the pavilion in the rain.'

'You think so? If she's taken a fancy to you, she'll probably hide in there and wait to pounce on you.'

Ben was about to laugh, but all of a sudden he had a most wicked vision of himself and Julia in the pavilion with the rain pouring down outside, curled up together under a cosy blanket with a fire blazing in the hearth… My God. Gilly was right. He was starved of female company—and for the time being at least, he needed to keep it that way.

Gilly was watching him with that particular look in his eye. 'Gilly,' Ben said, 'whatever you're thinking, you're a rogue.'

Gilly just smirked.

With a sigh, Ben carried on eating in silence. When he'd finished he rose and said, 'I'll perhaps spend an hour or two in my father's study.'

Gilly started gathering the plates. 'I suppose you're still wanting to find out exactly what happened over the business of the horse?'

'I want to know why my father's name was blackened. Wouldn't anyone?'

'Just make sure you don't waste too much of your own life doing so, my lord. After all, you might never discover the truth.'

'I will,' said Ben softly. 'Trust me, I will.'

But once in the study, the first thing he did was to pull out the girl's little book from his pocket and flick through it once more. This time, he saw something he'd missed earlier. Something she must have written today, with neat precision.

Our coach had a slight accident as we neared Linden House and a stranger came to help us.

There were some indecipherable squiggles and Ben guessed that Julia must have been crossed out several words. Then:

I wish that I had met someone like him in London.

He slammed it down in astonishment. 'No,' he muttered. 'No, this will not do!'

It would not do at all. The girl was most definitely a distraction he didn't need.

Pushing her book aside along with his memory of her, he unlocked the drawer where his father kept his most private correspondence and pulled out the letter he'd found in there after making the long journey from Austria to England, lame and travel-weary.

I am not a vindictive person, Lord Lambourne. I will not take the matter to the courts. But this was an act of fraud, not worthy of a man of your rank, and if the world gets to hear of this affair, then so be it.

Ben knew the man who'd written it. He held a high rank in society, his good reputation was indisputable. But Ben was not going to rest until he had proved his father's innocence—and forced this man, his accuser, to proclaim it also.

Chapter Five

Lady Harris was in her vegetable garden inspecting a row of leeks when Julia returned to Linden House. 'Sowerby,' her aunt pronounced, 'is not earthing these leeks up properly. Do you know what "earthing up" means, Julia?'

'No, Aunt,' said Julia politely. 'I've never had the opportunity to learn about growing vegetables. But I have brought you some burdock. I'll put it in the kitchen, shall I? Then I really must go and change my dress.'

'I should think so.' Lady Harris was scrutinising her. 'You look as though you've been fighting your way through a bramble patch.'

Julia laughed a little weakly before going inside to deliver the burdock to the kitchen. Then she scurried up to her room, where Betty was rearranging some of her clothes in the wardrobe.

'My goodness,' Betty exclaimed as Julia entered. 'You look as though you've been—'

'Fighting my way through a bramble patch,' said Julia. 'Yes, I'm afraid the path I chose was a little overgrown.'

Betty sighed. 'You shouldn't be going anywhere without me, my lady! You never know who you might meet. Now, let me help you out of that dress—dear me, the hem is all muddy. I'll try to clean it later, *if* I can get some hot water from that dragon of a woman your aunt employs.'

'You mean Miss Twigg? But she's a dear!'

'Not in my eyes she isn't,' said Betty darkly. 'I had a good talk with her earlier, telling her what you were used to eating, what time you usually took your bath and all the rest of it. Do you know what she said? She said she was the housekeeper here, so I was to mind my own business!'

Oh, dear.

'Betty,' said Julia, 'I shall be very happy with the way things are run here, I'm sure.'

'But you're the daughter of an earl, my lady, and don't you forget it! Now, I'm going to tidy your hair.'

Silently Julia submitted and reflected on her disasters so far.

Of course, she'd said nothing at all to her aunt about the encounter with Ben Smith the stonemason. How could she? She'd been sent here because she'd misbehaved in London and now she'd wandered off, dabbled her bare legs in a lake, then engaged in conversation with an unknown man who'd informed her that she was trespassing on a neighbouring landowner's territory. As for her diary, she shuddered at the thought that it might have been found—and possibly read—by Mr Smith.

At least Betty's mood improved as she helped Julia into a clean dress and restored her hair to order. Then Betty set off downstairs to clean Julia's muddy shoes and shortly afterwards Julia descended also, to be informed by one of the maids that Lady Harris was taking tea in the sitting room.

As soon as Julia appeared, her aunt began pouring out a cup for her. 'Well?' she enquired as Julia sat down. 'Have you recovered?'

'It was only a short walk.' Julia tried to laugh. 'I'm not tired in the least.'

'You can't fool me,' said Lady Harris. 'I know something happened while you were out there.'

It was no good. She had to confess. 'Aunt,' she said, 'I'm afraid I was caught trespassing this afternoon.'

'Trespassing? Good heavens.' Lady Harris peered at her over her cup of tea. 'How far did you wander, for goodness sake?'

'I only went as far as the lake, as you suggested. But apparently it belongs to your neighbour, Lord Lambourne. I truly didn't realise I had crossed into his land.'

Her aunt, far from looking dismayed, made a dismissive gesture. 'Pah, take no notice of that. Property is theft, after all, and most of the land was stolen from the people anyway.' She peered at Julia even more closely. 'Who told you this? Was it that young fellow who's hellbent on rebuilding the pavilion? You'd remember him if you met him. He has brown hair and walks with a limp.'

'Yes.' Julia steadied herself. 'Yes, I did meet him as it happens.'

Lady Harris was nodding. 'I believe he was quite badly injured, but he seems determined to fix that pavilion all the same.'

'And the pavilion belongs to Lord Lambourne?'

'I suppose so, though like I say, all property is theft.'

She looked around. 'Wherever is Twigg with that chocolate cake? I imagine you'll be hungry after your walk.'

Hungry? Not really.

Lady Harris was staring at her. 'Well? You seem a little lost for words. What did you think of the fellow?'

Julia attempted a smile. 'He appeared rather startled to find me wandering around.'

'I guess he'd expect you to be in London, being paraded in front of a bunch of foolish young suitors.' Lady Harris was vigorously stirring extra sugar into her tea, as if she was attacking the young suitors with her spoon. 'But what, Julia, did you think of *him*?'

Julia took a moment to sip her own tea. She said at last, 'I must say, Aunt, that I was a little surprised by him.'

'Why is that?'

'He seemed well spoken. Well educated. It also appears rather strange for him to be working so hard when he has an injured leg. I can only hope that Lord Lambourne is paying him well.'

Lady Harris had cupped her hand round one ear. 'What? What's that you're saying?'

Julia spoke a little louder. 'I said, "I hope Lord Lambourne is paying him well for his work on the pavilion!"'

'No good. I still can't hear you. It's all that clatter from the kitchen that Twigg's making. I suspect she's pointing out to us that she's hard at work while you and I natter.'

At that very moment Miss Twigg brought in a plate of chocolate cake and for a few moments she and Lady Harris argued over whether or not the tea was too strong. Then Lady Harris suddenly chuckled. 'I enjoy a good battle. Just think of the pig boys! Though I rather like pigs, as it happens,' she added thoughtfully. 'They are intelligent creatures. But will I let those boys trespass? I will not!'

She drank her tea and grinned. 'I am quite firm on the issue. Aren't I, Twigg?'

'You are indeed,' said Miss Twigg, slicing the cake for them with great precision. 'You're a terror, in fact. How I put up with you, I do not know.'

Lady Harris chuckled, then leaned across to Julia. 'You're maybe thinking my staff should call me "my lady". I can't stop people doing that if they wish, but I've no time for titles and all that flummery. I'm quite the revolutionary, you see.' She pointed to the cake. 'Help yourself, Julia. Generally Twigg's a pretty hopeless cook, but her chocolate cake, I must say, is not bad.'

Miss Twigg was on her way out, but she paused to raise her eyebrows at Julia as if to say, *You see what I have to put up with?* Julia, smiling at her, took a slice, then her aunt took one, too, and for a while there was a contented silence.

'Tonight,' said her aunt when there was nothing left on her plate but crumbs, 'once we've had our supper, maybe you'll play chess with me, Julia. Yes?'

'Yes,' said Julia. 'Most definitely.' She loved chess, but rarely had the chance for a game. Her sisters said that chess was dull beyond words, while Charles, who'd taught her in the first place, refused to play with her when she began beating him just a little too often.

Chess. And chocolate cake. She gave a little sigh of pleasure.

This really is a grand adventure.

But—Mr Smith. And her diary. Her optimism was dispelled. How ever was she going to get it back, without running the risk of bumping into the man again?

That evening Julia had won the chess game easily, much, she suspected, to her aunt's delight. But afterwards she went upstairs to see Betty, feeling a little guilty because earlier Betty had moaned to her, 'There's nothing for me to do here. No one for me to talk to either!'

She found her maid sitting on her bed, nursing a swollen wrist. 'Betty! Whatever have you done?'

'It's this house,' exclaimed her maid. 'Everything's so *old*. So full of twists and turns. I was exploring, that's all.'

'Why?'

'Well, I like to know where everything is. So I'd gone up some narrow stairs to the attic rooms and I heard that woman calling out from below. "Who's up there?" she was shouting in her ratty way.'

'You mean Miss Twigg?'

'Yes. I do. Anyway, I hid from her and she went away. But when I was coming back down those stairs, I slipped and hurt my wrist.'

'You poor thing. It isn't broken, is it? Here, let me see.'

Gently Julia examined it.

'I can move it,' Betty was muttering, 'so it's definitely not broken, but it will take days and days to get better.'

'I'll fetch you a cold compress,' said Julia decisively. 'I'll also see if my aunt has a soothing remedy.'

'No!' groaned Betty. 'I don't want any of her concoctions! And don't send that Twigg woman to look after me, or I'll bolt my door!'

Lady Harris looked up when Julia came downstairs again. 'What's happened?'

'It's Betty. I'm afraid she's sprained her wrist.'

'Send her home,' said her aunt decisively.

'What?'

'Send the woman home. She's neither use nor ornament. There's a carriage for hire in Lambourne village and Matthew—Dottie and Grace's brother—drives it. Matthew can take her to Bath tomorrow, for the next London-bound coach.'

'Are you sure, Aunt?'

'Absolutely.'

Feeling a little guilty at not raising more opposition, Julia went back upstairs—but the look of relief on Betty's face when Julia told her the news was almost laughable. Betty did manage to express some concern about Julia's dire fate in having to manage without her, but Julia quickly soothed her. 'Betty,' she said, 'I shall be fine. My aunt's servants will attend to me. You will tell my parents so, won't you?'

That night, as she lay in her bed, listening to the sound of the breeze softly brushing the branches of an old lilac tree against her window, she was thinking hard. If her mother knew that, in fact, Julia intended to call on her aunt's staff as little as possible, she would be horrified. If her mother knew Julia had been alone for an hour in the woods with Mr Smith, she would most likely faint.

Mr Smith. If Julia closed her eyes, she could still see the look of surprise on his remarkably handsome face as he caught sight of her sitting by the lake and writing in her book—

She opened her eyes abruptly. Her book. She had to get it back before he read it. She would have to go up there once more to get it back and, if she met him, she absolutely must refuse to talk to him, as was proper for a young lady of her rank. Yes, it was just not right for her to be on speaking terms with the man.

But the trouble was, she could still picture his smile as she finally drifted off to sleep.

The next morning Julia was woken by a great clattering sound outside in the yard. Scurrying to her window, she saw that a rather ancient coach had drawn up there and a man in a big caped coat was attending to the harness of two horses. This, she realised, must be Matthew, brother to Dottie and Grace. Dottie had explained to her last night that the coach belonged to the village inn, the George, where Matthew did various jobs and driving the carriage was one of them. Betty was out there already in her cloak and bonnet, with her packed valise at her side. Clearly she couldn't wait to be gone.

Julia dressed hastily. She took one look at her usual stays and corsets before thrusting them back in the chest of drawers with a shudder. Instead she put on her chemise and a blue cotton frock, tied back her hair and pulled on her stockings and shoes. Then she went downstairs and Betty saw her as soon as she emerged from the house.

'Oh, my lady,' she exclaimed. 'Why don't you come back to London with me?'

Julia shook her head, appalled. 'No,' she declared

firmly. 'I will be fine here, Betty. Truly, I will. Tell my parents that I will write, very soon!'

She stood and waved to the departing carriage until it was out of sight. The morning was crisp and fresh, the sun was shining and the whole day lay before her. The only shadow on the horizon was the business of her blessed notebook. She prayed it might be buried by falling leaves by now, or may even have slipped into the lake. He wouldn't have found it yet, surely? Even if he did, he surely wouldn't waste his time reading it. Or would he?

'Thank God she's gone,' said Lady Harris, who'd appeared at her side. 'Does the blessed woman ever stop talking?'

'No,' said Julia and laughed aloud. 'Oh, Aunt. It's lovely to be here with you again!'

'Of course it is,' said her aunt, with considerable satisfaction.

The morning held further surprises for her. After they'd both taken their breakfast, her aunt led her out to one of the barns to show her the two-seater gig she kept in there. 'Now,' said Lady Harris. 'What do you think of this?'

It was so unlike the elegant carriages in which the fashionable set toured Hyde Park each afternoon that Julia smothered a gasp. 'I think it's quite extraordinary, Aunt! Do you drive it yourself?'

'I used to. But now I have to get Sowerby to drive me and he just doesn't go fast enough.' She looked sharply at Julia. 'Do you fancy having a go?'

Julia didn't hesitate. 'Oh, yes!'

'Then grab yourself a coat and gloves. I'll tell Sowerby to harness up my mare, Nell, and we'll be off.'

Julia took scarcely ten minutes to pull on her jacket and leather gloves and then they were on their way, along an ancient farm track that threaded between mown corn fields. She'd driven a gig once before at their house in Richmond, when she'd begged the grooms to let her take it around the grounds while her parents were out. But when her parents got home, her mother had declared her a hoyden and the grooms had resisted every one of her pleas to repeat the experience.

The trouble was, she loved being a hoyden—and her aunt encouraged her avidly. 'That's the spirit, Julia my girl! Bit of a hill here, so Nell will slacken up. But then you can let her loose again. She's loving it as much as I am. Hoorah!'

Occasionally Julia thought of Betty and she felt a twinge of unease, picturing the surprise with which the maid would be received when she finally reached London. Would her parents send someone instantly to fetch Julia back home?

No, she told herself firmly. Her father would reassure her mother that even Julia could not get into trouble in Lady Harris's remote dwelling. No, no trouble at all. Apart from meeting with Mr Smith yesterday, which of course, would not happen again.

Except that she had to find her diary. That blessed diary—she really must retrieve it. She had to think of some excuse to go up there again, somehow…

She jumped as her aunt tapped her arm. 'You're daydreaming, girl. Nell thinks you've fallen asleep. Tighten the reins!'

* * *

Later, once they'd had a hearty lunch back at the house, Julia wondered briefly if she might be able to hurry up to the lake and back without her aunt noticing, but Lady Harris dashed her hopes by asking Julia to read to her. 'Let's have *Gulliver's Travels*,' her aunt declared. 'I do not want anything pious in the afternoons—sermons would send me to sleep.'

Julia resigned herself to the task, but she had scarcely read for ten minutes when her aunt broke in to say, 'Right. That's enough. Now, I've a feeling you would enjoy taking that gig out again while the light's good, wouldn't you?'

Julia, a little surprised, said, 'Yes, I would. But are you suggesting I drive it on my own?'

'Of course I am. You're competent enough, so you may as well make the most of this lovely afternoon. Why don't you go and find that young fellow you met and ask him if he'll play chess with me tonight? There's a good track up there that Nell can cope with.'

What?

Julia felt slightly stunned. At last she said, 'Do you mean Mr Smith, the stonemason, Aunt? But does he play chess?'

'Most certainly he does and very well, too. He's been over here for a game several times.'

Julia was floundering. 'What if he's not working there today?'

'Oh, he'll be around somewhere. He's living up at the Hall at present, I believe.'

'He's actually living in Lord Lambourne's house?'

'Yes. It's been badly neglected, so I guess he gets on with other jobs while he's there. He's a handy fellow.'

Julia's heart was bumping rather hard. 'Aunt,' she said, 'do you really think I should be going to see him on my own?'

'You're in the country now, my girl. No need to worry over all that silly chaperoning business here. I've got to know the fellow and you can trust him not to do anything he shouldn't.'

Yes, Julia thought, a little deflated. Of course. She was not one to tempt any man to distraction; in fact, she already knew how to put them straight off her, since all she had to do was speak her mind. Besides, this might give her the ideal chance to look for her diary. 'Very well,' she said. 'I'll go.' But Lady Harris didn't even answer, because she had fallen asleep in her chair and was snoring gently.

Chapter Six

It was around four in the afternoon and the warmth of the sun was dwindling, but Ben was still working at the pavilion. He'd brought a jug of ale and a pasty to keep him going till supper time and he was just finishing his food when he noticed a slight movement among the birch trees beyond the clearing. He stayed very still.

It was a young fox, he realised; nothing unusual about that, for these woodlands teemed with wildlife. But it was no wonder this particular creature had caught his eye, because its coat was spotted with patches of pure white.

Ben knew what happened to these rarities out in the wild. Their parents shunned them and they usually died young, prey to hunger, disease or predators. Indeed, this one had done well to survive for so long. Already it was vanishing into the undergrowth and Ben began to rise from the low wall he'd sat on, cursing slightly because his leg had stiffened up again.

That was when he realised that a gig was being driven up the lane that led from the valley. And driving it was a

slim, dark-haired girl in a blue frock and light jacket—
Julia. He rubbed his forehead. What now?

As soon as she spotted him, she drew the gig to a halt.
'Mr Smith?' she called out. 'There you are. I hoped you
might still be here.'

Her greeting was cheerful. Lady Harris must have
offered her the gig, but this really did break all the rules
of propriety. Reluctantly he went to help her down, making sure the physical contact was as brief as possible, but
even so he couldn't avoid inhaling the delicate scent
of her as he put his hands to her waist. He said, 'Julia.
This is a surprise.'

'Yes,' she answered lightly, brushing down her skirt.
'Yes, here I am again.'

He stepped back, shaking his head in disapproval.
'What,' he said, 'would your parents think, if they realised you were coming out alone to meet a man you
barely knew? They would be horrified, surely. You could
be taking a huge risk.'

His rebuke hit home, he could see that. 'What do you
mean?' she whispered.

He sighed then remembered he'd undone the top buttons of his shirt as he worked. Swiftly he reached to
fasten them. 'Your parents,' he said, 'must have warned
you often that if you were found alone with any man in
an unchaperoned situation, then your reputation might
be in danger.'

'But my aunt trusts you, Mr Smith. She sent me to
you.'

Devil take it, what was Lady Harris playing at? Why
hadn't she told the girl who he was? Because he'd told

her he wanted his identity kept a secret, he supposed, but then why was she sending the girl to him like this?

The silence hung heavily. He realised she was looking around, especially at the lake, and he thought he knew why. He said at last, 'I gather you've told Lady Harris that we came across each other yesterday?'

She met his gaze again. 'I suppose I felt I had to. But she just nodded and said I was safe with you.'

'Your aunt,' he said, 'is a fine woman in many ways, but she is not noted for her observance of society's rules. Surely you realise that?'

He broke off because at that moment he'd noticed her hands. She wasn't wearing gloves and he could see that her palms were chafed and stained by the leather reins. With a suppressed exclamation, he reached to touch them. 'Your hands! Why on *earth* didn't you put on driving gloves?'

She whispered, 'I don't know. I suppose I forgot.'

'No maidservant to remind you. Is that it?'

He saw her colour rise and he sighed, letting go of her hands. 'At least the skin isn't broken, but you do need to bathe them. I have fresh water and cloths by the pavilion—you can wash them there. Then I'll lend you some gloves to drive back.'

She followed him and sat where he'd indicated, on the low stone bench. He went inside and came out with a bowl of water and a muslin cloth and silently she began to wash her hands.

Then she looked up and said, 'You think I'm a fool. Don't you?'

Ben sighed again. 'No. I don't. But I'm certain your

parents would not be happy about you being here. They would be concerned about your future prospects.'

'You mean my marriage? Oh,' she said airily, 'lining up some suitors for me won't be a problem, believe me. Besides,' she added quickly, 'no one needs to know about this. Do they?'

'No. Except your aunt. Speaking of whom, why did she send you to find me?'

'My aunt wishes to know, Mr Smith, if you will come and play chess with her tonight.'

Once more Ben was completely thrown. Was this Lady Harris's idea of a joke? If so, it wasn't funny. He said, 'Chess? Is she serious?' He was suddenly suspicious. 'This wasn't your idea, was it?'

'No, indeed not!' she cried. 'How could I even have known you played?'

That was heated, most definitely. She rose to her feet and said, 'I told my aunt I ought not to come here. I knew this was a bad mistake.'

She was already heading for the gig, but he caught up with her. 'Julia. Wait. I'm sorry. Tell Lady Harris that, yes, I'll come—'

Suddenly he grimaced with pain. Damn, his leg had almost given way again and of course she'd noticed.

'What is wrong?' she breathed. 'Is it your leg? Is it troubling you?'

'Really,' he assured her, 'I'm fine.' He pointed to her hands. 'I promised to lend you gloves, didn't I? Don't go without them. And by the way, yesterday I found something of yours.' He pulled the notebook from the pocket of his breeches.

She looked frozen with embarrassment, so he pointed

to the bench and said, as gently as he could, 'Perhaps you'd better sit down again.'

As he gave it to her he expected her to snatch it from him, or maybe to question him fiercely. Instead she said very quietly, 'Did you read it?'

He suddenly realised that he very much wanted to spare this girl yet more embarrassment. He said lightly, 'Only to check that it was yours. It's for all your appointments, I gather. Reminders of your hectic London life.'

She took it back in silence, not even looking at it before slipping it into her pocket. Then she gazed around at the woods, which were tinted with gold by the setting sun, and she said softly, 'I love it here. It's so beautiful that I think I could live somewhere like this for ever.'

He said quietly, 'I think it's beautiful, too.' He was silent a moment, then sat down also, but kept his distance. He said, 'Julia. I wonder if you have maybe had one or two unpleasant experiences with London's gentry?'

She shrugged. 'Oh, most girls tend to get pestered from time to time. Insulted even. I'm told it's my own fault.'

He said sharply, 'Have your family told you that?'

'Not really. They're actually very kind to me.' She tried to smile. 'But I'm afraid I did say some foolish things recently, to a man at a party.'

'Did he deserve them?'

This time her eyes gleamed with humour. 'Oh, yes. Most definitely. I also spilled some champagne over his shirt.'

'Deliberately?'

'Of course. So my parents decided that until the fuss dies down, I should come here to stay with my aunt.

I've known her since I was small. When I was younger
we used to visit her often and I'm very fond of her. You
see, she's different. Like me.'

'What do you mean, different?'

He saw her screw up her eyes a moment in thought.
'Different in that I don't enjoy the things my sisters love,
like shopping for clothes, or having dancing lessons.
My older sister Pen is perfectly lovely and she's getting
married very soon, while as for my younger sister, she
already dreams of her wedding even though she's only
fourteen! But I'm not as pretty as them, though when I
try to say marriage may not be for me, everyone thinks
I'm mad.' She looked up at him with challenge in her
eyes. 'No doubt you do, too.'

Ben considered his next words carefully. 'Marriage
is a huge commitment and I believe it's your right and
yours alone to make that decision. No one should be
forced into a lifelong relationship because it's what society expects. If you feel it's not for you, then stick to
your beliefs.'

'Indeed,' she said in a lighter tone, 'that should prove
very easy, because so far no man has shown the slightest interest and I really do not care. My aunt has offered me some advice on how to drive men away, but I
think I have plenty of ideas of my own. As you'll have
noticed, I find it easy to appear positively eccentric!'

Ben pointed to her feet. 'At least you've remembered
to lace up your shoes properly this time.'

He'd meant it as a joke, but she looked mortified and
he felt a sharp pang of regret. Something about this
girl was puzzling him, badly. She'd declared she wasn't
pretty—well, he had to disagree with that. She had a

most attractive face, with sparkling grey-green eyes and high cheekbones. Her slender figure gave her a look of fragility that was outrageously deceptive, for she clearly loved the outdoors. Why on earth did she have such a low opinion of herself? What had people *done* to her?

He realised she was rising from the bench and preparing to return to the gig.

'You need gloves,' he said firmly. He went into the pavilion, calling back to her, 'I'm afraid they'll be huge on your small hands, but they'll do the job. You can give them to me tonight, at your aunt's house—'

He broke off, because he realised she had followed him in.

'Oh,' she said. She was looking round, amazed. 'Mr Smith, this is wonderful. It's like a miniature palace! Who painted all this?'

He had to smile at her enthusiasm. 'It was built and decorated decades ago.' He pointed. 'I believe the wall paintings were done by an artist from Bath.'

She was still gazing raptly round the room. But surely, for a girl of her upbringing, there was nothing much to admire? The furniture consisted only of two wooden chairs, a table and an old sofa. There was a fireplace, which he'd had to clear of the ancient debris left by nesting birds. But the octagonal interior was full of light, thanks to the south-west-facing windows. The scenes on the walls were exquisitely done in shades of ochre and cobalt blue, while framing them all were stencilled friezes in exactly the same colours.

'This is truly exquisite,' she murmured.

He nodded. 'I certainly intend to restore it fully, if I can.'

She looked up at him. 'For Lord Lambourne?'

He hesitated only briefly. 'For Lord Lambourne, yes. And now, it really is time for you to go.'

She was gazing at the stone lintel above the door, in which was etched the Lambourne crest of a phoenix. Then she pulled on the leather gloves he'd handed her, laughing a little at the size of them, and followed him outside.

She was really rather beautiful, Ben thought suddenly. All the more so since she was unaware of it.

He helped her up into the gig. 'You can tell Lady Harris,' he said, 'that I'll come down to Linden House later.' He added, 'Your aunt, I must warn you, loves nothing better than to tackle me at chess and she's rather a fine player.'

She chuckled as she gathered up the reins. 'I beat her, though. Last night.'

'You did?' He was astonished. 'Good for you.' He patted Nell's neck and stood watching until the gig was out of sight. Once again he recalled what she'd written about him in her little book.

I wish that I'd met someone like him in London.

He shook his head and returned to his work. She had better forget any thoughts like that as soon as possible, but he would be seeing her again, tonight! What was Lady Harris thinking of? More to the point, what on earth was *he* thinking of, in agreeing to go?

As Julia drove into the yard, old Mr Sowerby looked up from the logs he was sawing and came over to take

Nell's bridle. 'You've got an eye for this, my lady,' he said approvingly. 'Good to see a young lady taking the reins so well.'

Julia smiled as she hopped down. 'Nell's a dear.' She quickly removed the outsize gloves and stroked the horse's velvety nose. 'So easy to handle.'

'Aye, but you're a natural,' said Sowerby. 'Oh, and Lady Harris is out in the orchard picking damsons, if you want to find her.'

Goodness. Did her aunt ever stop? 'Thank you, Sowerby. I'll join her soon.' But first, Julia went up to her room, where she put the gloves and her notebook in the back of a drawer, then sat on the bed and tried to make sense of this latest encounter with Mr Smith.

Clearly he was trusted by Lord Lambourne, since he was working for the nobleman in his absence and even living in a part of his house. He spoke well and appeared well educated. But he was right—her mother would swoon away if she knew her daughter had been talking to him, let alone if she'd seen how her daughter's wandering gaze had strayed instantly to where Ben's shirt was unbuttoned at the neck. He'd quickly fastened it, but she still couldn't erase the memory of his bare chest, which was smooth, muscular, tanned…

Julia, she scolded herself, *the man must think you a complete idiot.*

Indeed, he'd looked positively horrified when he saw her approaching. She should be used to that, for most young men in London did find her a nuisance. But Mr Smith was definitely different to the men she met in town, because she felt quite odd whenever he was near. In fact, she could not help staring at his handsome face, especially his mouth, which curled up quite delightfully at the edges whenever he smiled.

Her diary, though! She was hot with embarrassment. How much had he actually read of it? Quite honestly, she couldn't bear to know.

After rolling over on her bed so she could prop her chin in her hands, she gazed out of the window and up into the woods. The light was fading fast and she couldn't see the pavilion, but she could picture it. She could picture Mr Smith, too, trying to hide his limp in a way that somehow twisted her heart. When he'd put his hands on her waist to help her down from the gig, she had not wanted him to let go.

Oh, dear. She'd always teased her older sister whenever Pen rambled on about her fiancé, Jeremy. But the stonemason was disturbing her mightily, which just would not do, especially as tonight he was visiting her aunt's house. There was only one answer—she would have to make sure that she stayed out of his way and didn't embarrass him or herself any further.

'Julia!' Her aunt's voice pierced the silence. 'Are you up there? Whatever are you doing? Did you manage to ask the young man to play chess with me tonight?'

Julia leaped to her feet and hurried out to the top of the stairs. 'Yes, Aunt. He's agreed.'

'Good. Come down and have your tea with me.'

A command from Lady Harris was enough to banish any girl's vaguely romantic notions. Quickly Julia went downstairs to the dining room where Grace bustled about serving the food while Lady Harris once more extolled the virtues of living in the countryside. No more mention was made of Mr Smith. Even when Julia rose from the table and explained she was going upstairs to write letters to her family, her aunt just looked at her a little curiously.

'Letters? Very well,' she said.

But once in her room, Julia didn't write a thing. Yes, she did sit at the little writing desk in the corner, but for heaven's sake, she had neither paper to write on, nor ink and a pen. Though a few moments later there was a knock at her door and Miss Twigg marched in bearing a tray, on which were all the writing implements Julia required.

'Lady Harris,' Miss Twigg announced, 'said you might need these if you're writing letters.' She set the tray down on the desk.

'Yes.' Julia was blushing to the roots of her hair. 'Yes, of course. Thank you.'

She hesitated a moment. She'd never had the chance to speak to Miss Twigg without her aunt being present. 'Miss Twigg,' she said, 'you've known my aunt for a long time, haven't you? Do you wonder if sometimes she gets lonely here?'

'Lonely? Heavens, no. She has me and Sowerby, of course, and the maids, and sometimes Matthew from the village drives her into Bath to do some shopping and take the waters.'

'Does she ever go to church? I know she didn't when we used to stay here.'

'Church? Not her. Her husband was a churchgoing man, but that didn't stop him having women galore.'

'No!'

Miss Twigg eyed her carefully. 'Yes. Didn't you know? Though I suppose it's not the kind of thing your parents would mention in front of you. But the rogue married her for her money, then after a year or two he headed off to Europe with some floozy or other. You can imagine how the experience of that man's so-called virtue put paid to any notion of religiosity on Lady Harris's part.'

'Yes,' said Julia, a little dismayed. 'I suppose it would, rather. But, Miss Twigg, my aunt is very independent, isn't she?—and perhaps just a little eccentric. For example, don't you think it's odd that she's befriended that man who's coming to play chess tonight? The stonemason working on the Lambourne estate?'

Miss Twigg's expression became guarded. 'I don't know him myself. But I do know your aunt is a good judge of character and she is particularly partial to a game of chess.' She took a step towards the door. 'Listen, I think that's her calling. Yes, indeed. I must be off.'

So Julia was left alone in her room, supposedly writing letters ,but instead sitting there thinking, *The life of an elderly single lady. No family, no children.*

Was that really what she wanted for herself? She certainly wanted freedom and the chance to make choices for herself…

She jumped up as she heard the sound of a horse's hooves clattering into the yard. Dashing over to her window, she carefully parted the curtains an inch and saw Mr Smith, on a rather good bay mare—he'd borrowed one of Lord Lambourne's horses, she guessed. She also noticed that he had smartened himself up for the occasion. He had taken the trouble to shave and his buff coat and buckskin breeches were quite respectable.

But those locks of hair falling over his forehead made

him looked quite wickedly handsome. Oh, dear. She dashed back to her desk and sat down, her pulse racing. It was as well she'd been sensible enough to isolate herself up here in her room. She began to write her letter.

Dear Mama and Papa...

What could she say? She could tell them about the journey. She could try to explain why she'd sent Betty home. Or—

'Julia?' That was her aunt's shrill voice coming from the bottom of the stairs, causing her to drop the pen and splatter her letter with ink. 'Julia,' her aunt called again, 'I'd like you to come down here, now!'

Chapter Seven

As Ben handed the reins of his horse over to Sowerby, the old fellow greeted him cheerfully. 'Evening, sir!'

Sir. That was just fine, for it appeared the man didn't recognise him in the slightest. Miss Twigg was a different matter, for she was as sharp as a new pin, but if Lady Harris was true to her promise, she would have made Twigg swear to keep his identity secret as well. Any other staff, he believed, came here by day only. But surely Lady Harris would have to tell the girl at some point who he was? He'd been wondering all the way here if Her Ladyship was maybe planning something for tonight, other than chess.

He soon found out. She was planning to have a headache, that was what.

Miss Twigg greeted him at the front door. 'Mr Smith. Good evening. Her Ladyship is expecting you in the drawing room.'

Mr Smith, she'd called him. That was it, then. Lady Harris was clearly intent on keeping his secret for now. He looked around as Miss Twigg led him into the drawing room, noting that a decanter of sherry and two glasses were on the sideboard, but there was no sign of Julia. Lady Harris was on her feet and raising a hand in greeting. 'Thank you, Mr Smith, for coming here to oblige an old lady! Twigg, you may go.'

Already his hostess was waving him towards the chessboard set upon a table, but there were matters to be discussed first. He waited until she sat down, then he said, 'Lady Harris. Why did you send your young guest with your invitation? You know I wanted no one to realise I was here.'

'Of course I know,' she retorted. 'I haven't told her who you are, young man, and I don't intend to. Now, do sit down. You make me feel quite uncomfortable, looking at me like that.'

He sat with a sigh. 'Yes, but don't you see? She is being misled and this is very awkward—'

He broke off as Lady Harris suddenly put her hand to her head. 'Goodness,' she exclaimed. 'I am the victim of an almighty headache. It must be Twigg's fault. That cake we ate earlier was far too rich for me and she should have known it!' She rose from her chair, marched through the open door to the foot of the stairs and called, 'Julia? Julia, I'd like you to come down here, now!'

Ben had followed her. 'Lady Harris,' he hissed. 'Why in God's name are you *doing* this?'

She said, 'Because the girl needs you.'

What? Ben was speechless. Whatever was she talking about? But it was too late for him to say or do anything more because moments later Julia was coming slowly down the stairs, rather unwillingly, he felt. But damn it, she looked so pretty that he almost forgot how awkward all this was.

Her dark, silky hair was pulled up into a loose top-knot, but most of it had fallen out from its ribbon and was fascinatingly untidy. Her lips looked pink and full and, whether she realised it or not, the simple dress she wore emphasised her delicate curves to perfection. But she was *not* pleased to see him, for she merely nodded to him and said tightly, 'Good evening, Mr Smith.'

He murmured a polite reply and wondered what came next, but Lady Harris did not hesitate.

'Julia,' she announced, leading the way back into the drawing room, 'Mr Smith would like a game of chess with you.'

'What?' This time Ben said it aloud.

'You heard me, both of you. As for me,' Her Ladyship continued, 'I must retire upstairs, since I feel distinctly unwell. Come to think of it, I've been poorly all afternoon. I really do not know why Twigg insists on serving such elaborate food; I am beginning to believe she does it to deliberately annoy me.'

Off she went—and Ben could see that Julia did not know what to say or where to put herself.

Heaving an internal sigh, he pulled out a chair and gestured for her to sit down. 'I'm sorry,' he said. 'Your aunt seems determined to push us together and this is rather awkward for you. But here we are. So how do you feel about a game with me?' He added quietly, 'You know, if you prefer it, I can always go.'

For a moment she stood very still and he realised he truly had no idea what thoughts were racing through her mind. At last she said, 'No. Don't go.'

That was when Ben realised that he shouldn't even have asked her. He should have come to his senses, made a polite farewell and marched—no, limped— straight out of her life. This was the start of a slippery slope and didn't he know it. But he nodded and they both sat down at the chessboard.

The game was absorbing, for he was an experienced player and so, he swiftly realised, was she. At first Julia made her moves primly, showing no emotion, and he, too, said hardly a word. But the game swiftly developed into one of intense concentration on both sides, giving him the chance to study her face and the fleeting expressions that crossed it: success, self-rebuke, pleasure in a particularly clever ruse.

When the end finally came and he had to submit, he leaned back in his chair and applauded. 'Julia,' he exclaimed, 'you are really rather good at this. Aren't you?'

He saw her almost glow in pleasure at his compliment. Rising to his feet, he went over to the sideboard to pour them each a small glass of sherry. 'I think we should drink a toast. To you, Julia, and your campaign for independence. As for chess, I acknowledge you as my better, absolutely.'

But as he placed the glasses on the table, he leaned too heavily on his injured leg and stumbled slightly. God damn it, he didn't want the girl seeing his weakness yet again. He strove to cover up the moment of agony, but Julia must have seen the pain etched on his face because she, too, was on her feet.

'Mr Smith. I'm so sorry. Does your leg hurt *very* much?'

'Only now and then,' he lied.

'And will it get better soon?'

He sat down again and tried to smile. 'I'll probably always have a limp. But the doctor tells me the stiffness should gradually ease, if I keep exercising it.'

'It must be horrid for you,' she blurted out, 'when you're clearly used to being active. If you don't mind me asking, how did it happen?'

'It's simple really.' He lifted his shoulders in a shrug. 'I fell off my horse and, in doing so, I managed to break my leg in three places.'

He saw her gasp. 'How awful! I broke my ankle last year in Richmond Park, because I fell off my horse when I was galloping—which I wasn't supposed to do. My mother was very cross. But at least it healed quickly and I was looked after, whereas you—haven't you any friends or family to help you?'

That was when he should have cast his resolve aside and told her who he was, in precise detail. But he didn't, and why? Because he was being a selfish idiot, that was why. He was enjoying her company more than he'd enjoyed anything in a long while and the way she was looking at him so earnestly, so compassionately, disarmed him completely.

How could he avoid being fascinated by those wide eyes of hers that were fringed by lashes as intensely dark as her hair ? All those stray locks tumbling around her face gave her an appearance that was sufficiently déshabillée to set any red-blooded man's pulse racing. It was certainly dangerous for his peace of mind and his body.

He said at last, 'I'm absolutely fine on my own. I was well cared for after the accident, even though it occurred when I was abroad.'

'Did you enjoy your travels, Mr Smith?'

'Most of the time, yes.' He smiled. 'In fact, until I fell off my horse I found foreign cities quite fascinating.'

Her face brightened. 'I would adore,' she exclaimed, 'to travel. My older sister is getting married very soon and afterwards her husband is taking her to the south of France, then Rome.'

'Is she happy about it? The wedding, I mean?'

'She is ecstatic. And I do envy her just a little, because I would love to go to the places I imagine you must have been. But not with a husband telling me what to do. I wish I'd been born a man. I do. I do!'

'Instead,' he said, 'you're intent on keeping men, or suitors at least, out of your life. Haven't you thought that you might some day find a husband who would sympathise with your longing for adventure and travel?'

She shook her head. 'He would still expect me to spend most of my time in London. Have you worked for rich gentlemen there, Mr Smith?'

'I've spent a fair bit of time in London, yes. But it's not my favourite place, I suppose because of the crowded streets, the smoke, the people... Well, some of them, anyway.' He pointed to her glass. 'Don't forget your sherry. Let's drink a toast. May you some day find exactly what—or whom—you are looking for.'

'I'm not on any kind of hunt!' she cried. 'I am quite happy as I am, thank you!'

'I'm glad to hear it,' he said gravely. He lifted his glass. 'Long may you remain content with your life.'

Julia raised her glass too but sipped only a little of the over-sweet sherry. Was she content? No. She wasn't.

She'd declared she was happy, yes, but she suspected he was mocking her. He'd seen right through her and she was troubled, because she knew she must sound ungrateful. She had loving parents and a beautiful home—how could she complain?

'I really should not grumble about London,' she said slowly. 'But there are some people I meet there whom I find detestable. They can be foolish and conceited and—'

She broke off, because she had suddenly remembered her notebook. Oh, heavens, how she prayed he'd not read her *Guide to the Gentlemen of London*.

But he still looked quite calm as he said, 'You are fond of your family, though, aren't you?'

She answered swiftly, 'Oh, yes. Very fond. But I wish my mother and father would listen to me when I tell them that I do not want a Season in the slightest. How on earth would I cope with it?'

'Like all the other debutantes?' he suggested mildly. 'I have heard that most girls enjoy it.'

She bit her lip and frowned.

Yes, she wanted to say. *Yes, they do.*

But not her, for she attracted trouble wherever she went. Her parents had assumed Somerset would be safe, but look at what an utter disaster her first day here had been—trespassing on private property, being caught by a stranger dangling her bare feet in a lake, and now here she was, talking about completely improper subjects with a man who—it was no use denying it—made her feel quite dizzy whenever he smiled.

He was still watching her when he said, with just a hint of that fatal smile, 'I take it that you're determined not to marry?'

'I am!' she cried, 'But how can I avoid it, when I'm soon going to be forced into this wretched Season?'

'But your parents will consult you on your choice of husband, surely? And hasn't the idea of romance ever entered your head?'

'I'm sure my parents would never force me to marry a man I loathed, but in my world, Mr Smith, marriage is a business arrangement. My older sister Pen is suitably betrothed, but my father still has two daughters to marry off and he will be assessing every proposal very carefully.' She looked at him. 'I cannot blame him. But I do need more ideas to put men off me!'

'Wear the most hideous gowns you can?' he suggested. 'Eat garlic?'

She felt herself cringe.

Sir Frederick Timms. Breathes garlic everywhere.

Oh, no. She'd written that in her notebook. *Had* he read it? She really could not bear to ask so instead she laughed a little weakly. 'My mother wouldn't let me make myself unpresentable. She would scrub my mouth out if I ate garlic and burn any hideous clothes or bonnets I tried to wear. But maybe—' and she was sounding, she knew, a little desperate '—maybe I could think of a topic so dreadfully tedious that I could bore them to death when they tried to court me.'

'Such as...?' he prompted.

'Chess!' she cried out in triumph. She pointed to the board in front of them. 'I could recount, step by step, some of the cleverest moves made by the chess masters. I've read lots of books about chess, you see.'

'That doesn't surprise me,' he murmured.

'Or I could talk about obscure literature. I remember that when my sister Pen came out, there was another debutante who had an obsession with medieval poetry. She used to go round parties reciting *Piers Plowman* and Pen said she could empty a room in five minutes.'

Ben looked intrigued. 'Is this literary lady still single?'

'I'm glad to say she married a man who is a professor of history and they are very happy travelling around Europe in search of obscure old manuscripts.' She sighed, feeling a little crestfallen again. 'I think I might enjoy that kind of life, too. But I don't think I'm likely to find another professor of history at a London society ball, do you?'

'I should think it's highly improbable,' he agreed.

'So,' she said with an air of resignation, 'I shall make the most of my freedom here while it lasts. After all, I could never have talked with you like this in London. It's funny, though, isn't it, how my aunt wanted you to come here to play chess with her, then said she'd been feeling poorly all afternoon? But she does seem a little absent-minded at times. How, may I ask, did you come to meet her?'

She was surprised to see him choke slightly on his sherry. At last he said, 'Oh, I've come across her a time or two chasing off those boys and their pigs.'

'Ah, yes.' Julia had to smile. 'I believe the boys only do it to annoy her. But I am truly sorry about her disappearing and you having to play with me.'

'It's been a pleasure,' he said politely.

'You are very kind to say so, Mr Smith. And you

will, won't you, tell me if you think of any other ways in which I can repel any suitors? Oh, dear me. I seem to have spilled a little of this wretched sherry on my dress!'

Ben waited patiently as she sprang to her feet, turned her back on him and fetched out her handkerchief to rub at her skirt. The material, though, was flimsy and he realised that as she bent over to deal with the stain, the view he got of her pert bottom was startlingly delectable. That, he thought, was definitely not the way for her to repel suitors. Why Julia was so convinced of her own unattractiveness was a mystery to him. Maybe it was because her older sister, Pen, was forever outshining her?

Yes, Julia was different. Unconventional. But the funny thing was, he couldn't remember ever having enjoyed a conversation with a girl so much.

She didn't want to get married. Well, neither did he, at least not yet, so that was another thing they had in common—though he certainly couldn't see her surviving her Season without a multitude of proposals. Damn it, as she wriggled around, sorting out her dress, he longed to pull her in his arms and kiss her right now...

That was the moment when he heard the rattling of pots and pans out in the kitchen. Julia heard it, too. 'That will be Miss Twigg,' she said. 'My aunt's housekeeper.'

Ben nodded. Miss Twigg's nearby presence reminded him that he really ought not to be here alone with Julia and probably Miss Twigg thought it, too.

'I think,' he said, 'that it's time for me to go.' It was also, he warned himself, time for him to make a firm resolution not to see her again.

But as Julia was leading him to the door she suddenly said, 'I envy you your ride through the woods at night. Sometimes, when my sisters and I used to stay here, we would creep out of the house in the dark and walk up into the woods. It was wonderfully alive. We saw owls, badgers, foxes…'

That was the moment when he made his biggest mistake yet. For he began to tell her about the young fox he'd seen, alone and undernourished.

She was clearly upset. 'Why is the poor thing in such a state?'

'Because he's rather unusual. His coat is patched with white, which sometimes happens, and those markings mean he'll always be spotted by predators. He'll have spent most of his short life in hiding.'

'What will happen to him?'

Ben hesitated. 'He's done well to survive so far. But he'll find it difficult once winter arrives and he'll probably die, I'm afraid.'

'Oh, no!' She clasped her hands tightly together. 'Surely you can do something to help the poor creature?'

'I've left out some food for him, by the pavilion. But really, it's almost impossible.'

'Please!'

He was already shrugging on his coat, but he hesitated again. Often interfering with the course of nature merely prolonged a creature's sufferings, but her eyes were so pleading that once more an unfamiliar feeling tugged at his heart. 'I'll carry on putting out some food for him by the pavilion,' he said. 'The little fellow seems to like it there. You could maybe come to see him, too.'

Now, that was unbelievably foolish of him, but the words were out before he could stop them.

'I would love that.' Her eyes positively shone. 'What can I do to help?'

'Bring a little food,' he suggested, 'Scraps of bacon, some bread perhaps. I'll put out water, too. But, Julia, I'm afraid the young fox still might die. He's clearly been in a bad way for months.'

'I'll come tomorrow with food…' She stopped, suddenly looking anxious again. 'That is, if you don't mind me foisting myself on you?'

He shook his head. 'Not at all.' How could he have said otherwise?

'Thank you,' she whispered.

Then she jumped, because there were loud footsteps in the hallway behind them and Lady Harris's familiar voice boomed out, 'So, have you thrashed him at chess yet, young lady?'

'I did win our game.' Julia smiled at her. 'But Mr Smith is rather good.'

Lady Harris looked sternly at Ben. 'I hope you played properly? No deferring to the fairer sex or any of that kind of nonsense?'

'I assure you,' said Ben, 'that I would not insult her skill.' He nodded politely to them both. 'I really must be off. I sincerely hope your headache is better by tomorrow, Lady Harris.'

'My what? Oh, yes. The headache. Dratted nuisance. But at my age, what can one expect?'

Outside, Sowerby fetched his horse and Ben set off into the night. The moon was full and as he rode up the woodland track towards Lambourne Hall he was aware of the faint rustlings in the undergrowth that indicated the scurrying of small creatures, while from overhead came the eerie cries of the owls.

Lady Harris had invented that headache, he was quite sure of it. What was her game?

Ben needed to have it out with Her Ladyship at some point, but she would probably be awkward as hell.

'She pretends to be an eccentric old lady,' he murmured to himself. 'But her wits are as sharp as a new carving knife. What can she be up to? Why is she pushing the girl and me together like this?'

He was not interested in any kind of courtship, not yet. He was well aware it was his duty at some point in the future to look for a suitable bride and to provide the estate with an heir, but his priorities for the moment were to secure the family fortunes, give his leg time to heal and, above all, to clear his father's name. As for Julia, he could rest assured she wasn't fixated on men and marriage like most girls of her age and class.

But he hated the fact that Julia was being deceived—and the worst of it was that the girl seemed to trust him. As for him, seeing her so often was doing very little for his peace of mind.

Back at Linden House, Julia said goodnight to her aunt, then went upstairs to her room, where she lay on her bed fully dressed and sighed aloud. She'd placed her solitary candle so it illuminated the model sailing ship and now she remembered how that same little ship had made her dream of adventures whenever she stayed here as a child.

Meeting the stonemason, Mr Smith, was her biggest adventure yet—and quite possibly the most foolish. She told herself she was being extremely sensible about him. She was fortunate to have found a man with whom she could hold a friendly conversation, without worrying if he was imagining her as a possible bride. But the trouble was that she felt warm and unsettled in a most disturbing way whenever he was near.

At first she'd been horrified when her aunt left her alone with him tonight; embarrassed, too, because surely he hadn't expected to be landed with her yet again? But he'd been kind. He'd been considerate. During the chess game he had taken her seriously as an opponent from the beginning and he'd shown no vanity, made no brazen flourishes as he'd moved his pieces. Instead he'd made her feel they were silent equals in a situation where rank and wealth did not matter.

As for the moment when he'd applauded her victory, she'd felt the thrill of that compliment tingle all the way down to her toes. For a moment she'd been quite unable to speak.

Back in London, she had resigned herself to the fact that she just wasn't interested in the things other girls relished, like courtship and flirtation and stolen kisses. She truly thought she was indifferent to all that—but with Ben, she felt less certain. It happened every time she saw him and was struck anew by his handsome face, or noticed without meaning to how his arm muscles tightened beneath his shirt as he casually went about his work at the pavilion. He made her feel hot and awkward and not like an earl's daughter at all.

Maybe it was being in the country and free of society's rules that caused her to act and think so foolishly.

But tonight, during the chess game, she'd had difficulty pulling her gaze away from his brown eyes and his rare but delightful smile. It was a wonder, actually, that she'd managed to move her pieces, let alone win.

She also loved the way he wasn't conceited about his appearance. Yes, he'd smartened himself up a little for tonight's visit, but his hair was still tantalisingly unkempt and he obviously couldn't care less that his clothes were old. But the odd thing was that he sounded and behaved like a well-bred gentleman, so why was he a stonemason? Had something tragic happened in his past, maybe? A financial calamity, perhaps? She had already guessed he must have secrets, because sometimes he looked sad, though often he looked as if he might be laughing at her, just a little.

She sighed aloud. Who could blame him? She was rather ridiculous, after all. Who had ever heard of a girl who dreaded her Season and wanted to drive her suitors away?

'Why on earth do you not wish for a husband?' an objectionable acquaintance of Pen's had once said to Julia at a tea party. Her name was Georgina Sheldon. 'Do you really wish, Julia, to be on your own, for ever? No husband, no children, just a sad old lady?'

A sad old lady. Like her aunt?

But Lady Harris wasn't sad. Her marriage had been a disaster, but now she was very happy, ordering around the servants who clearly thought the world of her, condemning society in very round terms while actually loving to read the latest scandal sheets that Sowerby picked up for her from the village. Her aunt acted like a lady who owned the world, because she was free and independent—just as Julia intended to be.

But she couldn't wait to see Mr Smith again tomorrow. The thought rose in her chest like a bubble of excitement. Meanwhile, it was clear she wouldn't get to sleep, so perhaps she should try to write a letter to Pen. She hopped up from her bed and sat at the little desk on which Miss Twigg had earlier laid out fresh ink and paper.

Dear Pen... she began.

> *I am here at last. It is quite delightful to be with Aunt Harris again. By the time you receive this letter, Betty will no doubt have arrived in London and I hope Mama is not too cross, but poor Betty hurt her wrist and was of no use to me at all.*
>
> *I am being well looked after here by my aunt's staff...*

Oh, dear. That was Lie Number One, for as a matter of fact she was being allowed to do whatever she pleased. She ploughed on.

> *My aunt is most welcoming. The countryside is beautiful, as you will remember, and Linden House is as pretty as ever.*

Her thoughts wandered. She sat with the pen dangling in her hand, then wrote on.

> *While I was walking in the woods, I met a man. Tonight I played chess with him. He is a stonemason and I like to think he is my friend...*

Oh, no. She slammed down her pen. She could not possibly send that! But then again, why not? Mr Smith worked for his living, but he wasn't what everyone would assume. He was a man of the world, he had travelled and no doubt been employed by rich men throughout Europe. And oh, she did love the way his brown hair strayed so wilfully across his forehead and the look of approval in his eyes as they'd played chess tonight! If she wasn't careful, she'd be thinking yet again of what Pen whispered to her, about the things young women weren't supposed to think about until they were safely married.

She added to her letter.

Do not, on any account, tell Mama and Papa about Mr Smith.

She could trust Pen, she knew she could. Tomorrow, Mr Sowerby would take her letter to the post, but now it was time to get changed into her nightdress. As she did so, she couldn't help but glance at herself in the full-length mirror. Maybe she was just a little pretty? She sighed. What did it matter? Mr Smith wasn't interested in what she looked like, she was sure. He was just being kind to her.

She buttoned up her nightgown, blew out the candle, climbed into her bed and was soon fast asleep.

Chapter Eight

The next morning Julia woke to find the sun pouring through her window. She knew she should have rung for Dottie or Grace to help her dress, but instead she chose a comfortable brown frock that she could easily button up herself, then she brushed her hair and tied it back loosely. It was truly a blissful relief not to have a maid fussing around, telling her she must look like a lady before even getting out of bed.

During breakfast, her aunt alternated between reading one of her news-sheets and grumbling to Miss Twigg about the dire state of the world. 'It's truly dreadful, Twigg, what goes on these days! Dreadful!'

For a while nothing could be heard but the rustle of paper and Lady Harris's mutterings. But as soon as Miss Twigg departed to the kitchen to tell Dottie to make more toast, Lady Harris turned her beady gaze on Julia and said, 'I forgot to ask you last night—did you challenge that young fellow to another game of chess?'

Startled, Julia put down her cup of tea. 'No, I didn't. I really don't think that men like to lose at anything, especially to females. My brother certainly doesn't.'

'Mr Smith,' declared her aunt, 'is not like Charles, thank God. What an almighty fuss your brother makes about his blessed cravats. How long does it take him to get them right, do you think?'

Julia smothered a smile. 'Often an hour, I believe.'

'Hmph. I guessed as much.' Suddenly Lady Harris turned towards the kitchen. 'Twigg! Twigg, where's the sugar for my tea? Really, do I have to do everything for myself?'

Julia said swiftly, 'I'll get the sugar, Aunt.' She rose and fetched the sugar bowl from the sideboard, then settled in her seat again and drew a deep breath. 'Aunt,' she said, 'I was just wondering. No one seems to talk at all about your neighbour, Lord Lambourne.'

Lady Harris looked up swiftly. 'Eh? What was that?'

'Lord Lambourne,' Julia repeated patiently. 'Mr Smith works for him, doesn't he? Have you ever met Lord Lambourne? I don't recall you ever mentioning him.'

Lady Harris cupped her ear. 'What did you say? I didn't quite catch that.'

'I was asking about your neighbour, Lord—'

'Pah, I never see any neighbours. Would I live in this God-forsaken place if I wanted to be bumping into people every time I left my front door, like you do in London? I visit Bath to see my doctor and take the waters, and that is quite enough for me.

'Anyway, you know I've no time for titled men, be they viscounts, earls or whatever—meaning no disrespect to your father, of course.' She turned impatiently towards the kitchen door. 'Twigg, get a move on with that toast, then come and read me this piece about whatever the Prince Regent is up to, will you?'

Miss Twigg appeared moments later with a plate of toast and a pot of fresh tea. She winked at Julia as she sat down and said, 'Here you are, my lady. Now, where's this article? Is it the one about the latest squabble between Prince George and his wife?'

'That's the one—nice and loud now. I'm feeling particularly deaf this morning.' She pointed at Julia. 'It looks like a lovely morning, so why don't you go for a nice walk? While you're out, I'd like you find me some blackberries. Yes, blackberries—there should be plenty of them up in the woods. I use them to make a cure for winter colds. Off you go, now!'

Julia didn't need any more encouragement. She went to fetch her jacket, then after saying a cheerful 'good morning' to Grace, who was sweeping the tiled hallway, she sneaked into the well-stocked larder to cut a couple of slices of bread. Carefully she wrapped the slices in a napkin and put them into a small basket together with some scraps of cold bacon, then she called goodbye to her aunt and set off for the path up the hill.

'This is all perfectly correct,' she told herself. 'I'm going to find blackberries for my aunt. But I also promised Mr Smith I would bring some food for the fox cub and I am doing so. I will, of course, speak to him calmly and decorously, as is proper.'

The sun shone down from a perfect blue sky and crisp leaves crunched beneath her feet as Julia climbed steadily through the woods. She stopped when she heard the rhythmic chink-chink of a hammer and chisel—and there was Mr Smith in the clearing, chipping away at a block of stone. His white shirt was loose at the neck, he'd rolled up his sleeves to display his muscular fore-arms and for a moment she was transfixed.

He hadn't seen her, so she stood very still at the edge of the clearing and felt her heart tighten in that peculiar way again. She also felt a little breathless, even though the walk hadn't tired her in the least. Oh, my. His obvi-ous strength together with the skill he used in shaping the stone fascinated her exceedingly. Then he saw her and straightened up.

'Good morning, Julia.'

It was time to act with decorum. 'Mr Smith. Good morning,' she said very politely. 'I've brought some food for the young fox. Have you seen him this morning?'

'Not yet.' He looked around, then smiled at her. 'I'm afraid the noise I've been making here probably made him wary, but I wouldn't be surprised if he's lurking nearby. Foxes are intelligent creatures and he'll have re-alised I'm not his enemy. Why don't you put your food out at the edge of the clearing there?' He pointed. 'Then we can sit here by the pavilion and see if he appears.'

She hesitated. 'Are you quite sure I'm not holding you up in your work?'

'No. Oh, no. I'm ready for a break.'

She set out the food as he suggested, then sat on the stone bench. She said, 'I wish I knew more about wild animals. I suppose you've learned a good deal on your travels?'

He laid his hammer and chisel carefully in his tool-box, then settled himself on the bench also, at a respect-ful distance. He said, 'I suppose I learned most of what I know about animals from my father. He was especially good with horses. He used to talk to them and, believe it or not, I really think they understood him.'

He spoke calmly, but something in his voice made Julia ask, 'Is your father dead?'

This time he looked at her directly. 'He is.'

'But he can't have been terribly old! Was he ill?'

'He was fifty.' He looked at her and his eyes were suddenly dark. 'He died earlier this year—and I think he died of despair.'

For a moment she couldn't speak. Then she whispered, 'Oh, no. Whatever happened?'

Ben had never spoken about his father's disgrace to anyone except Gilly and he'd certainly never intended to tell this innocent girl about it. Why should he? But incredibly, as she gazed up at him, he found himself revealing more. 'My father,' he said, 'was accused of selling a horse that was unsound—for a large sum of money.'

'That is a dreadful accusation.' She said it very softly. 'I can imagine how hurtful such a thing would be to a man of honour.'

He nodded. 'My father was indeed an honourable man,' he said tightly. 'But he was accused of fraud by a man of considerable power. My father could not prove his innocence, nor could his accuser truly prove his guilt, but my father's life was ruined.'

He realised that she had reached out to put her small hand on his. 'I'm sorry,' she whispered. 'Really, I am.'

'Yes.' He could hear that his voice was still bitter. 'So am I, especially as I wasn't there for him when he passed away.'

'What about your mother?'

'She died when I was six.'

'Oh, *no*.' She was looking up at him and her expressive eyes were wide with distress. She shook her head. 'I really should not grumble about my family. I'm so lucky to have them.'

Gently he eased his hand away from under hers. 'They will know that you love them,' he said. 'Trust me.' Suddenly his attention was caught by a movement nearby and he pointed. 'Look, Julia. Over there. I can see the fox.'

Indeed, gazing at them from the edge of the clearing where she'd put the food was the white-spotted fox, who had seen them and was wary. But after a moment he began eating very quickly and once he'd finished he stood very still, his eyes fixed on Ben. Then he turned and trotted away.

Ben realised he'd been holding his breath. He saw that Julia, too, was still gazing at the place where the fox had been, then she said to Ben, very quietly, 'Thank you. I'm truly grateful for all of this. Being able to come up here on my own has been wonderful. But I mustn't keep you from your work any longer. I really ought to go.'

She'd risen to her feet and he rose also. 'Do you want to go, Julia?'

'Not really.' She smiled a little shyly. 'I love it here.'

Once more he found that his common sense—his instinct for propriety and society's rules—had vanished. Because he said, 'Then stay. Why not?'

He saw the hope in her eyes. 'May I? Really?'

He was already pointing at the pavilion. 'Do you want to look inside again at those paintings? I've brought the original stencils and the paints from the Hall and some day I mean to have a go at restoring them.'

Julia followed him inside and was gazing raptly at the faded frescoes. 'Would you let me help you? Please?'

How could he say no?

He continued to repair the outside of the building while Julia worked inside for over an hour. Whenever he looked through the windows he could see her, mixing the paints and applying them with the utmost care. She looked, he thought, as happy as he'd yet seen her. She concentrated so hard that she hadn't even noticed she had a large splodge of blue on her cheek and maybe she'd almost forgotten he was there, because she jumped as he entered the pavilion.

He said, 'You've done this kind of thing before. Haven't you?'

'Oh, you startled me! No, I've never actually worked with stencils, but I always used to love painting.' Her expressive face fell a little. 'My sisters and I once had an art tutor, but he was dismissed after two months because he fell in love with Pen. Everyone falls in love with her.'

He was curious. 'Are you jealous?'

'No!' She laughed. 'How could I be? Pen is perfectly lovely.'

And so are you, he thought silently.

He pointed to the door. 'Come and sit outside for a while. I have a flask of lemonade I brought from the Hall.'

He was fascinated by that splodge of blue paint on her cheek. He knew it was wicked of him, but it made her look so delightful that he didn't want to tell her about it. He waited for her to follow him outside to the stone bench that caught the afternoon sun, then decided his conscience would allow him no rest until he mentioned it.

He pointed to her face. 'You have some blue paint on your left cheek,' he said. 'Just a little. It should come off with a damp cloth.'

Her hand flew up to her face in horror. 'Oh, no. And I would never have known!' Her happiness had vanished. 'I'm ridiculous, aren't I?' she said in a low voice. 'Truly ridiculous!'

'Of course not.' He rose and fetched a clean cloth which he dipped in the fresh water barrel nearby. 'Here. You can wipe it off with this.'

She did so, but she still looked utterly despondent, so he took the cloth from her and put it down. 'Julia,' he said, 'I do not find you ridiculous. But I do think it a pity that you think so little of yourself. You are different, perhaps, but is that so dreadful?'

'It is if you're about to be put on the marriage market,' she said glumly. 'My brother keeps introducing me to his friends, but they usually back away as soon as possible.'

He poured her some lemonade. 'That marriage market again. It really worries you, doesn't it? Have you ever wondered if the fault maybe lies with your brother and his friends?'

'I would be foolish to say or even think so, since they are considered very eligible by most other girls!'

Ben hid a smile as he remembered her comments on various men in that notebook.

Waddles like a walrus.
Breathes garlic at you.

Instead he said, 'That's because they're rich, presumably. Heirs to peerages. But I wonder, have you confided in your mother about your worries? She might give you a little more time to grow used to the idea of a Season.'

She picked up her lemonade and laughed. 'My mother? She's very sweet, but she's the worst of them all, believe me! I am a tremendous worry to her, I'm afraid, since she finds the idea of a dedicated spinster in the family truly appalling.'

His mouth quirked a little. 'A dedicated spinster? You're sure about that? How old are you?'

She looked defiant. 'I'm eighteen!'

'Ah,' he said with mock solemnity. 'Then your fate is sealed. Clearly you will spend the rest of your life knitting by the fireside and tending a multitude of cats.'

She'd been sipping her drink, but she gave a splutter of laughter. 'I don't think I'm ready for that!'

'Of course you're not,' he said briskly. 'And let me tell you this, Julia. If those men in London have any sense at all, when your Season begins they'll be fighting over you.'

This time, Julia almost dropped her drink entirely. What? *Fighting* over her? She really didn't know what to say—as a matter of fact, she suddenly felt very odd indeed. Of course, she'd met lots of young men, but all in all she had found them a complete nuisance with their noisy talk and their efforts to impress everyone around them.

Ben was different. She supposed it was because he wasn't rich, which meant, of course, that he had no airs or affectations. But there was something else—something that made her feel a little breathless whenever he was near, because she thought he was, well, *nice*.

That was it, she told herself firmly. *Nice.* He probably still thought she was slightly mad, just as her brother's friends did, but he was at least trying to be kind about it.

The trouble was that she found him exceedingly attractive, too. She couldn't stop herself sneaking sideways glances at him whenever he wasn't looking, admiring his profile and his stubbled jaw. She was doing it *now*, for heaven's sake. She dragged her gaze away and pretended to be looking at the surrounding scenery instead.

'Julia.' Ben's voice was touched, she noted, with more than a hint of amusement. 'May I ask, are you practising some new idea to put men off you?'

'What?' That shook her back into looking at him.

'You were,' he announced, 'staring into the distance— somewhere over there, in fact.' He pointed to the horizon. 'Are you trying to tell me that I'm boring you rigid and you'd rather I was anywhere else?'

'Oh, no, no!' she cried in dismay. 'I was just thinking that I really should not be here at all. It's not that I don't trust you. Of course I do! But I'm afraid my mother would be appalled.'

He nodded gravely. 'Do you think she would worry that I might take advantage of you?'

She jutted her chin. 'Well, I don't think you would for one minute.'

'Good. And besides, you can probably run much faster than I can.'

Smiling, he pointed to his lame leg. He was brave, she thought, to joke about it, because she guessed he was often in pain.

She said, 'I'm sorry, I didn't mean—'

'I know you didn't,' he broke in gently. 'And please believe me when I tell you I have no intention whatsoever of taking advantage of your trust.'

Of course. He was tactfully trying to indicate that he didn't find her tempting in the least. Besides, her parents would never, ever permit her to be courted by a stonemason, but even so she felt suddenly desolate at the thought that soon he would be gone from her life completely.

She rose to her feet, picked up her basket and spoke as brightly as she could. 'Dear me, how foolish I am. Do you know, I'd almost forgotten that my aunt asked me if I would find some blackberries for her.'

'Blackberries?' He rose, too. 'What is she making this time?'

Julia laughed. 'She's concocting a medicinal syrup, I believe, for the winter months. She said there would be some blackberries in the woods, but I really don't know where to start.' She hesitated. 'I don't suppose you…?'

Ben smiled. 'There are plenty of blackberries along the path just above the lake.' He pointed. 'Shall we go and look together?'

Ben found he was rather sorry that Julia was back to being her prim and proper self. As they walked, her gaze never met his but was firmly fixed on the path ahead. She'd withdrawn once more into her tight little shell of formality.

She must, of course, come from a wealthy family, quite possibly a very distinguished one. He'd always been aware that Lady Harris had many aristocratic relations, but Ben wasn't going to ask any more questions on the topic because he'd decided that he didn't want to know the answers.

But he felt angry with her parents. He feared she'd been brought up as many well-bred daughters were, to be decorative, polite and subservient to her parents' and her future husband's wishes—which was all *wrong*. Here she was, active and independent and curious, yet she felt that the only way she could be her true self was to remain unmarried. What a criminal waste.

By now, she was some way ahead of him on the path and was looking all around for blackberries. He knew where there was a bramble patch bursting with ripe fruit and he could have guided her there immediately, but he was deliberately dragging it out. Yes, he was being wicked because, damn it, he was enjoying her company. Enjoying also her complete unawareness of the way her print dress—which she probably thought the epitome of modesty—clung to her pert hips as she walked along the path before him.

She was so graceful and slender that he guessed she would be a delight to dance with. Even more of a delight to hold and kiss...

Just then he realised she'd found the blackberries for herself because she turned to call back, 'Look, Mr Smith! Here's a fine patch of blackberries. Gorgeous ones.'

She was already gathering them avidly so he joined her as she started to fill her little basket. 'They are delicious,' she breathed as he drew nearer. 'Try one.'

Her expression brimmed with delight. Her lips were stained dark red and, when she licked them and gave a little sigh of pleasure, his pulse thumped. He said quietly, 'My name is Ben. Please call me Ben.'

Then he reached out and brushed away a bit of blackberry that clung to the corner of her mouth. He could have sworn a slight tremor ran through her as his finger touched her skin, then she gazed up at him and whispered, 'Ben.'

His hand still hovered. He felt an overwhelming urge to haul her against his body and kiss her senseless. His pulse was pounding and his loins throbbed warningly. She would never, he hoped, guess at the willpower it took him to step away. He said, in a voice that was harsher than he intended, 'It's time, I think, for you to go home.'

Time, too, for him to come to his senses. Time to remind himself why he'd come to Lambourne Hall in the first place. Why he'd intended to keep himself isolated from company while he concentrated on finding out exactly why the sale of his father's fine horse had gone so wrong.

Every day since he'd arrived, he'd spent hours each morning and evening, combing through his father's papers, especially those relating to his father's stables. He came to the pavilion in the afternoons because he found the physical work a way of making reparation for his neglect of his duties in the past.

But his prime concern was to find something that would clear his father's name. Anything else—anyone else—was a distraction, especially this lovely girl.

Ben guessed she was deeply wounded by his apparent dismissal, even though she nodded and said lightly, 'Of course I should go.' But as she pulled on her jacket, she added, almost in a whisper, 'Ben. Please tell me. Have I done something wrong again?'

'Wrong?' he said sharply. 'How do you mean?'

'You know. Something odd. Something to add to my list of how to put men off me—like being good at chess.'

Damn it. She'd done nothing wrong—he was the one at fault, he was the one who was totally to blame! 'You haven't,' he said at last. 'Not at all.'

She still looked a little anxious, but she nodded. 'Good. I've enjoyed this so much,' she said, more steadily now. 'Please may I come and paint again? Of course, I'd hate to stop you working and get you into trouble with your employer, Lord Lambourne. But it's so lovely here, and in London I hadn't quite realised—' She broke off.

'What?' he said. 'What, Julia?'

'I hadn't realised,' she said quietly, 'that I could be so very happy.'

Christ. That really did almost fell him. He was getting in deep, far too deep. 'I'll walk you home,' he said.

Not another word was spoken on the way and he told himself, *This is it. I must not see her again, and it's for the best.*

But as they approached Linden House, she turned to him and said, 'You didn't give me an answer. May I visit you again?'

What could he say but *Yes*?

Chapter Nine

After that, each day after lunch Julia said to her aunt, 'I think I'll just go for a stroll.'

Every time, she expected Lady Harris to say *No*, or *Why?* or *Where are you going, exactly?* But she didn't. She mostly said things like, 'Hmm. You may as well enjoy this fine weather while it lasts', or 'Do what you like. You're only young once.'

Lady Harris never mentioned Ben; in fact, only Dottie and Grace showed any curiosity concerning Julia's wanderings. Julia enjoyed her chats with the two sisters, who never ceased to ask her about London. 'We've heard such stories, my lady, about what a wonderful place it is! They say there are palaces on every street and fine ladies and gentlemen parading everywhere!'

Dottie particularly enjoyed brushing Julia's long hair. 'I would love to put it up for you, my lady, with fancy pins and ribbons, as if you were going to a grand ball.'

Julia smiled, but shook her head. 'No, Dottie. Just tie it back plainly with a ribbon, if you please. Do you know, I find it amazing that here I can be ready to go out in ten minutes, while in London it can take hours.'

'But that's because in London you'll be making your-self beautiful to catch the eye of some fine gentleman,' exclaimed Dottie, securing the ribbon with a neat bow. 'It's a pity that there's no one for you here. Such a shame that the new Lord Lambourne hasn't arrived at the Hall yet.'

Julia felt her pulse jump. 'The *new* Lord Lambourne? Why do you call him that?'

'Because the old Lord, his father, died only recently. No one saw him very much, but he was good to every-one around here and he really loved the horses he kept at the Hall's stables. Didn't you realise?'

Julia said slowly, 'No. I didn't.'

Dottie sighed. 'He died suddenly in the summer and his heir still hasn't come back. This new Lord will be a catch, though, when he does come home—I've heard he's lovely and handsome, but it's wicked to leave that huge old place lying empty. There now, I'm letting my tongue run away with me.' She gave a last tweak to Julia's hair, then stood back. 'How pretty you are, my lady. I'm sure you have plenty of admirers in London.'

Julia felt her breath catch in her throat.

Not really, she thought. *Besides, there's no one that I want as much as Ben.*

She sighed. She was also doing as much as possible to put him off her, whether she intended it or not. Trip-ping over her own feet. Going around with blue paint on her face. Letting him find her embarrassing book—*had* he read it?

Oh, dear. There was no doubt that kind as he was, he must think her ridiculous.

Every afternoon though, as she walked up to the pavilion, Ben always greeted her with courtesy. He continued to repair the pavilion's crumbling stonework, while she did her best to complete the faded stencilling. Always, at around three, they would settle on the bench overlooking the valley to share the bottle of lemonade that Ben had brought with him.

He often brought scraps of food, too, to place close to the undergrowth that surrounded the clearing and the young fox would appear to swiftly eat Ben's offerings before vanishing into the woods again.

She found herself telling Ben more about the happy times she'd spent as a child here at Lady Harris's, while he spoke of the cities and countries he'd visited in his travels. But he never told her about himself, she realised. He never told her any more about his father, or his mother who had died when he was a child—and she was careful not to ask too much. Not to pry.

It was as if there was an unspoken pact between them—*we know we each have secrets*.

She did not want him to know her father was an earl and guessed his silence about his own background was because of the gulf between them. Often she was aware that what she said or did betrayed her naivety—for instance when she asked him to explain exactly what one of the faded wall paintings was about.

'Is it a party?' she asked, eagerly pointing at the wall. 'Or perhaps a Greek or Roman bath house? These people don't seem to have many clothes on…'

Her voice trailed away, for suddenly she'd realised they were all enjoying themselves very much and very intimately. 'Oh,' she murmured, blushing a fiery red. 'How foolish of me.'

Ben didn't bat an eyelid. He said politely, 'Not to worry. After all, the painting is so faded that the details are far from clear.' Then he added, 'And perhaps they had better remain so.'

Julia turned back hurriedly to her stencilling, but she could hear Ben at work outside whistling cheerfully and suddenly thought, *I am going to miss him terribly when it's time to go home.*

Something even worse occurred to her. She didn't really want to go home—because it meant she would never see him again.

Almost a week had passed by swiftly and the October weather stayed fine. Each afternoon Julia went up to the pavilion and Ben kept his distance, continuing to repair the exterior of the pavilion. But just knowing that he was near filled her with a kind of quiet contentment.

Then one afternoon, as she was preparing to put away her painting things, she remembered that her aunt had asked her to look for more blackberries.

'You're usually heading back for your tea by now,' warned Ben. 'Will you really have time?'

'I'm sure I have.' She was putting on her jacket and picking up her basket. 'It's not far, is it? I can remember the way.'

So off they set, a little reluctantly on Ben's part because his leg ached from all the work he'd done that day, which slowed him considerably. Julia was well ahead when she turned and called back to him over her shoulder, 'I think I need the path to the left, Ben. Don't I?'

Then she was off again, walking briskly.

Damn it, muttered Ben. She'd come to the place where the track divided into three and already she was heading up an overgrown path that hardly anyone used these days. 'Julia,' he called. 'That's the wrong way. Wait.'

But she didn't hear him. 'Julia,' he called again. 'Julia—*no*.' He cursed himself for letting her outpace him. 'Not that way. For Christ's sake…'

Somehow he managed to catch up with her just before she reached the edge of the old stone quarry. Here, the builders had carved out quantities of stone in order to construct Lambourne Hall a century or more ago, but the great, excavated hollow still gaped like a deep wound in the hillside and the drop to the bottom was sixty feet or more. The place was lethal and didn't he know it—for this was where, earlier in the year, they had found the body of his father.

Ben clutched Julia's shoulders and almost shook her, so overwhelmed was he by the mingled fury and powerlessness that had seized him. At last he ground out, 'You could have been killed.'

She was very pale. 'I'm sorry. I—I didn't know.' She glanced in disbelief at the quarry's edge. 'I never guessed that it was here.'

'I told you to wait for me,' he said between gritted teeth. 'You should never have gone rushing off on your own, do you hear me? Don't *ever* do that again.' He was furious. He was also holding her as if he would never let her go and he was frightened by the power of the emotions that coursed through him.

She was searching his face, as if trying to comprehend his rage. 'I'm sorry, Ben,' she repeated. 'But I would have seen it in time—the quarry, I mean.'

'I didn't know that, though, did I? All I could see was you, dashing onwards into a situation where you might have been killed!' He shook his head, trying to calm himself. Then he added more quietly, 'You shouldn't be wandering in these woods anyway. Lady Harris shouldn't be sending you up here and I'm a fool for letting you do so.'

'You're angry with me,' she said. He saw now that her wide, wonderful eyes were glistening with unshed tears. 'And you're hurting me, Ben. Just a little.'

He knew that he was still holding her far too tightly, knew, too, that he was putting her in another kind of danger entirely and he released her so suddenly that she almost stumbled. It was as if he had no control over his own body. This place had terrible memories for him, but the helplessness he'd felt when he feared he might lose this precious girl was shattering.

She was safe from tumbling to her death in the quarry. But maybe—just maybe—she wasn't safe from *him*.

The problem was that she looked so damned lovely. Her eyes were wide and vulnerable, and when she moistened her parted lips with the tip of her tongue, he wanted to kiss her—or so he told himself, though to be honest, he wanted a good deal more.

'Should we go back now?' she whispered.

He realised she was still stunned by his anger, shocked and even a little frightened. So he attempted to quell his raging thoughts and the fierce arousal that had come about when he held her tender body next to his and he said, in a voice that was still gritty with tension, 'You came here, didn't you, to collect some blackberries?'

She nodded, still looking crestfallen.

'Then follow me,' he said.

At last they reached the copse where the blackberries grew. There weren't many left, for the birds had eaten most of them. But he helped her gather what remained, then said, 'Right. It's growing dark, so I'd better walk with you back to your aunt's house.'

'But your leg!'

Damn. She'd noticed his limp was worse. He shrugged. 'I can manage.'

They walked back together in silence, but as soon as Linden House came into view she stopped and said to him in a low but clear voice, 'What was it, Ben, about the quarry? You were so angry. I've never seen you like that. It wasn't just because of me, was it?'

'Someone I once knew died there,' he said.

For a moment she shut her eyes. 'Oh, *no*. I'm so sorry. I was an idiot to have dragged you there.'

He made a gesture of dismissal. 'You shouldn't blame yourself—after all, how were you to know? I'll leave you now. Your aunt will be wondering where you are.'

He turned to go and walked—no, get it right, man, he *limped*—back to Lambourne Hall. Once there, he called out to Gilly that he'd be with him shortly. Then he went straight to his father's study and began hunting once more through all the documents his father had kept about his beloved horses. He was almost desperate now. He had thought he'd found everything there was to be found about every horse he'd owned: their sires and dams, their age and health and indeed the details of their sale if indeed they'd left his father's stables.

He'd found nothing at all about Silver Cloud's ill-fated departure. But this time, as he leafed through the same old files yet again, a loose sheet of paper fell from the rest of the documents.

He picked it up and read it with growing wonder. It was the final bill from the man who had been hired to transport Silver Cloud from Somerset to Richmond, in Surrey. There was little enough about him: he was simply referred to as 'Francis Molloy of London'.

Ben had always known it would be hard to prove any wrongdoing on the part of the horse's buyer, for he was an eminent man of high reputation. But could this fellow Molloy have had a hand in the deception?

Ben tapped his finger on the paper, thinking hard. The conveyance of valuable thoroughbreds was an expensive business, requiring the use of wagons that were fitted inside with barriers and slings to keep the animals secure. Frequent stops had to be made on the way to exercise and water them. There would be records, surely, of the men who organised these transports—and Mr Molloy of London could well be worthy of investigation.

That night Julia was challenged by her aunt to a game of chess, but she played atrociously. At first Lady Harris made no comment, but when Julia dropped her knight on the floor, her aunt finally said, 'I think, young lady, that you could do with a change of scene.'

Oh, no. Was Lady Harris going to send her home? That would mean she would never see Ben again. But would she dare now to visit him anyway? This afternoon she'd done something awful by going near that quarry and he'd been terribly angry with her. It almost broke her heart because when he'd held her in his arms, she'd wanted to stay there for ever.

She said, as she put her knight back on the board, 'Are you thinking of sending me back to London, Aunt?'

'Good grief, not yet.' Lady Harris chuckled. 'Nothing as dire as that. You've only been here a couple of weeks. But I intend to go into Bath tomorrow, to see my doctor.'

Julia looked up quickly. 'I do hope you're not ill?'

'Of course not. I'm never ill, but the wretched man insists that I see him every so often and insists, too, that I take some of those dreadful spring waters. You'll come with me, won't you?'

Julia was no stranger to Bath, for when her family visited Lady Harris in the old days, her mother often took her daughters there. Julia had always thought it was a beautiful city, with its elegant buildings and glorious parks. Lately London's fashionable set had taken to visiting Brighton instead, but Bath still fared well, especially with elderly visitors.

'I would love to come with you,' she said.

Early the next morning Grace and Dottie's brother Matthew arrived with the carriage from the George Inn nearby. Of course the conveyance was nothing like her father's magnificent carriage and its lack of springs meant that it bounced and rattled all the way to Bath. But they arrived there with an hour and a half to spare before Lady Harris's appointment with her doctor, so there was time to stroll among the shops and to drink mineral water in the Pump Room.

'This is quite foul stuff,' declared Lady Harris loudly.

Nevertheless, the room was packed with genteel visitors who'd come to take the waters, converse with friends and generally ignore the small string orchestra that played valiantly in the background.

When the time came for her aunt to visit her physician, Julia decided to remain there and listen properly to the music. But it wasn't long before she became aware of a young woman with a determined expression heading her way.

Oh, no. It was Miss Georgina Sheldon from London, known by Julia's sisters as The Gorgon. She was due to have her come-out next year, just like Julia. Some said she was nearly as pretty as Pen, but she had a tongue like acid. Julia pretended to be concentrating intensely on the rather dirge-like piece the string players were wading through, but within moments she felt a tap on her shoulder.

'Lady Julia Carstairs,' pronounced Georgina. 'Fancy seeing you here—though now I think of it, you did make rather a fool of yourself at Lord Bamford's party, so doubtless your parents thought it best to get you out of the way for a while. Dear Tristram found the incident most amusing, I can tell you. He's been telling everyone.'

She sat on the chair next to Julia's. 'I wonder if you're going to brave the Season next spring? Personally, I cannot wait. There's Christmas first, of course, with all the country house parties—I've had so many invitations! Then when I make my debut, there will be such a choice of eligible men—with your brother Charles being one of the foremost, of course.'

Julia almost gagged. Georgina and Charles? The thought of Georgina Sheldon as her sister-in-law was appalling. No. Please, just *no*.

She said, 'I'm surprised to see you here, Georgina. I thought you would be in London.'

Georgina looked around, pursing her lips. 'Yes, Bath is quite dreary nowadays, isn't it? So many old people. But my older brother Henry has a house on the Royal Crescent—you'll remember Henry, of course?'

Julia nodded. Henry was one of Charles's friends.

'Mama,' continued Georgina, 'really wished to visit Henry and his wife to take the waters.' She pretended to yawn as if bored, then suddenly said, 'Your aunt's house lies close to Lambourne Hall, doesn't it? I wonder, have you heard any news of when the new baron will return?'

Lord Lambourne—*again*. Julia shrugged, realising that the proximity of any new heir was bound to cause speculation with girls like Georgina. 'I've heard nothing at all of the man,' she said.

'Of course,' mused Georgina, 'he will be quite a catch. I was hoping to meet him while we were here in Somerset, but my brother has no news of him either. Which is most peculiar—'

Just at that moment Lady Harris sailed into view and Georgina broke off to giggle behind her hand. 'Such an oddity, your relation,' she murmured. 'Everyone laughs at her. How you stand her, I don't know—ouch!'

Georgina's giggle changed into a shriek of pain because Julia, on rising, had managed to stand on Georgina's foot.

'I'm sorry,' said Julia airily. 'How dreadfully clumsy of me.'

'You might have broken my toe!'

'I doubt it. But I do hope you weren't going dancing tonight.' She smiled sweetly and went to meet her aunt.

'Is everything all right?' asked Lady Harris, glancing sharply over at Georgina.

'Absolutely fine, Aunt.'

'I saw that Sheldon girl talking with you. Georgina's like a dose of poison. Shall we go home now? Have you had enough of Bath?'

'Yes,' said Julia, linking arms with Lady Harris. 'I've had enough of Bath. Let's go home.'

The sun shone from a clear blue sky all the way back to Linden House, making the autumn colours of the fields and woodlands quite glorious. At the slightest breath of wind, more leaves would come fluttering down from the trees and Julia remembered how, when they stayed here as children, she and her sisters used to run around laughing as they tried to catch them.

'You'll have one lucky day for every leaf you catch,' Lady Harris had told them.

Had they believed her, the three of them? Maybe. But that was years ago, and she knew now that no amount of lucky leaves could save her from her fate next spring, when she would face balls, parties and people like Georgina Sheldon and Tristram Bamford.

As for Ben Smith, he'd had enough of her. His harsh words to her at the quarry had made that all too clear.

Chapter Ten

The next morning, it began to rain. In fact, the showers continued for five days and the skies were heavy and grey. Julia browsed the books in her aunt's library, as she did when she was a child. She wrote letters to her parents and Lizzie, telling them about the trip to Bath. She also wrote again to Pen.

> *I have met with my stonemason quite often, Pen. I have grown to truly like him. He is kind and respectful, but I'm afraid I have made him angry and I might not see him again. I know you won't say a word of this to anyone else, but I miss him.*

She gazed out of the window at the pouring rain, then gave her letters to Sowerby so he could post them in Lambourne village.

One afternoon the sun came out at last and as they sat in the drawing room after lunch, Lady Harris took Julia completely by surprise.

'Now,' said her aunt in her decisive way. 'Since that infernal rain has decided to stop, I think I'd like you to help me collect some frogs.' She rang the bell. 'Twigg! Are you there? Or Dottie, or Grace! Please come and remove this tea tray!'

As Dottie hurried in, then out again with the tray, Julia's eyes were wide with astonishment. 'Did you actually say "frogs", Aunt?'

'Indeed. I usually see plenty of them in the two ponds in my woodland garden, but this year there aren't any. I would guess they've migrated to conduct their reproductive rituals up by that lake in the woods, so I thought you and I could take a stroll in that direction and bring some down here in time for their winter hibernation. A fine idea, don't you think? It's no use asking Twigg to accompany me. The woman faints at anything that wriggles.'

'But the lake…'

'I know. It's on Lambourne's land, but it's not as if the frogs belong to the man, is it? All wild creatures are meant to be as free as the air around us. They are owned by no one.'

The lake. The pavilion. *Ben.*

'Aunt,' Julia said, 'I'm actually a little tired. I was thinking of taking a rest.'

But Lady Harris was already heading for the door. 'Come along. Put your boots on, because it will be muddy around the lake after all that rain. We'll tempt the frogs with some titbits. Let's be off!'

With a feeling of acute apprehension, Julia climbed with her aunt up the familiar path to the lake, armed with a large mixing bowl from the kitchen and a bag of breadcrumbs. If Ben was here, what would he say? He might think this was her doing. She decided she could probably start filling another notebook with ways to deter admirers.

Men will not be attracted to girls who do eccentric things like attempting to move frogs from one lake to another...

'There'll be frogs here,' hissed Lady Harris in a dramatic whisper as they approached the lake's edge. 'Look, Julia. They adore the sunshine.'

True enough, Julia could see a dozen or more frogs basking sleepily on some low, flat stones that were half-submerged. 'Throw a few breadcrumbs,' whispered her aunt. There was no sign of Ben so Julia, feeling a surge of relief, swiftly obeyed and the two of them ventured closer.

'Now,' instructed her aunt, 'pick a frog up, very gently, and pop it in the bowl with more crumbs. It will be quite happy.'

Julia reached for the nearest one, but goodness, it was too quick for her! Immediately it jumped into the water and swam off, while the others stayed where they were, gazing up at her. She could swear they were finding all this highly amusing. Sighing, she prepared to try once more to coax the frogs a little nearer. 'Here you are,' she whispered. 'Breadcrumbs. Don't you like breadcrumbs? Do you prefer worms? Because if so—'

But one by one they dived into the lake and she nearly toppled into the water herself when she heard

Lady Harris calling out, 'Mr Smith! Yoo-hoo! Julia and I are over here!'

Oh, no.

'Hello, Lady Harris. Good afternoon, Julia.' It was Ben, looking effortlessly handsome as usual.

Julia's heart bumped to a stop at his husky familiar voice. Then she glanced back at the lake in horror, because she realised she had let her bowl roll into the water. Still kneeling at the edge of the lake, she tried to retrieve the dratted bowl and failed, while getting her gown wet into the bargain. How *could* she keep doing such unutterably stupid things whenever Ben was around?

Lady Harris, meanwhile, was greeting Ben warmly and explaining in great detail about the frog mission. Ben was nodding politely, but she guessed he was highly amused. Then he came over to her, crouched down beside her, rolled up his shirt sleeve and reached to pull in the bowl, giving her an awe-inspiring view of his bare forearm that was corded with muscle. She swallowed hard.

'In trouble again?' he said, rising and helping her to her feet. Then he added with a smile, 'How are you, Julia? I've missed your visits these last few days. I suppose the rain was a problem?'

Oh, no. He was being nice to her. It would have been so, so much easier if he wasn't. She had to make a huge effort to summon her normal voice. 'Of course the rain kept me mostly inside,' she said. 'I've also been rather busy. I've been helping my aunt and writing letters home, that kind of thing.'

Just at that moment Lady Harris called out, 'Julia! I must return to the house now!'

Julia was flustered again. 'Very well, Aunt. I'll join you,' she called back. 'I can do this another time.'

But Lady Harris raised her hand in a most definite gesture of refusal. 'No, you jolly well won't join me. You'll get some of those frogs for me—I'm sure Ben will help you. But I'm going home. I need to check that Twigg isn't making a hash of telling those maids of mine how to clean my precious silverware. I'll see you at the house later.'

She marched off.

Julia, hugely embarrassed, turned back to Ben. 'I know this sounds, ridiculous, but the fact is, my aunt asked me to help her collect some frogs to put in her two garden ponds. I explained we'd be trespassing, but she took no notice.'

Ben nodded, looking serious. 'She has little heed for the law, I'm afraid. Normally it doesn't matter, but as for stealing frogs from a lake—well, maybe the magistrates should be informed.'

'The magistrates? Oh, no.' Julia put one hand to her cheek. Then she gasped. 'Ben! You're teasing me, aren't you?'

He grinned. 'Of course I am. Shall I help you continue with your villainous theft? By the way,' he added, 'frogs don't eat breadcrumbs.'

She was forgiven. They were still friends. She felt such an enormous surge of relief that she couldn't stop smiling, and neither could she stop looking at his lovely strong hands as he set the bowl on its side, then managed to guide some inquisitive frogs into it.

Yes, she couldn't help but imagine his fingers warm on her bare skin, but that was quite enough of such nonsense. She ought to be practical. She ought to be sensible, for heaven's sake. She said, 'I must apologise again for causing you such anxiety the last time we met, by wandering off to that quarry.'

He leaned back a little to look straight at her. 'I should apologise, too. I overreacted.'

'Because somebody died there?'

'Yes,' he said very quietly. 'Yes. Because of that.' Suddenly he smiled and once more her heart inexplicably soared. 'Anyway, let's put all that behind us. You know, our little fox has really missed you and I see him looking for you, every afternoon.'

She laughed. 'Oh, Ben. Now you're teasing me again.'

He shook his head. 'I am not. I swear, he's been positively pining. In fact—' and he looked beyond her, then pointed '—he's already noticed you. You see?'

She could indeed see the white-spotted fox watching them from behind a tree. She clasped her hands together in delight. 'He's looking very much better. Do you still put food out for him?'

'Just a little, though soon I'll stop, because he'll be able to fend perfectly well for himself.'

Julia was quiet for a moment. Then she said slowly, 'I absolutely love it here. I do not want to go back to London.'

'No one is unkind to you there, are they?'

'No. Oh, no!' she exclaimed. 'My parents only want me to be happy! But they would not approve of all *this*. After all, just look at me. Collecting frogs for my aunt's ponds, for heaven's sake!' She tried to say it breezily.

But he was looking at her and she knew what the real problem was.

Quite disastrously, she had fallen in love.

Ben waited for her to say something else, but she didn't. Silently he bent to pick up the glass bowl in which several frogs now sat, looking comfortable but also rather puzzled. Julia was peering at them, too.

'I think they're perhaps worried,' she said, 'that this tiny world is going to be all they'll see. I wish I could explain that they will be perfectly content in their new home.'

'Just as you might find yourself happy to enter London society next spring,' Ben said quietly.

Her face fell once more and she whispered, 'If only.'

Ben's heart ached for her. 'You're quite young, you know,' he said gently. 'And a good deal can change in a few months. Most girls, I've heard, love their come-out. Surely you want to have a little fun? Enjoy a few flirtations?'

He saw her shake her head almost fiercely. 'That kind of thing is not for me! Besides, I'm no good at it, I've told you that. You've seen it for yourself!'

He felt a desperate impulse to help her. To comfort her. She was different, but she was beautiful—and someone needed to tell her so. He put his hand on her bare wrist, where the blue of her veins could be seen beneath her delicate skin, and he felt her trembling. He said, 'If I can help you to think differently, I will. And, Julia—'

He halted, because he'd seen that two fat tears were

forming in her lovely eyes. Oh, no. She was crying. 'Please,' he said. 'Julia, don't do that. Please stop.'

'I'll stop,' she promised, 'yes, of course I will.' But still the tears rolled down her cheeks. 'Oh, Ben, I'm such a fool. Only I truly love being here, with you and—and—'

She was pulling out a neatly folded little handkerchief and pressing it to her face. He touched her on the shoulder. 'You will be all right,' he urged. 'And you are not foolish. Believe me.'

But *he* was. And suddenly he couldn't bear it any longer.

This was crazy of him. This was *wrong* of him. This girl had grown to trust him and he was deceiving her badly. He had to tell her who he was—but not now. Not when she was upset and vulnerable.

Soon, though, he ordered himself. *It must be soon.*

'I'll take you back to your aunt's house,' he said quietly. Carefully he picked up the bowl of frogs.

They walked in silence down the path, but as they reached Lady Harris's extensive and rather wild gardens, he realised the lady herself was out there with her aged manservant, Sowerby. She was busy clearing a large pond of weed with a net fastened to a pole, while Sowerby's job was to untangle the soggy mass of greenery from the net each time she lifted it.

Lady Harris looked up when she saw them approach. 'You've got some frogs for me,' she said, pointing her net at them with a flourish. 'Excellent.' She put down the net and came marching forward to collect the bowl, which she lowered to the edge of the water. 'Here you go, my beauties,' she crooned, tilting the bowl on its side so several of them could clamber out.

Then she rose, peering into the bowl she still held. 'That's six of them left. Now, I've another pond up behind that clump of willow trees. Take the rest of them there, will you? And, Sowerby, you can spread all that slimy stuff on my vegetable plot. It will be excellent for the beans next spring. As for me, I'm going inside to clean myself up.'

Ben and Julia looked at each other as she marched off, then both burst into laughter. 'Oh, dear,' said Julia, as they walked to the other pond and watched the rest of the frogs crawl happily in. 'I feel this is a dreadful imposition, Ben. You don't deserve it.'

He was still smiling. 'Why?' he said.

For a moment she hesitated. Then she said, 'I fear my aunt has been thrusting me into your presence ever since I arrived. I don't know why—I really don't understand. It must be very awkward for you.'

He was shaken yet again. Awkward for him? She was so sweet. So modest. 'It's no hardship to be in your company, believe me.'

'That's just what I mean!' she exclaimed. 'Whatever I say, however foolish I am—you are just so very kind to me!'

She spoke as if he'd just offered her the best present in the world—merely by being kind to her. But then, she completely took his breath away because she stood on her tiptoes and kissed his cheek.

It was a mere butterfly touch of her sweet lips, but it stunned him. It broke down his defences against the raging desire that had been simmering inside him for days and his whole body tightened with raw male need. He stepped back from her and tried to fight it down, saying almost harshly, 'Be careful, Julia. How can you be sure that I'm trustworthy?'

The sudden change in his voice must have shaken her because he saw how those wondrous grey-green eyes widened in surprise. She said, haltingly, 'You are my friend, aren't you?'

Her friend?

Good God. This lovely girl had just kissed him and, light though the caress was, the warmth of her, the sweet scent of her was sending the blood pounding to his loins, heating him and hardening him down *there*. Didn't she realise what she was doing? Probably not. He said at last, aware that his voice was sharp with the effort to control his desire, 'Julia. I think you are very innocent, aren't you?'

A faint blush rose in her cheeks. 'I do know what happens between a man and a woman, if that's what you mean.'

'Have you ever been kissed?'

She met his gaze steadily now. 'Of course not. In London, I'm guarded night and day.'

'Yet your parents,' he almost growled, 'sent you here without a chaperon. They made a big mistake. And Lady Harris should be protecting you better.'

Now she had gone rather pale. 'My father did his best! He sent a maid with me, but she…she…'

Her voice trailed away. He said, 'What did she do?'

'Betty never stopped talking,' she replied defiantly. 'Then she sprained her wrist, so I sent her back to London.'

He wanted to laugh. He wanted to scold her. Damn,

most of all he wanted to make love to her, though it appeared that she did not regard him as a threat in the least.

He rubbed his hand across his temples, then looked again at the girl. Who was she, exactly? She was clearly from a wealthy family and she was beautiful, too, with her silk-soft dark hair and delicate features. She had also somehow worked her way past his defences and into the dangerous territory of his heart—dangerous because he was in no position to take anything further. He had sworn to clear his father's dishonoured name before he thought even remotely of settling down.

Every day, he'd been seeking new ways to discover anything more about Francis Molloy. He'd been scouring his father's bills and records, writing to friends in London and soon he knew he would have to go there himself, to follow up various leads. Maybe he should tell her this now, but not just yet, for he couldn't bear this countryside idyll to be broken.

But she must have mistaken his silence for disapproval, because she said at last, in a very quiet voice, 'Ben. Please tell me if I've done something wrong again. We are still friends, aren't we?'

His heart—yes, his damned heart again—twisted within him. Dear God. Her friend? He didn't want to be her bloody *friend*. He felt himself reaching out for her, he couldn't stop himself, because his hands weren't his to control any more and he was grasping her shoulders, pulling her towards him while her eyes, her beautiful grey-green eyes were raised to his in surprise and something else. Longing. Desire even.

So he kissed her. He held her closely, until her slender body fitted intimately against his powerful one; his arms tightened around her and he kissed her. He heard her give a faint sound of shock and he moved back, just a little, though his arms still clasped her.

He saw that her eyes were asking a thousand silent questions, so he answered in the only way he knew, by pulling her close again and letting his lips brush hers before caressing them more firmly. When he realised her mouth was beginning instinctively to open to him he let the tip of his tongue tease and lick her until her tentative but sweet response drove his body into the full madness of male desire.

Ben was losing control. Cupping the back of her head with just one hand, he used the other to clasp her tiny waist, pressing her against his hard frame until all he was conscious of was the overwhelming need to make love to her—here. *Now.*

'Julia,' he whispered. 'Dear God. Julia…'

She muttered something incoherent, then her hands were on his shoulders and she was kissing him back, driving him even wilder. When she paused for breath he let his lips trail hungrily down along her jaw to her neck, licking and nibbling, and now he could feel the exquisite softness of her small breasts as she nestled against his chest. Hell, the urge to hold those breasts in his hands was all but overwhelming…

No. No, you brute. Ben pulled away abruptly. She stood there, looking confused and uncertain.

Well, he was certain of quite a few things. She was gorgeous. She was passionate and sensual. Her parents thought she would be safe, out here in the country; her parents were very, very wrong. Doubtless she was ignorant of the very physical and very risky response she'd aroused in him, although she still had a soft glow in her eyes that told him she, too, had forgotten her self-control. This must not happen again. She did not know what she was doing and he, Ben, was badly in the wrong to take advantage.

He was aware of her gazing up at him. Her eyes looked wounded. 'That was a mistake, wasn't it?' she said quietly.

He hadn't thought so at the time. His body still didn't think so; the hardness at his loins still throbbed. But she was right. Talk about heaping fiery coals on his head. He dragged his fingers across his stubbled jaw. 'Yes,' he said. 'Yes. I'm sorry. It was.'

This girl deserved far more than what he could offer her. He was damaged, both physically by his accident and mentally by the bitterness he harboured over his father's tragic end. She deserved to have her Season, she deserved to enter London society and to realise her own true worth. He'd been a blundering fool to befriend her and a fiend for kissing her like that. The problem was that he could not bear the thought of another man taking her in his arms and making her his.

She whispered at last, 'Will I see you again?'

'Julia,' he said abruptly, 'how long are you staying here?'

'At my aunt's? Maybe for another two weeks.'

He nodded. 'Then it isn't goodbye yet.' He ground the words out. 'But now, you had better go.'

Yes, he needed her to go before he kissed her again. Before he made sweet, glorious love to her, which his whole body was aching to do.

'I'll leave,' she said. 'But please remember this. I don't care who you are, or how other people judge you. And I never will care, I swear it.'

Julia walked very slowly back to Linden House, thinking. Ben had kissed her. Really, truly kissed her. It had only lasted a few moments, but she was still reeling from it. When his mouth had caressed hers she'd felt herself trembling with wanting him. All of him. Everything.

She knew now what Pen and her friends whispered about. When Ben pulled her close, there had been that hardness pressing against the softness of her abdomen which betrayed his physical need and stirred her, too, filling her with a sweet yet almost unbearable kind of ache. She'd wanted him to touch her lips, her breasts, she'd wanted him to touch her *everywhere*, even in her most secret place.

Of course he'd had the sense to end it quickly. She knew she ought to be burning with embarrassment because she'd kissed him first, so it was her fault. Her shame, because he'd had to almost push her away. Well, that gave her something else to add to her list of ways to put men off.

Make yourself appear far too eager for their attentions—even to the point of kissing them first.

The trouble was, she didn't care. Yes, he was a stonemason, but she didn't care about that either, because his kiss had made her feel so warm and wonderful that if he'd asked her to, she would have agreed to run away with him tomorrow and live anywhere.

As if he would ever do such a thing. She shook her head and tried to smile instead of crying.

You fool, Julia. You fool.

When she reached Linden House her aunt was dozing in the sitting room with *Gulliver's Travels* in her lap, but she sat up with a start when Julia came in.

'Well?' she said. 'Did the two of you get those frogs nicely settled?'

Julia nodded. 'They seem very happy.' She sat down in another chair.

Take deep breaths. Calm yourself.

'Aunt,' she said, 'I asked you soon after I arrived about Lord Lambourne. But I hadn't realised that the former Lord had died and there's now a new heir. Do you know anything about him?'

For a moment her aunt went very still. But then she waved her hand in the air and said, 'You know me, Julia. Titles and all that are nothing but nonsensical privilege. I'm quite the revolutionary, you know.'

Just at that moment Miss Twigg entered with the tea tray, which she set down on a table at Lady Harris's side. Julia could have sworn she winked at her before departing once more.

'But, Aunt,' said Julia, once the door had closed again. 'My father is an aristocrat and you always appear very fond of him.'

'Well, yes! That's partly because he's family and also because your father is a decent man.'

'What about the new Lord Lambourne, though?'

Julia persisted. 'Have you heard if he is what you would call a decent man?'

Lady Harris had reached for the teapot and was lifting the lid to poke at the contents with her spoon. 'I believe he travels often, which means he spends hardly any time here.' She gave an exclamation of disgust. 'Twigg has made this tea far too weak. We need a fresh pot and I will tell the woman so.'

She rose and went towards the bell pull, but as she did so she happened to glance out of the window and stopped abruptly. 'Bless me,' she cried, 'if I don't spy those wretched boys with their pigs again, up in my woods and after my acorns! Come along, Julia! Let's be after them!' Within moments she was at the front door, where she grabbed her purple cloak and was off.

Julia managed to keep up with her, but of course by the time they arrived the boys were already scurrying away, laughing. Once again, she'd got nowhere with her questions, but Lady Harris wasn't telling her everything, of that she was quite sure.

That evening she made her way to the library at the back of the house, for she'd remembered that in there she had spotted a volume called *Notable Families of Somerset*.

Laying it on the table and pulling up a chair, she sat and searched the book's index—where under the letter *L* she found 'Lambourne'.

Among the most distinguished landowners of our region are the Barons of Lambourne Hall, who can date their ancestry back to the time of King

Charles II. They have played a prominent part in Lambourne's history and in London society also. The Fourth Baron, Robert, born in 1767, has emulated his ancestors in his duty to the responsibilities of the title. In addition, he keeps a stable of fine horses. His wife, Lady Sophia Lambourne, is a younger daughter of the Viscount Huntingdon. There are no children as yet...

No children. Julia looked swiftly for the date the book was published—it was 1789. So the book was printed almost thirty years ago and of course there would be nothing about the heir who'd recently inherited the title. She went slowly up to her room and looked again at the letter she'd received this morning from Pen.

How is your handsome stonemason? I do hope, darling Julia, that you are not getting yourself into trouble.

Oh, but she was. Deep, deep trouble. She settled at her little desk and tried to write back, but she struggled to say a word. She was thinking, *I kissed him. He kissed me and it was wonderful.* And how could she possibly write *that*?

Ben had returned to Lambourne Hall, knowing what he ought to do. He could not go on lying to Julia like this, so he should go to her tomorrow and tell her exactly who he was, together with the problems he faced ahead. Soon, within weeks maybe, he would be re-entering London society, where they were bound to meet. So wasn't it the right, the only thing to do?

Gilly met him at the door; he must have been watching for him, which was unusual. But Gilly was blunt, as always. He put his hands on his hips and said without preamble, 'I guess you've been seeing that girl again?'

'Yes.' Ben walked into the kitchen with Gilly close behind and poured himself some ale. 'Don't read me the riot act, Gilly. I mean Julia no harm.' He sat on a wooden chair and began pulling off his boots.

Gilly, however, wouldn't be deterred. 'My lord,' Gilly said.

Ben looked up sharply. His valet didn't often use that tone.

'There's something you ought to know,' went on Gilly. He folded his arms. 'I think you should be calling this new friend of yours *Lady* Julia.'

Ben sat very still, with one boot off, the other half on. He said, 'Lady Julia?'

'That is correct. My lord—she is the Earl of Carstairs's daughter.'

Ben thought that if the world could spin and change utterly, this was what it would feel like. He stared at Gilly in disbelief. 'If this is a joke, I must tell you that I'm not finding it amusing in the least.'

Gilly shook his head. 'It's true, I'm afraid. I learned it when I went to the village this morning for your post.'

Ben closed his eyes. His leg was hurting again, really hurting. *Damn.* The terrible row over the horse. The slur on his father's integrity that had ruined his father's final years.

The man responsible for that was none other than Julia's father.

Gilly said quietly, 'Brandy, my lord?'

'Yes.' Ben grated the words out. 'A large one.'

Gilly brought the drink, then picked up Ben's boots from the floor. 'I'll take these outside and give them a clean,' he said. It was an action performed, Ben guessed, to give him time to absorb exactly what Gilly had just said.

Ben knew that the Earl of Carstairs and his father had been friends, meeting often at the races in Brighton and Newmarket. Yes, friends—until around a year and a half ago, the Earl had made an offer for a promising young gelding that was the pride of the Lambourne stables: Silver Cloud.

The rest was a story that Ben had gone over and over in his mind. When Ben had visited his father for the very last time here at Lambourne, his father had told him everything. He'd told him how the valuable gelding, on delivery to the Earl, was inspected by the Earl's veterinary surgeon and was found to have a twisted tendon and could never race. The animal had been like that, the vet said, from birth.

Ben's father could not understand it, for he'd had the animal thoroughly inspected before it left his stables. He felt he'd been unendurably maligned and after despairing of ever proving his innocence, he'd sold nearly all of his horses and started to neglect the Hall badly. The quarry fall in which he died was pronounced by the justices as an accident, but Ben believed it was an act of utter despair. His father had quite simply lost the will to live.

Ben knew that life could be cruel, but this news about Julia's father was something he could never have imagined. It seemed that Julia was ignorant of the bitter rift, but if Ben showed his face to her family, she would learn about it swiftly enough.

Did Lady Harris know of the feud? She was no fool and surely she'd heard about it. Perhaps that was why she hadn't told Julia who Ben was—she wanted to keep from her the fact that their fathers had been enemies. But Julia would find out some time soon and it would be all the worse.

Gilly had come back into the kitchen and was silently placing a platter of sliced ham and bread on the table, but Ben didn't want food. He wanted Julia. He felt as if she had brought light into his life with her innocent trust in him. They'd shared their love of the countryside, they'd shared tender moments, then there had been that kiss—that wonderful kiss that made him ache for so much more.

But to fantasise about any kind of future together was impossible, because Julia's father was involved in destroying his own father's life.

Gilly was eyeing him in that way of his. 'I get the feeling I've given you bad news about your new friend.'

'Yes. You have.' No more. He couldn't say another word.

Gilly gave a sympathetic grunt but added, 'Then it's as well you found out sooner rather than later, isn't it? Best eat up your supper, my lord. Going without food will mend nothing. By the way, there's a letter for you.'

Ben opened it to find that it was from a friend of his, in London.

You wrote asking me about a man called Molloy, who had a finger in many aspects of the world of horses. I've found no trace of his whereabouts, but I do believe that Tattersall's may have records of the man.

Ben drew a deep breath. Of course. Tattersall's auction house close by Hyde Park was known not only for its sales of fine horses, but as a fount of information regarding every consequence of those sales: contract negotiations, funding, even the transport of valuable thoroughbreds all around England.

This, then, was the next stage of his quest. He would go to London in search of Francis Molloy—and he had to tell Julia he was leaving.

Chapter Eleven

As Julia walked up to the pavilion the next day, she clutched the note she'd received that morning from Ben.

Please come. We need to talk properly.

He must have called at the house very early to push it under the door. He'd sealed it, then written her name on the outside—*Julia*—and Miss Twigg had handed it to her without a word.

She felt sick with apprehension. For days, she'd been telling herself that she and Ben were just friends, until that kiss yesterday. But from the curtness of his note, it seemed they were not even friends now.

She could see him up by the pavilion, carefully smoothing in fresh mortar between the stones where it had crumbled away. He must have heard her footsteps because he turned to face her, but there was no lovely warm smile for her. Instead he said, 'You got my note, then?'

Julia nodded. She lifted her head almost proudly. 'I can guess what you want to say. You don't want me here. Do you?'

She saw his hesitation and, oh, that was hard to bear, for she wanted him to hold her as he had yesterday, with his eyes full of desire. She wanted him to kiss her again; yes, even now she felt the longing unfurl deep inside her. She'd never thought she could feel like that about any man, ever. Yet now her stonemason, who'd awakened her heart in a way she'd not thought possible, was saying wearily, 'I'm sorry. But it's just not appropriate that we meet like this—Lady Julia.'

She felt his words fall on her like hammer blows. Shakily she took a step back. 'You've heard, then? That I'm an earl's daughter?'

'I have. Oh, Julia. Why didn't you *tell* me?'

She tried to lift her chin defiantly. 'Does it matter?'

'Yes.' He'd put down his pail of mortar and seemed to speak with a great effort. 'Of course it matters and you and I should not have been meeting like this anyway. I blame myself for that, very much.' He was silent a moment. Then he added quietly, 'All the same, I wish you'd explained to me from the beginning who you were.'

Julia felt a great lump rising in her throat. She realised she'd crumpled his curt note into a tight ball in her hand.

I want you, Ben, she said silently to herself. *Only you.*

'Can we pretend,' she whispered. 'just for a day or two more, that I'm not an earl's daughter?'

She saw Ben bracing himself. He said, 'I've told you, it's not possible. Besides, I have to go to London now, for several days. So it seems an appropriate time to say goodbye.'

This was the end. He was telling her she would not see him again. Of course, he was right. But she had been so happy during her days here with him and she'd thought he'd been happy, too; she'd even thought that perhaps he was beginning to care for her. One by one she tried to think of all the arguments she could present, all the words she could say, but it was like preparing to fight a battle that she had already lost.

She said, in rather a choked voice, 'May I stay just for a while? I could maybe do some more painting.'

He sighed. 'If you wish. But really, Julia…'

'It's all right,' she said. She smiled, even though she was fighting back the tears. 'I'll just finish what I was doing yesterday and then I'll be on my way.'

Damn. *Damn*, thought Ben. Julia looked utterly forlorn, but it really, really was no good. He remembered again the letter that the Earl, her father, had sent to his father.

> *I am not a vindictive person, Lord Lambourne. I will not take the matter to the courts. But this was an act of fraud, not worthy of a man of your rank, and if the world gets to hear of this affair, then so be it.*

It was likely that the Earl's bitterness over the affair would poison any hope of reconciliation, even if Ben succeeded in proving his father's innocence. He watched, riven with conflicting emotions, as Julia went into the pavilion to collect her paints, then came out again to mix them in the sunlight. She loved her family dearly. He could not force her to choose between them and him.

Suddenly she lifted her head and said, 'I've heard that your employer, Lord Lambourne, is unmarried. Is he looking for a wife, do you think?'

He said, *'What?'*

She began again. 'You must know him a little, through your work here. I was just wondering—do you think that maybe he wants a wife?'

He was astounded. He said curtly, 'Doubtless he'll marry some day. It's the duty of all aristocrats, after all. Why are you interested in him all of a sudden?'

'Because I've been thinking. I've told you that soon I'll be thrust into my London Season and, as you say, I must resign myself to it. I will have a large dowry when I marry so men are never going to leave me alone. So perhaps I should get the business over with.'

He was stunned. 'What business? What are you talking about?'

'Why, getting married, of course.'

He could hardly speak. 'But who to?'

'I'm trying to suggest,' she said, tossing her head a little, 'that maybe I could marry your employer. Lord Lambourne.'

Hell. That nearly floored him and it must have shown, because she looked even more defiant. 'You'll think I'm ridiculous. People often do. I suppose there's some problem, is there? Perhaps you've heard that he has a mistress to whom he is utterly devoted?'

'Julia! I mean, *Lady* Julia…'

She held up her hand to silence him. 'All right. I realise you think I shouldn't understand about men's mistresses, let alone talk about them, but you see, I wouldn't care if he did have a mistress. In fact, I would be very glad, because I don't think I would like that side of marriage at all, I don't think I would be any earthly good at it—' She broke off. 'Ben! What *is* it?'

He was trying to point, subtly, at the bodice of her dress. He'd realised that she must have fastened the buttons up wrongly when she put it on and some of them had come undone, revealing the delicate swell of her bosom.

As she glanced downwards her expression changed to one of absolute horror. 'Oh, no. My buttons. I am utterly mortified!' Desperately she tried to fasten them, but her fingers fumbled and her cheeks were turning a fiery red. 'I really think I must go—'

He grabbed her as she turned. 'Julia. Lady Julia. Stop.'

She did. She was gazing up at him, her eyes wide and wounded. He should have released his grip instantly but he didn't, because something had robbed him of his willpower. As the low autumn sun lit her face with touches of gold, he had to fight the longing to pull her into his arms, wind his fingers through her long dark hair and kiss her senseless.

He thought, *This intelligent, unusual girl sees herself as an outcast. What has society done to her, to let her think that her only way to lead a fulfilled life is to sacrifice herself to marriage with a man she's never met?*

And what kind of a man was he, not to have told her straight away that *he* was Lord Lambourne? Why didn't he tell her *now*?

Because any action on his part was far too late. For

her father had been his own father's worst enemy, that was why.

She was young and very innocent. She needed to return to her family, who would surely help her to enjoy her Season and give her a fair choice in who she could marry. Plenty of men would find her as irresistible as he did, God help him. When he finally re-entered London society and saw her surrounded by suitors, he would feel like punching them—but bear it he must. For her sake. Her happiness.

He let her go at last. She said in a low voice, 'You think I'm foolish. Don't you?'

Ben was appalled for her. 'You're not—' He stopped, gathered himself, then carried on. 'Julia. Let me assure you that you deserve every kind of happiness.'

There was a long silence. Then she looked around and said, 'I could be happy here. I suppose that's why I had my stupid idea of marrying Lord Lambourne. At least I would have his gardens and this countryside to enjoy and, from what you say, he would probably be away most of the time. A marriage of convenience, that's all I'd be after. Whoever I marry, I shall be an extremely tolerant wife and I shall be very happy if my husband spends time in London with his friends.'

He burned with frustration of all kinds. 'I do not understand why you expect so little for yourself. Don't you think you deserve a man who respects you? A man who loves you?'

She lifted her head proudly. 'Oh, no doubt I'll attract a good number of offers. As I said, my dowry, I believe, is substantial.'

He exploded. 'For God's sake, Julia! London's bachelors won't just be after you for your money. You're beautiful, don't you realise? Many men will desire you!'

She met his gaze steadily. 'But not you. I'm right, aren't I?'

What could he say? Some day he hoped she might understand, but at the moment he could say absolutely nothing, because he had to distance himself; he had to push her away, before he was tempted beyond endurance to kiss her again.

'Julia,' he said at last. 'There are many reasons why we cannot be together.'

'Then I'll spare you the trouble of having to think up any more of them,' she said softly.

'Julia. Listen—'

'Goodbye, Ben.'

He watched her as she set off down the path without a backward glance.

'You're exceptionally silent tonight, Julia,' said Lady Harris.

They were playing chess again in the drawing room and Julia forced a smile. 'Am I? I'm sorry, Aunt.'

'No need to apologise. Thinking about your family, are you? They'll be missing you.'

'Yes,' she said. 'I must write to them again soon.'

But she wasn't thinking about her family. She was thinking about Ben's warm brown eyes and the way his mouth curled up a little at one end when he was trying his best not to smile at something she'd said. She was remembering the way he'd kissed her, only yesterday…

'Julia! Are you daydreaming, girl?'

She realised her aunt had just taken her bishop. 'I

wasn't concentrating,' she said quickly. 'How foolish of me.'

She was trying to force Ben from her mind, for she guessed she would never see him again. He must always have known she was wealthy, but the discovery that she was an earl's daughter had shocked him badly. He'd been so very angry, too, when she suggested she might set her cap at Lord Lambourne. She knew it was stupid, of course she did, but she'd half done it to provoke him into...what? Another kiss?

Thus, you stupid creature, prolonging your misery.

'Julia!' chided her aunt. 'Don't you realise I'm about to capture your king? What's wrong with you, girl?'

'I'm sorry, Aunt.' She smiled. 'I congratulate you on your victory.' But she was still miles away. She was in love, she realised, and how it hurt.

Oh, Ben, she thought silently. *I wish I was just a serving maid or a farmer's daughter. You wouldn't turn me away then, would you?*

For the next two days Julia was kept busy helping her aunt and Miss Twigg to make jams and chutneys with the autumn harvest. But when she put a ladleful of flour instead of sugar into a pan of apples, her aunt said, 'For heaven's sake, girl. Your heart's not in this, is it? Why don't you go off into my library and find yourself something to read?'

So Julia headed once more to the library and went inevitably to the book called *Notable Families of Somerset*. She turned the pages until she reached the chapter about the Lambourne family and realised that there was also a section describing the Hall.

Lambourne Hall is a fine example of late Stuart architecture and the gardens were designed by a follower of Capability Brown. Everywhere, even in the gardens, the family crest of a phoenix rising from the flames can be found.

She frowned. She'd seen the phoenix carved into the lintel above the pavilion door, but she'd also seen it somewhere else, on something she couldn't quite remember...

Yes, she could. It was on the tool box Ben used. The box's mahogany lid had a bronze panel on which the phoenix symbol was etched. She put the book down, pondering. Of course, the tool box would belong to the Hall, so it was natural that Ben would use it while he worked here.

Suddenly she rose and put the book firmly back in its place. Whatever happened at Lambourne was none of her business. Soon she would be going home, where she would do what was expected of her. She would brace herself for her Season and maybe soon she would be planning her wedding, just like Pen.

But she guessed she would never meet anyone like Ben. Never.

Chapter Twelve

Ben had begun his journey to London the very next day. Gilly drove him to Cheltenham in the light chaise stored in the Hall's coach house and from Cheltenham Ben travelled by mail coach, stopping twice overnight at posting inns. On reaching London, he hired a cab to take him to the Pulteney Hotel in Piccadilly, where he gave his name as Ben Smith.

The family did have a town house in Clarges Street, but his father had let it out several years ago and the family lawyer, Thomas Rudby, managed the tenancy. Ben found himself comfortable enough at the Pulteney, where the staff were discreet and his bedchamber luxurious. Indeed, often in the past when he'd returned briefly to England from Vienna, he'd chosen to stay at the Pulteney instead of making the journey to visit his father.

He remembered with bitter regret how his father never complained about his son's rare visits, but on the occasions when Ben did make it to Lambourne Hall he would welcome him warmly. 'You're busy, Ben. Enjoy yourself. I'm fine.'

Always, he said that. Always.

That evening Ben knew he could have gone to dine at his club, where there would be old friends to meet. Instead he ate alone at the hotel, thinking of three people: his father, the Earl of Carstairs and Francis Molloy.

The next morning he went to Tattersall's sale yard at Hyde Park Corner, where there were daily auctions of fine horses. As ever, the place was crowded and the familiar scents of horses and hay brought back powerful memories for Ben of his father's stables at Lambourne, where the grooms had once cared for all his fine animals.

He straightened his coat and entered the office, where he approached a clerk. 'I'm looking for a man called Francis Molloy,' he said. 'He used to transport valuable horses around the country. I think you sometimes recommended him to your clients?'

'Just a moment, sir.' The clerk went over to a large register and brought it to the desk, but after a few moments of scrutinising the pages he looked up, frowning slightly. 'It appears, sir, that Francis Molloy is no longer on our list of recommendations.'

Ben snapped to attention. 'Why?'

The clerk hesitated. 'There were certain doubts raised about him. Nothing was proved, you understand. But we decided we no longer wished to be associated with Mr Molloy.'

'An address,' Ben said. 'Have you his address?'

'Sir, we are not allowed—'

At that moment a man in expensive clothes bustled through the door and spoke loudly to the clerk. 'Hey.

You there. I need to speak to someone about a horse. Am I going to be kept waiting for ever?'

Ben said to the clerk, 'You'd better see to him.'

The clerk followed the man out of the room, but the register still lay open and by the time the clerk returned to his desk Ben had memorised Molloy's address and departed.

Fernley's Lodgings, Goslett Yard. Ben vaguely knew the name, knew also that Goslett Yard was in St Giles, one of the roughest areas in town. He hired a cab outside Tattersall's and paid off the driver in Soho Square, then walked onwards, noting that though it was still daylight the sun was blocked out by high tenement buildings. Ragged children played in the street and outside a nearby drinking house, several men with ale mugs in their hands watched him with narrowed eyes.

A faded sign hung above a door: *Fernley's Lodgings*. He rapped until the door was opened by a woman in a patched dress and shawl.

'I'm looking for Francis Molloy,' Ben said. 'Can you tell me if he lives here?'

She looked him up and down. 'He left last winter without paying his debts. Are you going to pay them for him?'

'I wasn't—'

She slammed the door in his face.

He looked around, realising that those men outside the drinking house were still watching him. He walked up to them. 'Do any of you know a man called Francis Molloy?'

They looked first at each other, then at him, saying nothing. But just as he was turning to go, one of them spoke up. 'Listen, mister. We don't like strangers asking questions and usually we deal with them in our own way. But we reckon you're either brave or mad, nosing around these streets when you've a crocked leg. So as long as you leave sharpish, we'll not harm you.'

Ben met the man's gaze steadily. 'I believe Molloy may have wronged my father,' he said.

The man laughed. 'For God's sake, most of us here don't even know who our damned father is. Now, we'll give you five minutes to get out of here—no, make that ten, since you hobble so.'

Ben walked on to Soho Square. He felt sure those people knew Molloy, but where was the man now? He hailed a cab to take him to the office of his lawyer, Rudby, who ushered him to a chair with a broad smile on his face.

'My lord! I was about to write to you. I have excellent news about your London house. The long-term tenant was a problem to us with payments, but we've taken action on your behalf and he is finally leaving. From next week, you can take up occupation of it whenever you wish.' Rudby rooted among the papers on his desk. 'I fear the interior might be somewhat neglected, but I'm delighted to say I've made considerable progress in recovering further sums of money for you.'

Ben frowned. 'How?'

'I believe I warned you that your father was rather remiss in his handling of his affairs. However, I've now discovered large sums owed to him by various people and I've already retrieved many of these debts. Here you are.' He passed some financial documents across to Ben. 'Believe me, my lord, there will soon be enough money in the estate for you to fully refurbish both your town house and Lambourne Hall! Let me explain some of the figures to you...'

Ben was there for over two hours. He was rich, he realised. He had wealth which, together with his title, gave him the status to live among the elite.

He dined that night at one of his clubs and would have been content to remain alone, but some old friends spotted him and eagerly invited him to join them. They sympathised over both his bereavement and his injury, but soon enough the invitations were pouring in, to parties in London and to house gatherings in the country. He resisted them all, telling his friends he had much to do yet to sort out his affairs. But he didn't tell a single one of them that his overriding mission was to clear his father's name.

The next morning he visited his bank, then in the afternoon Rudby came with him to inspect the Lambourne town house in Clarges Street.

'As I said, some rooms need repair and renovation, my lord,' said the lawyer apologetically. 'But it really could be very fine.'

Ben nodded, gazing around the spacious drawing room in which they stood. 'I have to go to Somerset first,' he said. 'But after that I'll be back here to make plans. No doubt I'll be hiring builders, decorators, whomever I need.'

They returned to Rudby's office to finalise some paperwork, but the lawyer hadn't quite finished with him yet. 'There is something else, my lord. We hold various documents for your father, as you know. But I've found an old file relating to your father's purchases and sales of horses. Would you like to see it?'

Ben looked through the papers swiftly. There did indeed appear to be details of buyers and sellers for the last twenty years or more, but he guessed there was nothing he'd not already found at Lambourne Hall. He replaced the papers in the file. 'I'll take it with me,' he said, 'back to Somerset, to add to the records in my father's study. But, Rudby, there is something else. See if you can find out for me, will you, where a man called Francis Molloy might be living? He was a well-known transporter of fine horses, but he was struck off Tattersall's lists a while ago and appears to have vanished.'

Rudby nodded. 'I'll do my very best, my lord.'

Ben spent one more night in London, catching up with old friends and their news. But the following day he rose early, for he had decided it was time to return home.

He reached Lambourne Hall at around three, after two days of travelling. Gilly served him a cold meal, then Ben decided to walk through the beech woods to the pavilion, just as his father always did whenever he had been away. Even during his brief absence, the days appeared to have grown shorter and there was a chill in the air. More of the trees had lost their leaves and already the distant horizon was streaked with pink.

As he approached the pavilion he saw that a family of squirrels were scurrying around after beech nuts. So absorbed was he in watching them that he didn't notice until he was almost there that the pavilion's windows flickered with light.

Slowly he drew closer, but he somehow knew exactly what to expect. Julia was in there.

The doorway was wide open so he could see that she was working with absolute precision on the wall stencils, using her brush to dab paint on to the wall plaster. She wore an apron that was far too big for her over her gown and every so often she stepped back to assess her progress. It hit him like a hammer blow that she looked unbelievably lovely in that ridiculous apron with her long hair falling, as usual, out of its ribbon.

He steadied himself and went inside. 'Julia,' he said. 'Julia, what are you doing?' It was an utterly foolish question, of course, when he could see the answer for himself.

'Ben!' She whipped round, almost dropping her brush and stencil. 'I—I started working up here again on the day after you left.' He saw her hesitate. 'I suppose I just wanted to do something to thank you for your kindness to me while I've been here.' She put down her things and added anxiously, 'You don't mind, do you?'

She was glancing back at her work, hesitant, vulnerable. Briefly Ben closed his eyes. He had money enough now to have this pavilion rebuilt and fully decorated by the finest craftsmen in the country, but the thought gave him no pleasure.

She was the daughter of the man who had accused his father of fraud. Oh, God, he wanted her, but it could never, ever work. He said, fighting back the longing to take her in his arms and kiss her senseless, 'How could I mind? But you must have been working on this for days.'

She nodded. 'Ever since you left! Though I came up here only for an hour this afternoon and soon I must go. The problem is, you see, that my aunt is unwell.'

'Your aunt? What is wrong with her?'

'I truly don't know. She tells me not to fuss; in fact, she practically ordered me to come up here and, of course, she has Miss Twigg with her. But she is just not herself, though she refuses to let me send for the doctor from the village. She is hardly eating and she seems tired all the time.'

Ben, trying to lighten her mood, said, 'Whatever it is that bothers her, I guess she won't be ailing for long. She'll soon be after those boys and their pigs again.'

'True,' she said, allowing a brief smile to illuminate her face. But she still looked anxious.

'You're worried, aren't you, Julia?'

'Yes,' she admitted. 'Yes, I am.'

'Then I shall come and see her. Right now, if you like.'

'But you must have only just returned from London!'

'That's no problem,' he said. 'Let's go.'

Julia had made one resolution after another while Ben had been away. She'd vowed not to bother him in any way again and she knew that now she should tell him it was none of his business if her aunt was ill.

But she couldn't. She didn't even try. He waited while she removed her apron and pulled on her jacket, then they walked down together to Linden House. By the time they got there it was dark and beginning to rain—and her aunt was worse, Julia realised. Much worse. Julia had left her sitting in a comfortable armchair by the fire in her bedchamber, but now she was lying on her bed with her eyes half-closed while Miss Twigg hovered anxiously nearby.

Julia hurried to her aunt's side. 'Aunt, I've brought Ben. He has come to see how you are. Can I do anything at all for you? Would you like a drink of your honey and chamomile tea, perhaps?'

'Stuff and nonsense,' muttered her aunt, 'all this fussing. And why have you brought young fellow-my-lad here? I thought he was in London. Do you think I want *him* seeing me like this?'

But when Ben drew closer and took her hand in his, Lady Harris let him. She trusted him, Julia realised. She, like Julia, was glad he was here.

'Lady Harris,' Ben said. 'I can see you're being as stubborn as a mule, as ever. You appear to have a raging temperature and you're driving poor Julia and Miss Twigg mad with worry. I am fetching a doctor from the village right now.'

Julia drew him aside to murmur, 'I believe the only physician there is Dr Barnes. My aunt says he'll never move from his fireside after sunset. It's almost dark now.'

'I'll manage something,' Ben said. 'Miss Twigg, would you find Sowerby and ask him to saddle up Lady Harris's horse?'

As Miss Twigg hurried off he said to Julia, 'I'll be back very soon. Keep Lady Harris warm and try to get her to drink something, will you? Even if it's only a little tea.'

'Oh, Ben…' Julia's voice broke a little. 'I should never have left her, even for a minute!'

'Nonsense.' He touched her cheek lightly. 'You came to the pavilion and you met me, remember? Which is fortunate, because I'm going to help.'

Julia went to the front door to watch him ride off into the darkness. She hadn't expected him for days. She'd even guessed that she herself might have been summoned back to London by the time he returned. But when he'd arrived at the pavilion, her heart had been filled with both relief and despair. *I love him*, she'd realised. She could not bear to think of life without him—and that was disastrous.

She went slowly back upstairs, where Lady Harris, that indomitable source of humour and energy, was looking more and more frail while Miss Twigg did nothing but fuss and fret. Julia asked her to make some chamomile tea.

But while Miss Twigg was down in the kitchen, Lady Harris began to grow restless and started muttering to herself. *'I should have done something about the two of them sooner. Yes, much sooner...'*

Julia took her hand. 'Dear Aunt, whatever are you talking about?'

Lady Harris opened her eyes, suddenly alert. 'Me, talking? Nonsense, I've been asleep.'

'But you said—'

'Must be all this being treated like an invalid. It makes me thoroughly confused.' She tried to haul herself up. 'There's a great deal to do. Remind Twigg to keep a lookout for those dratted pig boys, will you? She always forgets!'

Julia shook her head. 'It's dark outside, Aunt, and

starting to rain. They won't be coming to your woods at this hour.'

'Rubbish. They're bound to come if they know I'm confined to my bed in this ridiculous way.' She sighed and lay back against her pillows. 'Where's that fellow Ben? I could have sworn he was here a minute ago.'

'He was, Aunt. But he's gone for the doctor.'

'Hmm. Interfering, is he? I cannot bear people interfering!' But her aunt seemed soothed, because soon she was sleeping again.

Julia went downstairs to listen anxiously for the sound of Ben returning.

When she heard hooves clattering in the courtyard, she ran to open the front door and saw that Ben had a companion with him, also on horseback. Sowerby had already come to hold both horses' reins.

'This is Dr Barnes,' Ben said as the two men dismounted.

'Thank you,' Julia said. 'Doctor, my aunt—'

'It's all right, Julia,' Ben told her as he led the way in. 'I've explained everything.'

'I'll go up and see her now,' said Dr Barnes. He was taking off his riding coat, which was soaked with the rain. 'Then hopefully I can prescribe a course of treatment.'

Miss Twigg had come to join them and he gave her a nod of recognition. 'Miss Twigg, come with me, will you?' He added cautiously, 'Just in case Lady Harris is a little awkward, as I confess I've found in the past.'

They went upstairs and Ben smiled at Julia. 'There,' he said softly. 'You can relax a little now.'

Her heart shook. His smile always did that to her—always. She was such a fool. 'Tea,' she muttered. 'I shall make you some tea.'

Just for a moment Ben rested his hands on her shoulders. 'Julia. Listen to me. Your aunt is going to be all right. Do you understand?'

She nodded. But what about *her*?

Ben took off his damp coat, then followed Julia into the kitchen and watched her busying herself over the tea things. He had to smile to himself again. As an earl's daughter, she surely wasn't used to such mundane tasks and when she struggled to open the tea caddy, he tactfully took over. 'Allow me,' he said. 'In fact, let me do it all, will you? I hardly suppose you've made many pots of tea in your life. And don't worry too much about your aunt. Doctor Barnes is a good man and he'll be used to dealing with her.'

He realised his mistake immediately, even before she said, 'Ben. How do you know so much about the doctor and my aunt?'

He cursed himself silently. 'Oh, one learns things.' He spoke in what he hoped was a reassuring tone. 'Your aunt is, after all, a well-known character around here. As for Dr Barnes, I've heard from several sources that he's very kind. He'll probably tell her she's been overdoing her home-made remedies.'

In fact, Ben had known the doctor for many years and when Ben had explained as they rode here that for the time being he wanted his identity kept a secret from Lady Harris's guest, the doctor had agreed, though he'd added, 'I trust you have sound motives, my lord?'

'I do,' said Ben. 'Believe me, it's for the best.'

Now Ben saw a hint of a smile on Julia's face at the mention of her aunt's unusual remedies, though it quickly faded. 'Sometimes,' she said, 'I worry it's because of me being here that she's ill. She's been doing far too much lately.'

He shook his head. 'She always does too much—just ask Miss Twigg. As for it being your fault that she's ill, that's nonsense. She's very fortunate to have you here with her, though you're looking tired yourself. Sit down, will you?'

He pointed to one of the chairs at the kitchen table and she slowly sat. Suddenly she blurted out, 'She's lucky—*I'm* lucky—that you arrived back today. Did you manage to do everything you needed to do in London?'

'Yes.' He sat also. 'I had a few business matters to attend to, that was all.'

She suddenly rose again, walked to the window, then turned round. 'You're not going to tell me any more, are you? Ben, I know nothing about you. Your family, your childhood—you've told me so little and there are too many things I don't understand!'

He tried to appear calm. 'Such as?'

She sat down once more and briefly put her hand to her forehead. 'You are living—actually *living*—in Lambourne Hall. You're employed in physical work, which seems utterly wrong when you're hampered by your injured leg. I'm sorry, but it's true! You ride to fetch a doctor who is notorious for not coming out after dark, yet he comes, immediately. Who exactly are you, Ben? Why haven't you told me more about yourself?'

'Perhaps because the details of my life are not important,' he said quietly. 'Certainly not to you. Your life lies in London, with your family. You're only here for a very short while, after all.'

He saw her shake her head. 'I've realised from the start that you're eager for me to return and face my fate. But I hate the thought of what lies in store for me.'

'Julia.' He leaned forward. 'You deserve a wonderful time in London. You will positively shine among the other girls when you are presented at court—and you are bound to obtain vouchers for Almack's without any problem whatsoever!'

She stared at him. She looked disturbed almost. At last she said, 'So you are an expert on the Season, are you?'

Hell. He'd made yet another blunder. He said lightly, 'Oh, everyone knows that only the most privileged young women are admitted to Almack's. I've travelled, you see. I hear things. Perhaps I'm only trying to tell you I'd guess you are as pretty as anyone else who will have their come-out soon.'

Far prettier, he thought. Adorably so.

She still frowned a little. 'Oh, flattery is wasted on me,' she said dismissively. 'Anyway, I've decided to stay here until I'm quite sure that my aunt has recovered. But after that, I shall go home.'

Ben nodded. 'An excellent idea.' She deserved the life and the opportunities she'd been raised to expect. She would surely find a decent man to marry.

And whoever that man was, Ben felt like punching him.

Just then the doctor came down. 'I'm afraid I'm unable to identify her exact ailment,' he said. 'But I'll give you some powders for her.' He was reaching into his bag for a packet which he handed to Julia. 'Hopefully they'll soothe her and, of course, I'll call again tomorrow morning. I gather you're here for a little while yet?'

'Yes,' she said. 'Of course. I will be here for as long as my aunt needs me.'

Doctor Barnes turned next to Ben. 'By the way, Mr Smith, Her Ladyship was most insistent that she wanted a word with you.'

Ben nodded and headed for the stairs. Lady Harris appeared to be sleeping, but as he entered she shifted a little on her pillows and murmured weakly, 'Ben. I'm very glad you're here, you rascal.'

She reached out for his hand, which he gave to her. 'You,' she said, 'remind me of your father, do you know that?' She was watching him intently now. 'He missed his wife dreadfully, but he found great consolation in you.'

The guilt that always lurked returned with full force. 'Even though I was hardly ever here?' he said.

'Young man, he wouldn't have wanted you to be here! He wanted you to see the world, which you did—and he was immensely proud of you!'

He pressed her hand, finding that for a moment he couldn't speak. Then he said lightly, 'I believe you were always a good friend to my father. But why are you calling me a rascal?'

'Because the girl… The girl…' Her voice faded. She licked her dry lips and Ben, quickly reaching for a glass of cordial nearby, offered it to her. She swallowed most of it, pulled a face then leaned back against her pillows. 'The girl has fallen for you,' she whispered at last. 'Can't you see, you fool, that the two of you were made for each other?'

He drew a deep breath and sat down on the chair beside her bed. 'Lady Harris,' he said at last. 'You've been pushing us together from the start. Haven't you?'

She thrust the near-empty cup back into his hands. 'Well, of course I have!' She was almost her old brusque self. 'You have to marry some time, surely, and the match is obviously ideal.'

'You talk of my *marriage*? I've only been back in England for two months! My leg is a wreck and the estate requires a good deal of work. Obviously Julia is charming, but really, we barely know each other and her father and mine were enemies. Julia would have nothing to do with me if she knew about it.' Ben looked at her sharply. 'You've not spoken to her, have you? About who I am?'

'Of course not. But do you think she would actually care?' She tried to heave herself up a little. 'The girl has missed you dreadfully while you were away.'

'I'm sorry to hear it. But she loves her family very much—I'm sure of that. You know all about the feud— the anger her father felt towards mine, the accusations he made. I cannot forget any of it easily. And how do you think Julia would feel, if she had to choose between us? Because that's what it would mean if I asked for her hand!'

Lady Harris looked suddenly weary. 'You men and your grudges. I'm not sure how you'll do it, but you must find a way. Yes, the girl loves her family, but she also has a fierce sense of justice and might want to know your side of the story. She'll know they're not perfect—which of us is?—so show some sense and take action! The girl's been pining desperately for you while you were away. She would deny it, of course. But she's a lovely little thing and, believe me, someone else will snap her up double quick when her Season begins if you don't get in there first.'

Ben closed his eyes briefly. Then he said, 'You don't what know my feelings are for her.'

'Of course I do!' she snapped. 'I may be old, but I'm neither blind nor deaf. I've watched the two of you together. I've heard you, laughing and talking. Get on with it, man.' She rested back against her pillows again and waved her hand irritably. 'Now, send Twigg back to me, will you? I'm still an invalid, you know.'

'I do know,' he said. 'Lady Harris, you'll follow the doctor's instructions, won't you? Or I'll be back to scold you.'

She made a tutting sound. 'Of course I will. Off you go, young man—and do something, for heaven's sake, to comfort the girl.'

He found Miss Twigg waiting at the foot of the stairs and she needed no bidding to return to Lady Harris's side. Ben headed onwards, to where Julia was.

She looked up quickly when Ben came back into the kitchen. He appeared tired, she thought. She'd been searching the pantry, wondering whether he was hungry, but she guessed that all he really needed was to return to the Hall and get some sleep.

'How is my aunt?' she asked quickly.

'She is no worse.' He smiled then and his smile warmed her, as always. 'She's also actually agreed to take the powders the doctor left for her.'

'Thank goodness,' said Julia with feeling. 'But I hope she was suitably grateful to you, for fetching the doctor?'

'That? It was nothing.'

Julia put her hands on her hips. 'Nothing?' she exclaimed. 'But you rode all the way to Lambourne village, in the dark and the rain. I don't call it nothing!' She pointed to a glass of wine she'd poured for him and said in a quieter voice, 'I wondered if you might like some refreshment before you leave.'

'Thank you. That's thoughtful.'

He sat down and she waited until he had tasted the wine, then she sat, too, and said, 'Why are you being so very good to my aunt, Ben?'

'Maybe,' he said, 'because she has been good to me, in the past. I'm not going to go into details, but our paths have crossed, several times. I also feel that, in just a very small way, I'm perhaps making amends for some bad mistakes in my life.'

'We've all made mistakes,' she said softly. 'What exactly do you mean?'

At first he didn't answer and she found that her heart was thumping almost painfully. But then he sipped a little more of the wine and said at last, 'Julia. I wasn't with my father when he died. I wasn't even able to attend his funeral.'

His voice, she realised, was almost bitter with self-contempt and she struggled to find a reply. At last she said, 'Maybe it was impossible for you to be there, Ben!'

He held up his hand to silence her. 'My father suffered a great injustice towards the end of his life and never recovered, but I ignored it. I travelled abroad, enjoying myself—I'd convinced myself it was what my father wanted. But I should have realised how desperate he had become. I should have been there for him.'

Julia realised she could not bear to see him like this. He looked haggard. Distraught. 'Ben. Listen to me,' she said steadily. 'Your father would have been glad that you made your own, successful life and turned into such a fine person—'

He rose to his feet and shook his head. 'You're wrong, Julia. So wrong. You don't understand the half of it. I am not a fine person!'

She longed to hold him. To smooth his hair back from his forehead and to tell him—what?

That she wanted him so badly that her whole body ached with need?

He cared for her, she was sure of it. Maybe miracles just might happen. Maybe she could defy all society's foolish rules and marry Ben the stonemason, then they could live as her aunt did, far away from London and heedless of its whims and fashions.

But Ben would never accept that. She knew it without asking, because he had his own kind of pride. But the thought of losing him dug as deep as any wound to her heart.

She rose to her feet. 'Ben,' she whispered. 'Oh, Ben. I'm going to miss you.'

He came to take her in his strong arms then. He held her so close that she could feel his heart steadily beating, but there were no words. After all, she thought sadly, what could he say?

He let her go at last. 'I'm sorry,' he said. 'I think we both realise this is impossible.'

She did her very best. She swallowed down that great lump in her throat, looked around and said almost lightly, 'Of course. I am being utterly foolish and I'm quite confirmed in my resolve that I shall never marry, ever! Now, the doctor recommended weak tea for my aunt as well as those powders, so I'll take some up to her. And, Ben, thank you. I don't know how I'll ever repay you for your help tonight.'

He went to look out of the window, then said quietly, 'It's nothing. But it's probably time I returned to Lambourne Hall. It seems to have stopped raining and the sky is clear, so may I borrow Nell again, to ride up there?'

She nodded as brightly as she could. 'Of course. Sowerby will saddle her up for you.' She hesitated, then said more quietly, 'Will you come here tomorrow?'

'I will,' he said. He was already pulling on his coat. 'I'll have to bring Nell back, after all. I'm sure that the doctor will visit, too.'

Julia bolted the front door after he'd gone, then leaned against it, feeling cold and empty. He could have kissed her, then—kissed her and more. But he was wiser than she and no doubt it was as well that he didn't.

For the next three days, Ben visited Linden House and Julia found his presence both a joy and a torment. He was wonderful with Lady Harris, telling her stories that made her laugh, and as she rapidly grew stronger, he helped her downstairs so she could roam the house looking for dust or chiding Dottie and Grace if the kitchen wasn't spotless.

'We're glad to see you back in good spirits, my lady!' Grace said to her, making Lady Harris chuckle.

Ben kept his distance from Julia and she accepted it because she had to face reality. Any day now she expected a letter from London to tell her that a carriage was being sent to bring her home and she felt as if she was about to lose something infinitely precious. She wanted Ben, but it was impossible and she knew she shouldn't torture herself so.

'That Ben,' her aunt said as Julia was reading to her in the sitting room. 'I'm disappointed in him.'

Julia put aside the book, which was the inevitable *Gulliver's Travels*. Goodness, she felt she knew the first chapter by heart now. Ben had called earlier to check all was well and she couldn't see a single reason for her aunt's criticism. She said, 'What exactly do you mean, you're disappointed?'

Lady Harris stared at her. 'Well, knowing him as I do, I expected more of him.'

'But he's been here every day to help you. I don't know how we'd have managed without him! It was amazing how he persuaded the doctor to come out so swiftly.'

Her aunt murmured, 'If the doctor won't come out for him, I swear I don't know who he *would* come out for.'

'For Ben? But surely the doctor won't have met him before? After all, Ben's only been working here for a while.'

'Hmmph. Shows how little you know.'

Julia said slowly, 'Aunt, what exactly do you know about him?'

'Well,' huffed her aunt, 'he is a good man, whatever they say about his father.'

'His father? Did you know Ben's father? But how—'

Lady Harris waved her hand dismissively. 'Now, where had you got to with poor Gulliver? Please carry on before I lose the thread entirely. Later, perhaps, we can play chess. How glad I am that you're here, for you have a far better brain than most females of my acquaintance.'

And much good has it done me, thought Julia rather sadly.

Ben had arrived home from his latest visit to Linden House to find Gilly standing in the kitchen looking rather stern. He also noticed there was an array of documents laid out on the nearby table.

'I suppose,' Gilly said, 'you've been to Linden House to see that girl, yet again. But for the life of me, I cannot understand why you're taking such a risk.'

Ben pulled off his coat. 'I've been visiting Lady Harris,' he said. 'Someone needs to help her out. She is my neighbour, after all.'

'While that girl is a guest there?' Gilly was not impressed. 'You'll be getting yourself into real trouble if you're not careful.'

'I hope I have enough sense to behave myself with Julia, if that's what you mean.'

Gilly raised an eyebrow. '*Lady* Julia. Just remember who her father is.'

As if he could forget. Today he'd walked back home up the hill with his head full of wild dreams. For several deluded minutes he'd even wondered if he might visit the Earl, her father, to apologise for what had happened in the past and to ask for Julia's hand.

My lord, I love your enchanting daughter. I am wealthy and have a good position in society, so can we forget the past? Will you permit me to marry her?

But what if her father refused to accept that Ben's father was not guilty of deceit? Where would that leave Julia? She would be forced to make an impossible choice between her family and him. Even if Ben found positive proof that his father was innocent in the business of the horse, would the proud Earl be willing to accept that proof?

Suddenly he realised that Gilly was pointing to those papers on the kitchen table. 'There's something there you ought to look at, my lord,' said Gilly quietly.

Before leaving the house this morning, Ben had remembered the documents Rudby had given him in London last week, about the sales and purchases of his father's horses over the years. Truly he'd expected nothing new, but he'd asked his valet to check them and now Gilly's words brought him sharply to attention.

Ben sat down and pulled the papers towards him.

'I took a look at them,' Gilly was saying, 'like you asked me to. The sheet I've left on top is the one you want.'

Ben scanned it and realised instantly that this was a report written by a veterinary surgeon, a familiar enough document to Ben, for he knew his father always had one done whenever he purchased a new horse. Only this time, the report was about Silver Cloud—and it was drawn up by the surgeon employed by the Earl of Carstairs.

It was a copy, Ben saw, maybe sent by the Earl to

Ben's father in protest at the transaction. Ben had never seen it before.

'There are the usual illustrations over the page,' said Gilly. 'You need to look at them.'

Ben looked. As usual, there were some detailed line drawings of the horse viewed from all angles, with notes at the side listing height, colour and other details. Ben read the notes with care and said, 'What have you spotted, Gilly? This describes Silver Cloud pretty well, doesn't it?'

'That's what I thought, at first. But come and take a look, my lord, at the painting of the horse in the hall-way.'

Ben followed him and they both gazed up at the painting. Ben was still holding the report and as he looked down once more at the written description, he suddenly felt his pulse rate quickening. 'Silver Cloud,' he said, 'had a dappled grey coat and a silver mane. The report agrees. But according to the painting, there is a distinctive patch of darker grey, *here*.' He pointed to the picture and the horse's left hindquarter. 'It's shaped almost like a heart.'

Gilly nodded. 'Exactly, my lord. Now, look at the surgeon's report. Is there any mention of it? No. None whatsoever, even though reports like this are meant to be accurate in every detail.'

Ben felt a slow but steady sense of growing hope. Still holding that vital paper, he looked again at the painting. 'There can be only one explanation. My father hired Molloy to take Silver Cloud to the Earl's stables in Richmond—and Molloy delivered a different horse. Somewhere on the way, Silver Cloud was substituted

with a horse that looked similar, but was fatally flawed.
The question is—have we enough proof?'

Gilly said, 'I know someone who might help. When
I rode into Claverton the other day for supplies, I spotted an old groom of your father's, Jem Thornberry. Do
you remember him?'

'I do. He was a good man.'

'He's working now at the saddler's in Claverton. He
would remember your father's horse, in every detail.'

Ben glanced at the picture again, then at the report.
'I'll go there tomorrow.'

He rode to Claverton the next morning, and found
Jem Thornberry working outside the saddler's. 'My
lord!' Jem was effusive in his greetings, effusive, too, in
his description of the horse when Ben questioned him.
'Silver Cloud? Yes, he was the finest animal I ever did
see. Perfect almost in everything—in fact, the only fault
you could claim in him was that he had a darker patch
of grey, almost heart-shaped, on his left hindquarter.
But that horse was quality, my lord. Yes, real quality.'

'You'd swear to the magistrates about the flaw in his
colouring, Jem? The darker patch?'

'I would, my lord.'

Ben shook his hand. 'Thank you, Jem. I'll be in touch.'

Ben rode homewards. He knew that the time had
come for the truth to be exposed—which meant that he
must return to London and confront the Earl of Carstairs.

Chapter Thirteen

The next day, Lady Harris seemed downcast as they settled down to lunch. 'This morning,' she announced, 'I received a letter from your bossy father. He wants you back home. Apparently he's sending your brother Charles for you.'

Of course, Julia knew this had to happen. She had been expecting the news daily, but even so her heart quailed within her. 'How soon is Charles setting off?' she asked her aunt. 'Does my father say?'

Lady Harris was adjusting her spectacles and peering at the letter again. 'I can't see anything about dates. It's a downright pity, though, that your family are intent on dragging you back to London, which is a place—'

'You cannot abide,' filled in Julia, smiling in spite of herself. 'Yes, you have told me that, several times.'

'I can't say it too often, in my opinion. Oh, and I almost forgot. There's a letter for you too.'

Julia opened it. It was from Pen and she read it with growing dismay.

Julia.
Absolute horrors. Charles has somehow got hold
of your letters to me and realises you've met some-
one special. He's not going to tell our mother and
father, but he says the man you've been seeing will
regret it if he's laid a single finger on you!

Charles is setting off very soon to bring you
home. I'm afraid our brother is very angry with
you.

Slowly Julia folded the letter up again. She realised
her aunt was watching her and frowning a little.

'Well, my girl,' said Lady Harris, 'you've been making a big fuss over my health, but you're looking quite
peaky yourself. Do you want me to tell that family of
yours that you're not fit to travel?'

Julia attempted a smile. 'Of course not. I must have
been here over four weeks and I always knew I'd have
to go home. But truly, I've had a marvellous time!'

'Hmmph,' said Lady Harris. 'I'm going to miss you.'

Julia suddenly realised her aunt was dabbing a tear
from her eye. 'Oh, Aunt! I'm going to miss you, too.'
She rose and went swiftly to take her hand and Lady
Harris nodded.

'That's enough sentimentality.' She sniffed. 'You're
a good girl, Julia, that's for sure. Now, it's my opinion
that you need to go and find young Ben.'

'Aunt, I really don't think…'

'What? You don't think he deserves to know you're
leaving? That's up to you. But I would like you to tell
him that I'm finished with any mollycoddling and I
know he's got better things to do than come here and

fuss over an old lady! Now, I'm going to sit by the fire in the sitting room and go through the household accounts with Twigg.'

Once she had gone, Julia looked again at her sister's letter and those words of doom. Then she went upstairs to put on her jacket and her walking shoes, because her aunt was right. It was time for her to go and say goodbye to Ben.

As Julia climbed the path to the pavilion she noticed that in the distance the sky was heavy with rain clouds. Would Ben be working there today? He might have finished for good because as far as Julia could see, there was little more to be done. If he was at the pavilion, he might not be pleased to see her. Yes, he'd made daily visits to her aunt, but since that night when he'd fetched the doctor, he'd made sure he was never alone with Julia.

She pressed on, but the rain was starting to fall and as she neared the pavilion, it began to hammer down. How foolish she was, to have set off here at all! But it was too late to go back so she speeded up her steps, hoping to take shelter in the pavilion. Ben would never be there, not on an afternoon like this.

She reached the pavilion and ran inside. Her flimsy clothes were already soaked through; indeed, she had to brush the rain from her face and her eyelashes to see anything at all in the dark interior. 'Oh, my,' she muttered to herself. 'I am such a fool...'

Her voice trailed away—because she'd seen that Ben was there.

He, too, had clearly been caught in the downpour, because he had taken off his shirt and was preparing to put on another dry one. 'Julia,' he said. 'What on *earth*—?'

For a moment she couldn't speak. She thought that his tanned and muscled chest was perhaps the most glorious sight she had ever seen. But what she felt for him was far more than merely physical. In fact, he'd come to mean just about everything to her during this short time, but now her brother knew about him and that brutal fact reminded her how anything there might have been between them was over.

She had prepared herself to tell him that she was leaving for good, but for a moment the pain clutched so deep that she couldn't breathe. Couldn't move.

Ben broke the silence. 'Julia. Are you all right? For God's sake, why are you here?' He'd pulled the dry shirt over his head. 'Is your aunt unwell again?'

'She is fine,' she replied. To her relief, her voice was steady. 'We are all grateful,' she added, 'for everything you've done.'

'There's no need for thanks. It was no trouble at all.' He looked at her searchingly. 'But there's something else, isn't there?'

'Oh,' she said, shrugging, 'it's nothing I wasn't expecting. I've come to tell you that I'll be leaving soon.'

'For London?'

'Of course.' She tried to say it lightly. 'I'm returning to my family.'

He was silent a moment. Then he said in a quiet voice, 'Back to where you belong.'

With that, Julia's heart felt as if it was sliced in two.

No, she wanted to cry. *I belong here. I belong anywhere, as long as I'm with you, Ben.*

She couldn't believe he didn't see that. She couldn't believe, after all that had happened between them, that he could accept her departure so calmly.

But clearly he did accept it and, dear God, it hurt. She drew a deep breath, deciding that her only option was to act as she should have done from the very beginning, so she echoed his words firmly and brightly. 'Back to where I belong. That's exactly it, of course.'

He was keeping his distance, with his arms folded across his chest as if to deter her. But his shirt was still unbuttoned at the neck and his breeches clung tightly to his lean hips; his brown hair was tousled as usual and his jaw unshaven. He was her Ben, her stonemason, and she couldn't forget the way his lips had kissed her to distraction.

She lifted her chin to meet his gaze. She reminded herself that it was all over, of course it was, especially now that Charles knew. But wasn't Ben even going to fight for her? Her throat ached with unshed tears. She remembered his kiss and the strange things it had done to parts of her body she'd never even thought about.

Love of that kind—physical passion, physical intimacy—was not for her, she'd always told herself. But he'd proved her wrong, for everything about him made her long to know more of those strange feelings he could arouse in her with just one touch. At this very moment, her heart was thumping wildly and even when she lowered her gaze she was hardly able to breathe. Quickly she looked up again, but that was even worse because his eyes were glinting, his cheekbones were tanned and taut and his mouth reminded her of his kiss...

Too late. All far, far too late. She felt cold in her

heart, as cold as the rain clouds that were blotting out the sun. But she could not forget the intimate moments they'd shared, could not forget his smiles or his caresses. From the beginning, everything had seemed so *right* with Ben. But he regretted it, that was clear, and she had to agree that anything further between them was impossible. Pen's letter and her brother's fury had reminded her of the depth of antagonism her family would feel if a workman presented himself as her suitor.

She looked at Ben defiantly. 'I have to face reality sooner or later. Perhaps it's time I came to my senses and accepted who I really am. That's all I came to say—and you needn't wish me luck in my hunt for a husband, for I am never going to marry, ever.'

Lifting her head high, she began to walk towards the door. But as she stepped outside she stopped with a gasp—because of course the rain was still pouring down and at that moment lightning flashed across the dark sky. She stood there, shaking, while thunder rumbled overhead, unable to move until she felt Ben's strong arms around her and he was pulling her back inside.

'Oh, Julia,' he was murmuring, 'what am I going to do with you?'

And all of a sudden she realised exactly what she wanted him to do.

As for Ben, he knew he should have sent her home to Linden House the minute she appeared. Yes, it was pouring down, but he could have perhaps wrapped his large coat around her and hustled her back down that muddy path in the rain whether she liked it or not.

Now, though, it was too late. She was totally drenched.

She was shivering, she was distressed and what could he do but put his arms round her and cradle her against his warm body and kiss the top of her damp hair until she was nestling into him, clinging to him as if she would never let him go?

She needed his protection. But how could he even think about offering her his, when all he wanted to do even now was make love to her? The raging desire he felt was pounding through his blood this very minute. She'd declared she had no intention of marrying, but he had guessed already that there were depths of passion lying beneath her purity and the man who gained access to her heart and her body would be lucky indeed.

He longed for that man to be him. He longed to be the one to caress her lips and her sweet breasts with the ardour they deserved and to awaken her to the heights of bliss, but it would be wicked of him. For even if she hadn't already declared she would not marry, he knew that when he finally came face to face with her father—a meeting that must come soon—the bitterness between their two families might grow even worse.

But he couldn't send her out in this! The rain was still hammering down, so he let her go and went swiftly to light the fire in the hearth, fanning the low flames until the room lost a little of its chill. But when he looked up, he realised she was still shivering badly. Her hair and dress were soaked; she had her arms folded across her breasts and what he'd thought were raindrops trickling down her pale cheeks were in fact tears, even though she made no sound.

She looked so lost and lonely that he wanted to take her in his arms to comfort her—and more.

Be honest with yourself.

Much, much more.

'Dear God, Julia,' he breathed, 'I cannot bear to see you like this.'

She tried then to smile and he found it even more heartbreaking than her tears. 'You can rest assured,' she said, 'that you won't have to put up with me for much longer. I really was rather foolish to come up here like this, wasn't I?' She stopped and added in a quieter voice, 'Foolish—and rather scared, too.'

'Scared?'

'Yes.' She gazed up at him, her eyes brimming with emotion. 'You see, I realised that I'm very inexperienced. Very innocent. I know that I don't want to marry, but my parents won't take any notice. Soon I shall be flung on London's marriage mart and I'm afraid of what I'll face, Ben.'

'Oh, Julia.' He took her in his arms. 'What can I do to help?'

'Just hold me,' she whispered. 'Hold me, Ben. I'm truly dreading being paraded in front of rows of suitors. But when you kissed me, it was wonderful. Please tell me—could other men's kisses be like that? And what would they want from me in return?'

'You,' Ben said hoarsely. 'That's all, Julia. They'll want *you*.' His self-control was in pieces. He pulled her close—and he kissed her.

He was still trying to tell himself that this must be merely a gentle meeting of their lips, a gesture of comfort, no more, for surely this was wrong in every way. But then she flung her arms around his neck and the sweetness of her answering kiss took over his body, his mind and his senses.

* * *

The rain poured down outside and the fire in the hearth cast flickering shadows around the room, making the figures on the walls appear to dance like the Greek nymphs of old. Julia caught just a glimpse of their knowing smiles before Ben's kiss tore away the foundations of her world.

She would not have guessed that a man of such strength could also convey such tenderness. His powerfully muscled arms held her close and that was her last rational thought, because when his lips met hers she forgot who she was. Who she was supposed to be. Lady Julia Annabel Emilia Carstairs was no more; instead she was just Julia, she was in love with this man and, as his kisses cherished her lips, her face, her throat, she felt all the strength and heat of his body.

Her heart pounded like the thunder overhead. Could there be more? Yes. Definitely, yes, for his hands were wickedly at work, too. While one stayed tight around her waist, the other was moving down to clasp her bottom and draw her so close that she could feel the hardness of him through her scant clothing. *Oh, my.* She might be innocent, but she knew very well what it meant. He wanted her, badly. He wanted to make love to her, now.

She felt her senses swimming, along with a delicious hunger for more. Lifting her face to his to invite more kisses, she let her own hand stray to the opening of his shirt, allowing her fingers to brazenly explore the temptation of his smooth golden skin. When she heard his soft groan of pleasure, the sound set a pulse throbbing low in her own body. 'Ben,' she whispered. 'Ben.'

It was a plea and he answered it, because she felt his hand cupping her small breast, teasing and caressing its peak through the thin cotton of her dress. She felt herself melting into a hot puddle of desire. She knew that all her senses were under assault, for even the scent of his skin—heady, male, intoxicating—had robbed her of reason.

She lifted her hand to run her fingers through his hair, just as she'd always longed to do. He was beautiful, there was no other word for it, and if he let go of her now she thought she might die. But suddenly he was pulling away and gazing at her with anguish in his eyes.

'No,' he said in a low voice. 'Julia, this is not right.'

She met his gaze proudly—boldly even, for what had she to lose, when she had already lost her heart to him and knew she would never love anyone else? For answer she undid the top buttons of her damp dress. 'I'm cold,' she whispered. 'Please warm me, Ben.'

Then she reached up to lay her palms on either side of his face and stood on tiptoe to kiss him, shyly at first, but with growing courage, teasing his lips with her tongue as he had done to her, probing and exploring until she was shivering not with delight, but with new-found power.

For he was hers. Maybe just for this moment, maybe never again; but for now he was hers and she wanted to remember this for all of her life. Once more he was pulling her close, his body hot and hard against hers. Had she really undone so many of her buttons? It appeared so, for his hands were everywhere, cupping her breasts, stroking her nipples.

The next thing she knew, he was carrying her to the

sofa, where he held her and kissed her again as she fell back against the cushions. After that he lowered his head to her bosom and…oh, my…she felt his mouth on her breasts.

He was using his tongue to tease and caress first one nipple, then the other. *'Ben.'* It was a whisper of disbelief at the unbelievable pleasure, for as his lips were licking and sucking, she felt that secret place between her thighs hungering for him in a way she wouldn't have believed possible.

Down there she was tight with yearning and he must have known it, for now his strong hand was reaching down, pulling up her skirt and moving higher and higher until her trembling thighs fell apart and he was stroking the slick flesh of her most intimate place.

She gasped as his fingers teased her there, again and again. She was physically shaking with tension until he kissed her gently on her mouth, 'Julia,' he whispered. 'Julia. You're so beautiful.'

'Don't stop.' Her voice was urgent. 'Ben. I cannot bear for you to stop.'

She felt his hands steadying her for a moment. Then she gasped as he began once more to caress her. She clutched at him, her fingers digging into his back as the incredible sensations mounted. More? Surely there couldn't be more—she couldn't bear it, could she? Already, she could hardly breathe; but then, then she heard herself gasping aloud as he caressed her one last time.

'Please,' she cried, 'please, I can't…'

'You can,' he whispered back. 'Darling Julia, you can.'

At that very moment an exquisite torment gripped her entire body and she shook in his arms as wave after wave of delight rolled through her. He continued to hold her, murmuring words of passion to her, kissing her breasts, her forehead, her lips.

'Ben,' she whispered at last. She lay sated in his arms. 'Ben, I had no idea.' She was pulling his head down, trying to kiss him back. She loved this man and she wanted all of him. But carefully he was easing himself away. She felt cold when she heard the rain still pounding on the roof, colder still without his arms around her.

She drew herself up a little. 'Surely,' she said, 'there must be something I can do for you? What I mean is…'

She was confused, Embarrassed. She knew that he must be aroused, too, and must be in a state of torment.

'No.' His voice was harsh and he'd drawn a deep breath as if deciding what to say next. 'What I mean, Julia, is that what you suggest is *not* a good idea. Believe me.' He shook his head to emphasise his words. 'No more. Do you understand?'

She nodded because, yes, she did understand. She watched in silence as he went to pick up a folded blanket from a chair and came back to wrap it carefully around her shoulders, before going to put more logs on the fire.

The room heated up, but she was still cold inside. She had begged for this intimacy. She had begged for *him*. She knew that after she returned to London, everything would be as it was before. She would once again be the Earl of Carstairs' daughter, to be offered in marriage to the highest bidder. But there would never, ever be anyone like Ben.

Ben was still struggling to get much heat from the fire, but God help him, his body was in flames and his erection still pounded. He had self-control, yes, but it had its limits. He glanced back at her. She was sitting on the sofa trying to straighten her disordered clothes, but her eyes were still wide with the aftermath of desire and her lips were still swollen from the power of their kisses. He could see her small breasts heaving as she fought to recapture her breath. As for him, he was in a state of mental and physical torture.

It had been a dangerous mistake on his part to ever lay hands on this sweet girl who tasted of honey and wine. Didn't she realise what she was doing to him? She'd thrown any caution to the winds and clearly she'd longed to go further, longed perhaps for him to ruin her, which was what it would amount to.

He added some fresh kindling sticks to the fire, then gazed through a window at the rain pouring down outside. He had awakened her heart and it was completely wrong of him to have done so, for clearly she had no idea of how even her lightest caresses could fill a man with raging desire, even if the man in question—himself— knew it would be desperately wrong to take advantage of her. He should have put an end to all this at the very beginning. She should be back in London, with her family standing guard over her whenever she set foot outside her house.

He should have waited until he could speak with her father about the feud and only then, when and if peace was made between their families, should he have considered courting her with the delicacy and respect she deserved. Instead, he'd almost seduced her. Yes, she was sure she wanted him, but what would happen when she realised his deception? She might hate him then.

Perhaps she would meet someone else she could love. Perhaps she would change her mind about marriage and find herself an eminently suitable husband who would be welcomed into the heart of her family. But the trouble was that Ben couldn't bear the thought of it.

He realised she was speaking at last. She said in a low voice, 'I've made a fool of myself. Haven't I?'

He joined her swiftly and put his hands on her shoulders. 'No. Not in the least. But what happened between us just now must be kept between us, do you understand?'

'Of course.' She tried to smile. 'After all, my parents could never allow anything like this to happen, could they?'

'No,' he said. No, they couldn't, for reasons she didn't yet understand.

But he saw the heart-wrenching sadness in her eyes before she looked around and said, 'Well, I suppose I had better be off. It sounds as if the rain has almost stopped. But, Ben—do you remember how you found my rather foolish notebook, that I'd left by the lake? Did you read it?'

He couldn't deny it, for he'd told her too many lies already. 'Yes,' he said. 'I did.'

'Then you'll know,' she said softly, 'what I wrote about you.'

How could he forget it?

I wish that I had met someone like him in London.

Just for a moment, he allowed himself the cruelty of hope. If he could quickly resolve the issues with her father, could he approach her then? He would never trap her into a commitment she declared she loathed. But he would give her as much freedom as she wanted and he would give her love. So much love...

She was walking to the door of the pavilion, where she looked out. The rain had indeed stopped and a watery sun was gleaming on the trees and the lake. He followed her.

'Borrow my coat,' he said. 'You'll catch a nasty chill if you walk home just in those wet clothes. You can leave it by the gateway to your aunt's gardens. I shall collect it later.'

'Thank you,' she said. She spoke politely, as if they were strangers. 'So this is goodbye, Ben. Truly, I wish you well.'

Without another word, she pulled on his coat and it hung almost to the ground on her slender frame. But God help him, he found that she looked adorable even in that outsize thing. He wanted to run after her and hold her tight, to tell her who he was and why he'd lied to her. But might she not hate him for it? She might feel tricked, betrayed even. So what could he do, but stand there and watch her go?

Julia left Ben's coat by the gate as he'd instructed, though just for a moment she held it to her face, breathing in Ben's scent, Ben's warmth, and her heart ached as if it would break. After that, in her wet dress and boots, she hurried on towards the house, hoping desperately to get up to her room so she could have a few private moments to get changed and compose herself. But as soon as she opened the front door, she heard her aunt calling out, 'Is that you, Julia?'

Then Miss Twigg appeared in the hallway. 'You'd better go to her,' she said. 'She's sitting in the drawing room and she's in a bit of a tizzy.'

Indeed, as Julia went to find her, Lady Harris looked quite agitated. 'I've had another look at that letter from your father,' she announced. 'I do wish he would write more clearly. Apparently your domineering brother could arrive as early as tomorrow to take you home. I was not expecting him so soon.'

Julia sat down. Charles. Tomorrow. And he'd read her private letters to Pen, about her and Ben.

Lady Harris was looking at her sharply. 'Are you quite all right, Julia?'

'Yes,' she lied. 'Yes, of course.'

'Well, you don't look it.' Her aunt sighed. 'Do you know, I'm feeling rather weary with the world so I'd like you to read to me for a while. *Gulliver's Travels* will do—the bit where he finds he's captured by all those little people called the—the—'

'The Lilliputians? But, Aunt, I've read that to you several times already!'

'I know, but I like it. It's funny. Makes me chuckle, a big strong fellow like him pegged to the ground.' She pointed at a nearby table. 'The book's over there. See?'

So Julia settled down to read it aloud and her aunt shook with silent mirth, but her own heart still ached unbearably. She had told Ben she would never marry, but there was one man she would say yes to—him. She couldn't stop thinking about Ben's last kiss and the look in his eyes as he'd drawn away. He'd taught her to know desire and she had encouraged him, every step of the way. It was what she had longed for. It was something she would never forget.

But Charles was coming to take her home. Her brother, she was sure, would be watching her like a hawk once she re-entered the social life of London, ready to pounce if any other unsuitable stranger tried to steal her heart. But there was no need for him to worry in the least about that, thought Julia sadly. Because Ben had already stolen it.

Ben had walked back to the Hall from the pavilion and Gilly immediately detected he was in an awful mood. 'Is it your leg?' Gilly said.

Ben nodded. 'Yes.' It was true; his leg was hurting him, but he was in no mood for Gilly's sympathy. Instead he went straight to his study. He re-read the bill for transporting his father's valuable horse, carried out by the firm of Francis Molloy, who had vanished without trace. Then he once more studied the veterinarian's report, filled in when the horse arrived at the Earl's stables in Richmond. Superficially, all looked perfectly correct.

There was just one problem: the horse the Earl received was not Silver Cloud.

The watercolour painting of the horse proved it, as did the evidence of his father's old groom, Jem Thornberry. But Ben was going to try another tactic first. He had given his lawyer Rudby instructions to find out, if he could, the whereabouts of Francis Molloy and this morning, Ben had received Rudby's answer.

My lord.
On making enquiries, I have discovered that Molloy was committed to Newgate nine months ago.

He was convicted of various crimes, including horse thieving.

Ben's course was obvious. He needed to go to London again, because it was time for him to enter society as Lord Lambourne and to proceed with the business of clearing his father's name.

Chapter Fourteen

The next day Charles arrived at Linden House just before noon. Lady Harris had gone out with Miss Twigg to feed the chickens, so Julia was on her own, drinking tea in the sitting room, when he arrived. A very nervous Dottie showed him in and immediately Julia could see her brother was in a furious mood.

Her heart was sinking, but she looked up and said, 'Charles. How pleasant to see you. I hope you had a good journey?'

He slammed down his hat and gloves on a nearby side table. 'I trust, Julia, that you will be able to pack immediately, because I'm taking you home straight away.'

She rose to her feet. 'Surely you're in need of a brief rest. And wouldn't it be polite for you to spend a little time with our aunt, who has taken good care of me?'

'Are you joking, Julia? From what I gather, you have been unchaperoned for almost five weeks. You sent Betty home so you were without a maid and since then you've been wandering around the countryside all on your own. It is truly unbelievable!'

'Lady Harris does have staff, Charles!'

'But have any of them looked after you as they should have done? No! Neither, I gather, has Lady Harris!'

Julia bit her lip. It was clear that Charles truly had read every word of her letters to Pen. How wrong of him. How disastrous for her. She said quietly, 'You read the letters I wrote to Pen. Don't you think that's rather unforgivable?'

Charles showed no sign of softening his tone. 'I think,' he said grimly, 'that it's your behaviour that's disgraceful, not mine. I warned our father before you even left London that he was making a grave mistake sending you to our absurdly eccentric aunt. I did hope that since she lives at the back of beyond, there wouldn't be much mischief you could fall into. But you managed to find someone to make foolish eyes at, didn't you? Do you know who your stonemason really is?'

Julia was beginning to feel as if the air in this room had become difficult to breathe. She tried to speak, but couldn't, because already Charles's next words were washing over her like a cold grey tide.

'Your so-called stonemason,' he said, 'is none other than Lord Lambourne. I realised it straight away, because you told Pen, didn't you, about his work abroad and his broken leg? You also told her he was living at Lambourne Hall, yet unbelievably, you never guessed, never even suspected who he truly was! But I can see by your expression that you understand the enormity of it now. You've been cavorting with Lambourne, unchaperoned and unprincipled. How could you?'

Julia somehow stood her ground, but inside she was shaking. She was remembering suddenly the conversation she'd overheard between her father and Charles, on the night it was decided to send her to Somerset.

'*You do realise, don't you,*' Charles had warned her father, '*who might be staying close by?*'

Her father had dismissed Charles's concerns, saying that the man in question was still abroad. 'You needn't worry about him,' he'd said. But her father was wrong, because Ben, Lord Lambourne, was indeed back home.

There had been very many things about Ben that she'd found odd. For example, despite his workman's garb his manners were those of one used to living in the highest echelons of society. He knew this entire district for miles around; he knew her aunt, he even knew the doctor in the village—and was living at the Hall, for heaven's sake!

How could she not have realised his identity? She had visited her aunt often as a child and Ben must have lived close by. But he was seven years older than her. He would have been away at school, or at his father's London property. Besides, her aunt rarely talked about any neighbours; she wasn't one for formal socialising, though she must have known who Ben was, and she should, she really should have told Julia...

But Julia herself ought to have known. Instead, she had deliberately blinded herself to reality—because she had fallen hopelessly in love.

Now she lifted her head proudly. 'So he's Lord Lambourne. Isn't that good news, Charles? I would have thought you would be relieved that I wasn't meeting with a mere stonemason.'

'But this is *Lambourne*!' cried her brother. 'Did he tell you about his father's fraudulent deception of our own father? The bitter argument they had, when Lord Lambourne—your Ben's father—refused to apologise?'

She couldn't help it. Her hand flew to her mouth in shock.

'He didn't tell you, did he?' Charles spoke with grim satisfaction. 'I'm not surprised. He'll know full well that his own father's behaviour was disgraceful.'

'Charles, I knew there was some trouble, but Ben believed his father was innocent of any wilful deceit. There must have been a terrible mistake!'

'Oh, Julia.' Her brother shook his head. 'Don't you see that the man has been playing you for a fool? Let me tell you what really happened. Our father and Lambourne's were once friends, linked by their passion for fine horses. Lambourne agreed to sell a young gelding of his to our father, but when it arrived, it was unfit to be ridden, let alone to race. Father had paid Lambourne a high price for it—and it was worthless! Are you truly saying you believe that our father lied about this?'

She shook her head and said heatedly, 'No! Of course not! Papa would never do such a thing!'

'You are absolutely right. Why should he? The sum of money he paid for that horse, large though it was, would be nothing to him. What angered our father most was Lambourne's adamant refusal to admit to his deception.'

'But Ben swore that his father had deceived no one— and he told me that his father was broken by this, his life was ruined!'

Charles lifted one eyebrow in scorn. 'And Lambourne explained all this while he was pursuing you under a false name? Do you call that kind of behaviour either trustworthy or innocent?'

She could find no words to answer him.

'Has it occurred to you,' Charles went on relentlessly, 'why Benedict Lambourne might have decided to latch on to you?'

She was beginning to feel quite sick, but she answered clearly, 'He did not "latch on" to me, as you so crudely put it. For goodness sake, he didn't even know who I was. When we met—purely by chance!—he was kind to me.'

'You truly believe you met by chance? You call it "kind" of him to pursue you and let him kiss you? Yes, I know about that from your letters. What other liberties did you allow him, I wonder? Sit down, Julia.'

'No! I won't!'

'I think you'd better, because you're not going to like what I'm about to say. When his father died, Benedict Lambourne was abroad and in hospital. But when he returned, he stopped briefly in London before going on to Somerset—and he was heard to vow revenge on our father, for supposedly driving his own father to an early grave. I thought little of it at the time. I believed that he could do our powerful family no harm. But Lambourne's a cunning fellow, there's no doubt about it—because he's found a way through our defences, hasn't he?'

Julia sat down on the sofa, for she had begun to tremble inside. Charles watched her closely.

'Yes,' he said at last. 'He's sworn revenge on us and his strategy is to seduce you, I'm afraid. Julia, you've been taken for a fool—' He stopped, perhaps because he'd realised that tears were welling in her eyes, no matter how hard she tried to blink them back.

He came to sit beside her then, her big brother Charles, who used to play silly games with her when she was small and let her ride on his shoulders. He put his arm around her. 'Oh, Julia. You haven't fallen in love with him, my dear—have you?'

When she gave him no answer, he shook his head and held her tight. 'I will kill him,' he muttered. 'I will kill him for this.'

'No!' She pulled away and shook her head fiercely. 'No, Charles. I cannot allow you to even *think* something like that!'

His face darkened. 'You do believe what I'm telling you, don't you?'

Still she could not speak, but Charles must have seen her expression, for he hesitated a moment, then said, 'I'm sorry, Julia. I blame our aunt, Lady Harris, for this. She badly neglected her duty to you in allowing you the freedom to meet this rogue.'

With a great effort, Julia pulled herself away from him. 'No, Charles. You will not put the blame on her—or on Ben either! He has been completely honourable towards me from the start; indeed, when he realised who I was, he told me that we must stop seeing one another immediately. But I took no notice!' She shook her head emphatically. 'What happened between us was all my fault.'

Charles looked at her, amazed. 'What on earth do you mean?'

Her voice was steady now, even though her heart was aching with pain. 'I encouraged him,' she said, 'at every step. I told all the family before leaving London that I wanted a taste of freedom and I found it. Ben was working on his estate, close to Lady Harris's property, and I pursued him. Day after day, I went to find him and talk to him. I encouraged our intimacy, Charles. Let me make it quite clear: this was not his fault.'

Her brother was on his feet. He began to pace the room, then he swung round to face her. 'Julia,' he said at last. 'Do you realise that if you go around spreading this story, you will be utterly disgraced?'

She shrugged. 'I'm not going to be spreading the story. But if you try to blame Ben…well, I've told you the truth of it and I shall defend him if necessary. Please make no mistake about that. I believe, even if you don't, that he is totally honourable.

'If you try to raise the matter in public, then he could lay the blame for what happened entirely on me and I swear to you that I would not deny my behaviour. In fact, I would tell everyone what I've said to you—that I did my best to seduce him.' She still spoke clearly, but found she was feeling a little breathless, a little faint. 'Is that all, Charles? Shouldn't I go upstairs now and pack?'

Her brother stood there, looking both bewildered and angry. At last he said, 'Very well. Very well. But as soon as you're ready, I intend to start our journey. I've no wish for you to spend any more time with Lady Harris who, in my opinion, has let you down quite abominably. I'm hoping that you might have time to reflect on the problems you've caused yourself and, for the sake of our family, I shall mention none of this once we are in London. I also hope you've remembered that it's Pen's wedding in a matter of weeks. It's best if both of us aim to forget that any of this unpleasantness has happened.'

It was at that moment that Lady Harris marched in. She took one look at Julia's brother. 'Hello, Charles,' she said, untying her bonnet. 'Throwing your weight around as usual, are you?'

Charles was tight-lipped. 'Lady Harris. I'm sorry to have to say this, but I hope you realise that you've let Julia down?'

'Really? Have I?' She plonked her hat on a side table. 'Funny, but I thought it was her family who did that. Trying to squash this delightful girl's spirits, just because she didn't fit the accepted mode. Hah!'

'Aunt,' said Julia.

But Lady Harris was still glaring at Charles with her hands on her hips. 'Well, young man? I've known you since you were a boy. I guess you mean well, but sometimes you can be a pompous ass, did you know that? What have you to say for yourself, hey?'

To describe her brother as annoyed would be putting it mildly. For a moment Charles looked about to explode, but then he merely straightened his exquisitely knotted cravat and replied haughtily, 'I have nothing further to say to you, Lady Harris—except that I warned our father you were not to be trusted with a single member of our family.'

He turned to his sister and spoke more quietly. 'Julia,' he said. 'You mustn't ever think that we don't care for you. We do, very much—which means that we want the best for you.'

He examined his pocket watch. 'I must go and check that the horses have been properly fed and watered by the grooms. Julia, we shall set off in half an hour and I trust you will be ready by then. We can dine when we stop to change the horses.'

He gave a curt bow to Lady Harris and left the room.

'Pompous twit,' muttered her aunt.

Julia sat down again on the sofa, feeling exhausted. Her aunt came over to sit at her side. 'Chin up, my dear. Your brother's a fool and some day he'll meet a woman who'll teach him some sense. I don't believe he intends to be so hard on you—he thinks he's helping, that's all, and he really does care for you. So you go back to London with him—and who knows what lies in store?'

'I'm afraid,' Julia said, 'that my brother is determined to take me in hand, Aunt. But I want you to know that I've loved my time with you. Really I have!'

Her aunt patted her shoulder. 'Be true to yourself,' she whispered. 'That's my advice to you, my dear.'

Julia wanted to ask if her aunt guessed that meeting Ben and losing him had broken her heart. But what was the use? Yes, Lady Harris had contrived the first meetings between the pair, but her aunt had not ordered her to fall in love. As for what happened in the pavilion yesterday, she really could blame no one but herself.

She met her aunt's enquiring gaze. 'You knew, didn't you, who Ben was? Did you also know about the bitterness between his father and mine?'

'I heard something of the sort, yes.' Lady Harris sighed. 'But take my advice and trust the young man—he knows what he's doing. So be patient and have hope. Sometimes we must wait for what we most desire. Now, it's time for you to pack your things.'

With a heavy heart Julia went up to her room, where

Grace was already waiting to help her. It was almost, thought Julia, as if the maid guessed her despair, for Grace said very little as she quietly began emptying the chest of drawers and folding Julia's clothes on the bed. Julia tried to be of some use, but in the end Grace said, 'You leave all this to me, my lady.' She pointed to some books Julia had borrowed from her aunt's library. 'Why don't you take them back where they belong?'

Julia nodded and carried them downstairs, finding seclusion of a sort in the book-lined room. Her aunt spoke of trust and hope. But how could she hope for any kind of future with Ben when, as well as the fact that he would be totally unacceptable to her family, she had told him she was not interested in marriage, ever?

Of course, Ben would not have proposed anyway, despite her sad attempts to lure him. He would have realised, as soon as he discovered who she was, that even something as simple as friendship between them could affect his efforts to clear his father's name. But would Ben use her for revenge? Never!

She could see she would make an easy target for an unscrupulous rogue. But Ben wasn't unscrupulous. Ben was a man of integrity, of that she was completely sure. When he'd learned who she was, he had been genuinely horrified and had told her they must on no account meet again.

Julia believed in Ben. She loved him. But now, for his sake, she must never see him again, although they were bound to meet some time, at one of those society events in London that she hated. Slowly she returned upstairs, where Grace was packing her frocks into a leather-bound trunk. 'Are you all right, my lady?'

Julia forced a smile. 'I'm fine, thank you, Grace. But I'm sorry to be leaving you all.'

'We shall miss you, too, my lady. But you're going back to London, aren't you? How exciting!'

Yes, Julia was returning home. But she knew she would never meet anyone else like Ben, not ever. And when some day their paths did inevitably cross—how, oh, how could she bear it?

Chapter Fifteen

Three days later, Julia and Charles arrived back in London on a grey and misty afternoon. Throughout the journey it rained as only English rain knew how, making the roads muddy and enforcing a slow pace. But her brother had made sure there were always heated bricks in the carriage to warm Julia's feet and rugs to wrap around her. He was his usual commanding self at the inns where they made their overnight stops, swiftly securing the very best rooms and service.

When they finally reached London and drew up outside Carstairs House in Mayfair, all the family were there to welcome her—her father, mother, Pen, Lizzie and even her father's two Labradors. Her mother hugged and kissed her, then led them all into the drawing room, where dozens of candles were lit and a large fire blazed.

'Oh, my darling Julia,' Lady Carstairs exclaimed. 'It's such a relief to see you back safely! It was a mistake to send you so far away, I knew it!'

Charles intervened. 'Mother. Father. I've spoken with Julia and I gather that her stay in Somerset was quite an adventure. But she is back with us now and has come to no harm whatsoever.'

He smiled at Julia, a smile that she felt was more than a little forced.

She guessed he was really saying, *Your turn now, Julia. Put our parents' minds at rest, for heaven's sake, or there will be the devil to pay.*

So she spoke in the lightest of tones. 'Oh, I've had a lovely time! Of course it was very quiet at Linden House, although one day we had a delightful trip to Bath. But really, nothing of exceptional interest occurred, and it is wonderful to be back with you all!'

Pen and Lizzie were watching her anxiously. Pen, she guessed, would have told Lizzie about her letters and what she'd written about Ben. Pen would have told her, too, that Charles had read them. No doubt they would be questioning her soon and she dreaded it, even though she loved them dearly.

She smiled round at them all once more, but really she was exhausted and Charles must have noticed, for when her mother declared that they would all have tea and scones straight away and hear every detail of her stay in the country, it was Charles who said, 'I think Julia is tired after her journey, Mother. Perhaps we should allow her to go to her room and at least get changed out of her travelling clothes.'

'You are right, Charles!' cried her mother. 'Julia, I shall send one of the maids up to you—Betty, I think.'

'No!' burst out Julia. Then she spoke more calmly. 'Thank you, Mama. But may I have a little time to be on my own?'

Charles escorted her to the foot of the stairs, where for

just a moment he held her arm and murmured, 'I will say nothing whatsoever about Lambourne to our parents and neither, I hope, will you. It's our secret for ever. Yes?'

'Yes,' she whispered.

He looked at her searchingly and not unkindly. 'Is it really all over between you and him?'

She nodded. 'Indeed. It's all over, Charles.'

When she entered her bedroom it seemed desolate. Elegant, yes, beautifully furnished, yes, but there was no model ship to make her smile, no lilac tree brushing its twigs against her window in the light breeze. No distant view of the woods and the pavilion. No Ben.

Wearily she sat on the bed with her heart aching so badly that she wasn't sure how she would get over it. She rose again and had just begun to pace her room in despair when the door flew open and her sisters came in.

They took one look at her, then they came silently over to hug her, Lizzie first, then Pen. After that they drew her back to the big bed and they all sat down, with Julia in the middle.

'Oh, Julia,' said Lizzie, wriggling a little closer so she could place her hand on hers. 'Are you quite, quite sure you're all right? You look so sad.'

Pen said, 'You're still thinking about *him*, Julia, aren't you? That lovely man you told us about. The stonemason.'

'He sounds really nice,' said Lizzie with a sigh. 'Julia, did he kiss you *properly*?'

Pen reached across to poke her sister in the ribs. 'Lizzie! Don't be so inquisitive! And even if he did,' she added, 'it really is as well that you and I do not know, in case our mother decides to question us.'

'But, Julia, maybe you can tell us just a little about him?' pleaded Lizzie.

Julia tried to swallow down the huge lump in her throat. 'He is called Ben,' she whispered. 'He has brown hair and a lovely smile. He broke his leg badly in the summer and still walks with a limp, but he likes nothing better than to be outside, working in the sunshine. I met him almost every day.'

'No wonder you're missing him,' said Pen sympathetically. 'Poor you. But you must have known our father and mother could never approve of you marrying a stonemason.'

'I knew it, of course. But then I found out more.' Julia drew a deep breath. 'You see, I discovered that he's not a stonemason—he's a baron, Pen! His real name is Benedict, Lord Lambourne.'

Her sisters gasped in delight. 'Why, that's perfect!' cried Pen, 'Why on earth can't you be married? Unless...' she hesitated '...unless he's married already? Or a fraudster, or a terrible gambler?'

Julia almost smiled. 'Believe me, he's none of those. But the trouble is that his father was our father's enemy.'

Pen looked puzzled again. 'Why would our father bear a grudge against your Ben, for something his father did? Surely the argument, whatever it was, has been long forgotten?'

Julia shook her head. 'Charles says that it hasn't. I think the matter was very serious.' She was blinking back a tear now. 'Charles also says that during the weeks I was at our aunt's, Ben was using me to get revenge on our father.'

'Using you for revenge?' Lizzie gasped. 'How awful. Do you think it's true?'

'Not for a moment! Oh, Lizzie! I really liked him, so very much!' She had to stop and pull out her handkerchief because her tears were flowing fast.

Pen began stroking her hair gently. 'Darling Julia. You must have trusted Ben. You must have believed he cared for you. So are you positive there's absolutely no hope?'

Julia mopped up her tears and tried to speak calmly. 'I realised, I suppose, that even though we spent a lot of time together, Ben was trying to keep his distance. I thought at the time it was because he was a stonemason, though I understand the true reason now. He was afraid I would have to choose between him and my family, because of the feud, and I think he didn't want me to have to make such an awful decision. But I don't want anyone except him and I'm already missing him, so much!'

She felt her tears well up again. Ben. Oh, Ben.

Her sisters were silent. At last Lizzie said, 'We are sisters. Remember? And we shall stick by each other *always.*'

They held hands for a moment, then Pen said thoughtfully, 'Julia. You are a good judge of character and you've never been impressed by anyone's fancy words or boasting. I agree with you that Charles must be wrong about this "revenge" business. If you really like Ben and you know he likes you, then there must be some way the two of you can be together.'

Julia shook her head. 'I told him,' she whispered, 'that I never wanted to marry, ever, and it's true that I didn't—until I met him. Though I still carried on pretending. I was always saying, "Heaven forbid that I should lose my independence!" Of course, he believed me. So it's over. I've ruined everything.'

For a moment there was silence, then Lizzie said suddenly, 'You can't have ruined everything. There must be a way. Why not ask Papa *now* to tell you all about this horrid argument with Ben's father? You never know, you might find out it wasn't as bad as you think!'

Julia gave a faint smile, but shook her head. 'I know it was bad, Lizzie.'

'But you can at least hope!'

'I don't think so. Everything has gone wrong.'

There was silence. Her poor sisters were clearly at a loss as to how to offer any further comfort, so it was up to her to summon a smile.

'Now,' she said to them, 'that's enough about me. So please tell me all of your news. What's been happening in London? What have I missed? How are your wedding plans, darling Pen?'

'Oh, yes. The wedding!' exclaimed Lizzie. 'Julia, you wouldn't believe the fuss Mama is making about it. It's not far off and she is already in a state of panic about the church, about Pen's wedding gown and the extra servants we'll need—everything!'

Pen joined in eagerly, largely, Julia guessed, to stop her thinking about Ben. As if she ever could. As if the great void in her heart could ever be filled by anyone else.

Over the next few days she was swiftly drawn again into her former life as the Earl of Carstairs's daughter. Although she had not yet been formally presented at court, her mother was eager to take her to private balls or parties and Pen, of course, joined them, often with her fiancé, Jeremy.

Julia made the best of it, for Pen's sake. She smiled and made light conversation with the other guests, as was expected. Gradually, it started to occur to her that some of the men who were present at these affairs were actually noticing her. Admiring her, even.

She responded politely to their pleasantries, but why was this happening? It could, of course, be her exquisite attire, because her mother, after a lecture from Pen, had taken Julia to a stylish modiste who provided her with some wonderful gowns. She had expected the gossips might still be muttering over her sudden disappearance from London, after she'd emptied that glass of champagne over Tristram Bamford. But, no, her brother's high-living friends were looking at her with something she wasn't used to—admiration.

When she found herself trapped in a corner by a tedious baronet who was eagerly telling her about his homes and his wealth, she caught sight of her image in one of the many gilded mirrors and realised that, yes, she did look different, somehow. It was hard to pin down. But maybe her lips looked fuller and her eyes, whose colour had once been compared to the sea on a cold day in midwinter, were more vivid. More expressive.

Her mother was thrilled. 'Julia, my dear, we might be planning a wedding for you before too long! I believe your trip to the country has done you a world of good. You have acquired an air of elegance, an air of mystery even, which all young men adore.'

Julia was in despair. She knew she ought to be flattered, but she wasn't. She missed Ben dreadfully. Would he be missing her? She doubted it. Even worse, he was bound to return to London soon, to take his place in society. Would he be looking for a wife?

Of course he would. All men of his rank had to have an heir. But how would she bear it?

Then one day, as she and Pen and their mother returned to the house after yet another shopping trip, Charles beckoned her quietly to one side.

'Julia,' he said. 'I've heard that Lambourne's in town.'

For a moment she could hardly breathe.

'If,' Charles continued, 'you should come across him anywhere, I trust you will act as if the two of you have never met. Do you understand?'

Her heart still hammered. But she nodded and somehow said coolly, 'Of course, Charles.'

She said it for Ben's sake. She knew he would not want Charles stirring up fresh trouble and she owed him this, at least.

But— *Ben*, she thought. *I miss you, so very badly.*

Their meeting happened even sooner than she'd feared. Less than two weeks after her return home, some friends of her parents, the Duke of Danby and his wife, held a twenty-first birthday party for their oldest son in their magnificent house in Grosvenor Square. Julia went with Charles, Pen and their mother. Their father, who tended to avoid these large social affairs when he could, had made his excuses.

There was dancing, of course, in the ballroom. The

whole house was crowded, yet Julia had not been there for ten minutes when she saw Ben. He was dressed in the usual evening finery of gentlemen of quality, a black tailcoat and skin-tight buff breeches. He looked heart-breakingly handsome. He also looked completely at home in this aristocratic *milieu*, surrounded as he was by the fashionable elite: men who were clearly friends of his and of course young women, too, girls who gazed at him and fluttered their fans flirtatiously.

All around her she could hear people talking about him. 'Have you seen that Lambourne's back? They say he'll soon have his father's estate put to rights, then no doubt he'll find a wife. One of the Duke's daughters would make an excellent match for the man…'

Julia wanted to ask her mother to take her home, but Lady Carstairs was nowhere to be seen. She thought of hiding, but she felt as if she could not move. And then— then, she saw that Ben was coming towards her, a little slowly because of his limp. People were watching, but he didn't seem to care.

'Julia,' he said. 'I've only just arrived in London. No doubt you've realised by now who I am. I know you must be hurt and furious over my deception—'

She held up her hand. 'Please,' she said in a low voice, 'don't make this worse for both of us. I under-stand that what happened between us was a bad mis-take and nearly all of it was my fault.' Her heart was pounding painfully. 'I think you and I ought to forget everything about our time together in Somerset.'

He looked at her. He was pale, but his gaze was steady. 'I don't want to forget it,' he said. 'It's not over as far as I'm concerned. But if that's the way you feel—'

He broke off because at that moment, the musicians struck up a brisk waltz and a girl in a green satin gown and emeralds came eagerly towards them. She was Lady Eleanor, one of the Duke of Danby's daughters. Julia knew her because for a while they'd had dancing lessons together.

'Lord Lambourne,' Lady Eleanor exclaimed, putting her gloved hand on his arm. 'I know you are unable to dance, which is such a shame! But my father and mother are wondering if you will join us in the dining salon for a glass of champagne and some refreshments. We really must celebrate your return to London.' She glanced at Julia. 'Lady Julia. We haven't seen you for a few weeks, have we? Though of course we all know about your distaste for fashionable society. Come, Lord Lambourne. Let me take you to my parents.'

She led Ben away, chatting to him eagerly. Moments later Charles, looking furious, came to stand by Julia's side. 'Was Lambourne actually talking to you? I can't believe he had the audacity to approach you. I swear, if he said anything to upset you, I will not be responsible for my actions.'

'He will not speak to me again, I'm sure,' said Julia. 'Whatever there was between us is over, Charles—and now, I really want to go home.'

She couldn't hide the tell-tale break in her voice and Charles must have heard it. After making his apologies to their hosts, he led her to the front door and went to find a footman to summon their carriage. In the meantime Pen came hurrying up.

'Julia,' she whispered. 'Darling, are you all right? Why are you leaving?'

'Ben is here,' Julia said.

'Oh, no!'

'Pen, he came to speak to me. But it's no good. I know there's absolutely no hope. I realise I'll have to get used to seeing him everywhere, but I can't, not yet. Charles is summoning our carriage to take me home.'

Pen looked hugely concerned. 'Where is Ben? Is he still here?'

'Yes. He was led away by Lady Eleanor to the dining salon. She was clutching his arm as if she'd won a prize.'

Pen gasped. 'Is he the tall man with brown hair and the slight limp?'

'That's him.'

'Julia, he looks lovely. He looks kind—and you say that he came to talk to you? Are you quite sure that there's no hope?'

'This feud between our father and his will never be forgotten, Pen. Never. Charles is absolutely furious that he even approached me.'

'Oh, Charles can be so bad-tempered. Have you thought of speaking to our father about it all?'

Julia looked at her sadly. 'How can I do that, exactly? Can I tell him that I fell in love with Ben while I was supposed to be isolated in the countryside to preserve my good name?'

'Of course.' Pen frowned. 'I'd forgotten. You were already in trouble over that stupid Tristram Bamford, weren't you? Thank goodness he isn't here. But our father just might understand...'

'Pen, it's impossible. I can't allow myself to think that there's any chance of us being together, because it hurts too much, don't you see?'

Just then Charles returned. 'The carriage is waiting outside, Julia,' he announced. 'I'll come home with you. Pen, explain to our mother that Julia is a little overtired, will you?'

Chapter Sixteen

Ben had seen her leave with her brother and he felt close to despair. She was no longer his Julia. She was someone else entirely: she was Lady Julia, the highly eligible daughter of the Earl of Carstairs. She'd looked exquisite in her gown of pale pink, but he had preferred the simple frocks she'd worn in the country. He had loved the determination with which she'd walked along rough paths to gather blackberries and he'd loved the way she had laughed with him.

They had become so close. This could not be the end for them, it couldn't.

He had arrived in London just two days ago with Gilly and, after collecting the keys from Rudby, he'd gone to unlock the family's town house in Clarges Street, Mayfair. The previous tenant had left weeks ago, but the spacious interior had clearly been neglected for far longer. He could see dust and cobwebs everywhere.

There were also heaps of letters to be read and his first task was to skim swiftly through them. Some were from old friends in the diplomatic service. Others were gilt-edged invitations to various social events at the houses of London's aristocracy, making it clear that Lord Lambourne's return was widely known and widely welcomed in most of the *ton*'s drawing rooms. That was why he'd come to the Duke of Danby's ball tonight, for it was part of his duty to re-establish his connections with other members of the aristocracy. He knew it was his duty also to marry before too long. But seeing Julia arrive in that ballroom tonight had all but knocked the breath from his body.

Until meeting her, he'd told himself that nothing, absolutely nothing, could be more important than making it clear to the Earl of Carstairs that his own father had committed no fraud. But now his life was in turmoil. He loved Julia. But how could he ever overcome her family's hostility?

He looked at his pocket watch and groaned because it was scarcely half-past nine. He'd escaped from the Duke of Danby's daughter, but she would find him again soon. Did he really have to stay to the end? The answer came unexpectedly, in the form of a folded letter brought to him by one of the Duke's footmen.

'A messenger came with this for you, my lord,' he said.

Ben opened it quickly. It was from Gilly and it was about Molloy.

On the very first day of his return to London, after Rudby had written that Molloy was in Newgate, Ben had begun the process of finding out what exactly had happened to the man, so he'd gone there—only to be told that Molloy was no longer there.

'Was he set free?' Ben had asked sharply.

'No.' The surly gaoler shook his head. 'He was sent somewhere else. Don't know where, though.'

Ben had offered more money with no result, but the ever-loyal Gilly had taken it upon himself to make further enquiries. Ben knew he'd gone out again this evening and now he'd sent a message to the Duke's ball, telling Ben to meet him at a drinking house in Holborn on Fetter Lane.

Immediately Ben made his excuses to his hosts and hired a cab to take him there. He was thankful that his long, dark greatcoat covered his evening finery, for the inn was filled with working men: dockers and market traders, he guessed. Gilly hailed him over to the beer-stained table in the corner where he'd been sitting.

'I've been to the Fleet Prison,' he said. 'It's close by, as you'll know. A gaoler told me Francis Molloy was transferred there from Newgate earlier this year, but he died in August of the prison fever. Apparently the man was guilty of any crime you can think of involving horses. God alone knows how he got away with it all for so long. Here. I've written down what the gaoler said.'

Ben was already reading Gilly's notes. Clearly Molloy got up to all kinds of trickery for years—altering records, bribing grooms to put horses out of action before big races. He looked up at Gilly. 'Molloy must have been a cunning man. I would guess that when my father hired him to take Silver Cloud to the Earl of Carstairs, Molloy remembered seeing another horse that was almost identical in looks, but valueless because of its defects.'

Gilly was listening closely. 'So you're wondering if somewhere along the way, Molloy replaced your father's horse with another?'

'I'm sure of it,' said Ben softly. 'And no one realised until you and I did—thanks to that vet's report and the painting.'

Gilly sighed. 'I wonder where your father's fine horse ended up? Ah, well. There's no use dwelling on that. Besides, I'd guess you've got all the information you need now, my lord, to prove your father's innocence. I deserve another pint of ale for what I've discovered to-night, don't I? And you owe me money! I had to fork out a guinea to get the information.'

Ben beckoned the barman and ordered more drinks. 'I owe you a good deal more than a guinea and a pint, Gilly. But you probably know that.' He folded the sheet of notes and put it deep in his pocket.

Gilly was still watching him. 'What are you going to do next? Will you visit the girl's father to tell him what you suspect?'

Ben hesitated. The answer, he knew, was obvious. Molloy was a convicted fraudster and Ben should confront the Earl of Carstairs and tell him everything. Surely he had enough evidence to persuade anyone that his father was innocent? But the Earl, he'd heard, was a proud man and would still, surely, bear a grudge. He would hardly fling the past aside; he was unlikely to ever welcome Ben through his door as a visitor, let alone as a prospective son-in-law. Again Ben had to fight down the old bitterness as he recalled the Earl's letter to his father.

This was an act of fraud, not worthy of a man of your rank.

Their drinks had arrived and Gilly raised his tankard. 'To the memory of your father, my lord. And remember that whatever you do next, he would have wanted you to be happy.'

Ben lifted his drink also. 'To my father.'

They talked then of times gone by, of Ben's travels in Europe with Gilly always faithfully by his side. Some other men in there came to join them; they were old soldiers who'd noticed Ben's lameness and asked if maybe he'd been injured in battle. For an hour or so he was able to forget his title and his wealth as they told one another of the countries they'd been in and the people they'd met.

Ben drank his pint, then another and another, until Gilly said, 'Time to go home, my lord.'

He had realised that just for a while, he'd not thought of Julia. Maybe some day, if things didn't work out, he would get over her. But as he unlocked the door to his house, the silence of it enveloped him. He remembered again how very beautiful she'd looked at the ball tonight and how he'd loathed all the men who surrounded her.

'Please,' she'd said, *'don't make this worse for both of us. I understand that what happened between us was a bad mistake and nearly all of it was my fault.'*

It was a mistake, yes, but not her fault because he had behaved in an unforgivable way by deceiving her and quite possibly convincing her to stay away from men and marriage for good. The problem was that he realised his whole life would be quite empty without her, so he was not giving up. No, not until he heard her say she didn't love him, because he would swear that she did.

* * *

Ben woke the next morning with a well-deserved headache. At around eight Gilly brought him some coffee and the latest mail, in which were several more invitations, including one to the home of Lord and Lady Sheldon in Kensington for a musical soirée tonight.

'*Never,*' he muttered to himself.

Dear God, he remembered—how could he forget?—the Sheldons' daughter Georgina, who'd used to chase him with grim determination whenever he was back in London from abroad. Would she still be after him? No doubt.

He rose and began dressing himself. On their arrival in London Gilly had hired some housemaids and footmen, and on his way downstairs he saw they were already hard at work, sweeping and cleaning, opening shutters and polishing the big windows so the sunlight could pour in. Gilly was giving instructions to a pair of footmen as Ben entered the breakfast room, but Gilly sent them away and began to reproach his master instead.

'You should have allowed me to dress you, my lord. You ought to start living in a way that's appropriate to your rank.'

Ben had to grin. 'You can't wait to turn me into a fine lord, can you? It will be quite a while before I get used to all that again.'

'You can't deny you're enjoying the food.' Gilly looked on in satisfaction as the two footmen came back bearing a selection of hot dishes which they placed on the sideboard. One of them served Ben a plateful of ham, kidneys and eggs while the other poured him some coffee. Ben drank it with relish, feeling the rich and fragrant liquid restore his spirits.

Today marked the start of his new life. He had substantial evidence that his father was completely innocent of any wrongdoing. He was going to confront the Earl, even if it meant…

Losing Julia? *No.* He would do his damnedest to make things right between them. He would never forgive himself if he gave up on winning her love.

Later that morning he visited his bank to discuss the estate's financial affairs. 'You have considerable assets, my lord,' said his banker, 'together with income from rented property and various investments.' Enough, he was assured, to maintain his town house in some style and at the same time to completely repair and refurbish the Somerset estate.

Yes. He could open up Lambourne Hall. He could marry and have children, he could take them to watch the wild creatures in the beech woods and learn the joys of nature…

He stopped, because when he thought of the children's mother, he could picture no one but Julia. He saw her face vividly every night, before he went to sleep; he remembered her smiles and her shy laughter. Most of all he remembered her kisses. It was time, whatever the consequences, to visit the Earl of Carstairs and tell him about the crook Molloy. The Earl might be furious to have his word doubted, but the truth had to be known. He gave Gilly a letter to deliver to the Earl's house.

Lord Lambourne would welcome a meeting at a
place of your choosing.

And Gilly returned soon afterwards.

'I was told,' he said, 'that the Earl is at his estate in
Richmond for the day, but he's due back in town later
this afternoon. I left your message with his butler.'

Ben was restless. He attended to more letters and
invitations, then started to make notes about the work
to be done on this house, but soon realised there was
no peace to be found in any of the rooms, since there
were servants everywhere. In the end he decided to go
for a walk in nearby Hyde Park.

He had forgotten just how crowded the park could
be on a fine afternoon such as this. The autumn air was
cool, but the sun shone, and it seemed as if all the *ton*
had decided to come here, whether on horseback, on
foot or in elegant open carriages. He was dressed plainly
and kept to the quieter paths, but more than a few of the
passers-by glanced at him, then looked harder before
coming towards him to say, 'It's Lambourne, isn't it?
How good to see you back in town!'

They all, of course, noticed his halting walk and he
knew he would have to accustom himself to giving the
same explanations, over and over. 'Yes, I broke my leg
in a riding accident in Austria, but it should get better
in time. Yes, I'm back in London for a while and I'll
try to get to your party next week...'

Or ball. Or dinner. Or—whatever.

Very soon he'd had enough of the interrogations,
some of which were insistent. Besides, his leg was be-

ginning to ache so he decided to set off home. He had just managed to extract himself from a noisy group of former Oxford friends when he noticed two well-dressed girls—sisters, he guessed—walking towards him on the main path.

He noticed them because he was aware that they were casting curious glances in his direction. They must be well born, for a maid was following at a discreet distance. He was slightly annoyed because now they were staring at him openly.

'Good afternoon, ladies,' he said, touching the brim of his hat and attempting to carry on.

But one of them, the older one, spoke up hesitantly, 'Excuse me, sir. But aren't you Lord Lambourne? I saw you last night, at the Duke of Danby's ball.'

He frowned. 'Who are you, may I ask?'

The girl replied swiftly. 'I'm sorry. You must think my sister and I are dreadful for intruding like this. But you see, I am Lady Penelope Carstairs—'

'And I'm Lady Lizzie!' broke in the younger one. 'Julia is our dear sister and she has just returned home from Somerset, where she stayed with our aunt Lady Harris. Julia told us that, there, she met someone called Ben and she—'

'Lizzie!' Her older sister nudged her with her elbow. 'Lizzie, not so fast.'

Ben took a steadying breath. Julia must have told them all about him. 'I am Lord Lambourne, yes,' he said.

Pen nodded. 'I thought so. Why did you tell my sister you were a stonemason, Lord Lambourne?'

That was direct. They obviously knew a good deal. 'Ladies,' he said. 'It was never, ever my intention to deceive your sister. As a matter of fact, I had no idea for quite a while who *she* was. We met unexpectedly because, to be quite honest, she had trespassed on my land and I didn't wish to embarrass her by telling her so. Then...' he hesitated again '...then we became friends.'

Lizzie clapped in delight. 'Julia was trespassing on your land? Oh, isn't that just like her! And you became friends—perfect.' Then she frowned. 'Lord Lambourne. Are you married?'

The girl asked it so suspiciously that he had to laugh. 'No,' he answered at last, 'I am not.'

'Or betrothed, maybe?'

'Most definitely not.'

'Thank goodness,' said Lizzie. 'Our sister likes you very much, you know. She has been positively broken-hearted since returning home and Pen and I simply cannot cheer her up.'

'Lizzie,' exclaimed her sister, 'you really are saying far too much, as usual.' She turned to Ben. 'I gather, my lord, that you and Julia had some kind of disagreement and parted badly. Is that true?'

Ben made his decision. He had to trust these two girls. He knew Julia loved them and they clearly had her confidence. Their maid, he noticed, had settled herself on a bench, still watching, but too far away to hear a word. Julia's sisters were waiting wide-eyed for him to tell them more.

He said, 'It's a long story. To put it briefly, there was a bad argument some time ago, between your father and mine. I feared your father might be very angry with Julia if he knew she'd met me.'

The girls were looking at one another with growing

amazement. 'Our father?' said Pen. 'Angry with *Julia*? Oh, never! Papa can be stern with other people, but really he is the softest, sweetest father imaginable. In fact he's lovely, as you'll realise as soon as you meet him...'

He realised Pen must have seen his reaction to that, for she drew a deep breath and said, 'Lord Lambourne, our sister Julia is pining away for you. Truly she is! So unless you've done something truly awful, like robbing a bank or gambling away your inheritance—'

'Or drinking like a fish. Like some of our brother Charles's friends,' added Lizzie.

Ben had to smile. 'I can assure you,' he said, 'that I'm not guilty of any of those heinous sins.'

Lizzie clasped her hands together. 'Lord Lambourne, tell us honestly. Do you really, really like my sister?'

'Lizzie,' scolded Pen. 'For heaven's sake!'

But Ben said quietly, 'I shall answer your question, Lizzie. Yes, I think the world of her.'

'Then you must do something,' Pen said decisively. 'You must call on our father, straight away.'

By now Ben was feeling a little dazed by this joint onslaught. 'That is my intention. I did send a message to him earlier today, but I was told he was not at home.'

'Oh, Papa drove out this morning to our house in Richmond, where he keeps all his horses. But he'll be back soon, although he'll probably go first to his club in St James's Street.' Pen screwed up her brow in thought. 'Lord Lambourne, now that you're in London you must be sent a good number of invitations. Have you received one to the musical soirée tonight, at Lord Sheldon's house in Kensington?'

'I have,' he said. 'Although I was not planning on attending.'

'But you must!' cried Pen. 'Mustn't he, Lizzie? We are all going, Papa, too.'

Lizzie nodded. 'Even though the Gorgon is awful.'

'The Gorgon?'

'That's what we call Georgina Sheldon. I suppose some might call her pretty, but she's also rather a monster and our father thinks so as well.'

'Hush your tattle, Lizzie,' rebuked Pen. 'This is a very serious conversation. Lord Lambourne, if you promise you'll be there tonight, then Lizzie and I will contrive to arrange matters so that you can see Julia on your own, just for a short time. Then you can tell her...' she went a little pink '...well, you can tell her anything you want. Anything *at all*.'

'It will be exceedingly romantic,' said Lizzie breathlessly. 'You can make everything all right with Julia, then you can tackle Papa, but don't worry because Pen and I will have him all sweetened up. He gets a little grumpy at musical evenings because he detests them, but we'll make sure that Mama lets him retreat into the card room, where he and his friends drink champagne and the music can't be heard. So he will hopefully be in a very good mood and we shall let you know exactly the right time to approach him. Won't we, Pen?'

'I agree. That really sounds like a good idea,' Pen said. 'Don't you think so, my lord?'

Ben still felt rather dazed. 'So I'm to speak with Julia and then your father. But do you really think this will work? It sounds complicated.'

'Maybe,' suggested Lizzie, 'we need a secret sign to

help us communicate with each other. A special wave, or a wink, or something.'

'No.' Pen was clearly growing impatient with her sister. 'We shall just go up to Lord Lambourne and tell him what to do.' She turned to Ben. 'You absolutely must be there, my lord! We shall not breathe a word to Julia and it will be a wonderful surprise for her.

'Now, I think we had better go, since I imagine our maid is getting fretful because we've been talking to you for so long. I shall tell her you are a nobleman and most respectable, but I shall also tell her she is *not* to mention this meeting to our parents. We'll see you tonight.' She wagged her finger. 'And you had better turn up, for Julia is quite heartbroken. She fears she has lost you *for ever*!'

Ben watched the sisters leave arm in arm, both still talking eagerly over their plan. He hadn't said yes. He hadn't said no either. But they'd told him that Julia loved him and he felt both the exhilaration and hope—a hope that was kindled further when he returned to his house to find a message from the Earl of Carstairs himself.

Had his daughters spoken to him already? Impossible. This message would have been sent long before the girls arrived home.

He read it.

Lambourne, I received your note. Kindly meet me at White's in St James's Street at five, if you are free.

Shortly before five he set off to White's club, where he, of course, was a member, like his father before him. He entered the lounge and realised the Earl of Carstairs was sitting in there already, talking with some distinguished-looking colleagues. The Earl rose to his feet as Ben approached.

'Lambourne,' he said.

'Lord Carstairs.' Ben nodded slightly. 'Thank you for agreeing to see me.'

The Earl looked around the busy room, then pointed to another door. 'I believe we can find ourselves a little more privacy through there.'

He led the way and Ben followed, noting that the room in which they arrived was furnished with only a few comfortable chairs set around the fire. A footman brought them claret and, as soon as he'd gone, the Earl sighed a little and said, 'I imagine that you wish to speak to me about your father. You were absent from his funeral, I believe? The last I heard, you were somewhere abroad, working for our government.'

'That is correct,' replied Ben. 'I was in Austria, on diplomatic business. But I injured my leg and I've only recently returned.'

The Earl lifted his glass and took a sip of the wine. Then he said, 'I wish I'd known you were back, Lambourne. You see, I've been hoping to speak with you for some time, about that rather awkward affair between your father and me.'

Ben's pulse raced but he drank a little wine also and waited to hear more.

'Well, young man,' the Earl continued, 'the argument between your father and myself has always troubled me. We were once friends, you see, but the matter of that horse I bought from him was the cause of some bitterness. So lately I've started looking into it all and I found that the dealer employed to convey the horse to my stables in Richmond has been struck from Tattersall's books. His name, I think, was Molloy, but unfortunately I don't know where he is.'

'I do,' said Ben. 'Francis Molloy was imprisoned for multiple crimes of fraud. He died in the Fleet a short while ago—and I've discovered that all his crimes were linked to his dealings with valuable horses.'

He drew a deep breath. 'Sir, I have good reason to believe that the horse delivered to you was not the one my father handed over to Molloy at his stables in Somerset. Somewhere on that journey, Molloy must have replaced my father's horse with the one you received—one that was valueless. Molloy was a clever criminal who got away with his tricks for many years.'

The Earl looked at him sharply. 'You're quite sure about this?'

'Indeed, my lord. I have physical proof in the form of a painting. I've also seen a copy of your vet's report making it plain that the horse you received was most definitely *not* Silver Cloud. There is also a former groom of my father's, who is willing to give evidence about the horse in court, if necessary. But I hope you'll agree that Molloy's name being struck from Tattersall's books speaks for itself.'

The Earl had been sipping his wine throughout, but Ben could tell he was listening carefully. Now he put his glass down. 'As I said, I've grown to regret this whole business, especially since your father's death. Unfortunately I have another appointment shortly, so I'll have to leave you now. But I promise I shall consider carefully what you've just said.' He rose, as did Ben, and the two men shook hands. 'Will you give me a little time?' said the Earl. 'I'll be in touch.'

Ben watched him depart. Nothing was yet settled, but he had to press on. Tonight, he would attend the Sheldons' party and see if it might be possible to talk to Julia properly, on her own. The evening might turn out to be a disaster, but he could not wait any longer.

He drank the last of his wine and set off for home.

Chapter Seventeen

The Carstairs family had mixed reactions to the invitation they'd received to the musical soirée.

'We must all go,' Lady Carstairs had said to her family over breakfast. 'The Sheldons have a number of distinguished friends—though not as many as us, of course—and it will be yet another formal outing for Julia, after her long absence from society!'

Her enthusiasm had not been shared by the rest of them. The Earl had spoken up hastily, saying that after a trip to Richmond he planned to dine at his club and might not be back in time. As for Charles, he was as blunt as ever. 'Mother, you know I hate musical soirées. Besides, Georgina Sheldon is quite intolerable.'

'The Gorgon,' Lizzie chuckled in an aside to Julia.

Her mother had heard and looked at her sternly. 'Lizzie!'

'I'm sorry, Mama.'

'Well, I hope, Lizzie, that you remember your manners tonight, because we are all going. Charles, since your father might be a little late, I would like you to escort us, if you please!'

* * *

By seven o'clock that evening, Julia was close to despair. She was in her bedroom, where she was supposed, like her sisters, to be preparing herself for the outing. But she did not want to go. In fact, she was dreading it.

She had slept badly after the Duke of Danby's ball last night. Seeing Ben there—talking to Ben there—had been unbearable because she still loved him, so much. But why would he bother with her, when he clearly had his pick of the *ton*'s debutantes? Why would he want to marry her, and be reminded for ever of what his father had suffered because of the dispute with her own father?

She understood now why he'd come to Lambourne Hall wanting time alone to grieve in private. Why he'd become so cold to her when he found out exactly who she was. She'd even wondered in these last few days if she could speak to her father herself about it, but, no— it was best to accept it was all over. *Least said, soonest mended*, her mother would briskly say.

The trouble was, Julia believed her heart would never mend. Worst of all, she would have to get used to seeing Ben at all the main society events. Would have to face the fact that, some day, he would get married. Meanwhile, there was tonight to be endured.

Betty, who was helping her to dress, was trying her hardest to instil some enthusiasm in her. 'My lady, you look lovely in your new gown. Really lovely. Look at yourself in the mirror—you are so very pretty!'

Julia looked. She barely recognised herself these days. Tonight, the pale blue silk gown she wore shimmered like silver when she moved, while Betty had pinned up her hair with skill. She was an earl's daughter with her whole, privileged future ahead of her and she guessed that once more tonight she would attract many admirers. She had changed beyond recognition because she knew now what it was like to be desired and to desire someone in return. But how many of her admirers would notice the sadness in her eyes?

Poor Betty had gone to such trouble over her and her mother had employed the most fashionable modiste in town to make her gown. But what was the point, when she missed Ben so dreadfully?

Charles had reminded her this morning that she just might see Ben again tonight. 'The Sheldons have several daughters to marry off,' he said, 'and Lambourne's a catch they won't be able to resist. If he is there this evening, you must treat him with the disdain he deserves.'

She had drawn herself up to her full height, which admittedly wasn't great. 'Charles, I hope you'll remember what I told you. If anyone has to be blamed for what happened between Ben and myself, then you must blame me.'

'Julia, you are being ridiculous!'

'I am not,' she'd said proudly. 'Charles, do I need to give you the actual details?'

Her brother had stalked off.

She still did not believe that Ben had decided to use her for his revenge against her father; indeed, Ben had positively tried to dissuade her from making her frequent visits to the pavilion, but she had taken no notice.

I encouraged him to make love to me! she reminded herself. *I did, I did—but I do not for one minute regret it!*

She would never forget the memory of his wonderful kisses and caresses in the pavilion as the rain beat down. She would have allowed him to go even further, but he was honourable, he was the one with the will-power to hold back. She knew he had been right to do so. But the trouble was, she couldn't bear being without him. She really couldn't.

Nor could she bear the thought of attending the soirée this evening, where she would doubtless have to listen to Georgina boasting about her skill on the piano and how half the gentlemen in London were in love with her.

Turning back to her poor maid, she suddenly said, 'I'm extremely sorry, Betty. But I'm not going to the Sheldons' house tonight.' She started pulling the pins from her hair. 'I shall tell Mama that I'm unwell.'

Betty moaned softly in despair, but then they both looked at the door, for they could hear approaching footsteps. Julia braced herself. Was it her mother? Or— worst of all—Charles, coming to read her the riot act again? Please, *no*…

The door was flung open and Pen and Lizzie burst in. They were both dressed in their finery, for Lizzie was coming to the Sheldons' house, too, a rare treat for the fourteen-year-old.

Lizzie pirouetted around Julia's bedroom. 'Look, Julia, look, Betty. What do you think of my new gown? Isn't it perfect?' Then she broke off. 'But, Julia, you aren't ready! What's happened to your hair? Whatever is the matter?'

Julia said quietly, 'I'm not going tonight. I shall tell Mother to give the Sheldons my apologies.'

Pen and Lizzie looked at each other in dismay. 'Julia,' said Pen firmly, 'you must attend. You really must.'

Why? Julia wondered. Why should it matter so much to them? 'Pen,' she said, 'I didn't expect you to force me! I really do not want to go and it's not even as if it's anything important.' Normally her sisters were on her side in everything, but this time they looked utterly dismayed.

Pen looked at Betty, who was listening with interest. 'Betty, would you leave us for a few moments, please?'

Betty curtsied and reluctantly headed for the door. After it had closed, Pen turned back to Julia. 'Now, my dear sister,' she said. 'Lizzie and I are going to make you really beautiful for tonight.'

Julia was mystified. 'Why? I've said I don't want to go, so why don't you take my side as you usually do? What mischief are you up to?'

Instead of providing an answer, Pen started looking for some face powder and Lizzie explored Julia's jewellery casket. 'No mischief,' said Pen firmly. 'But, Julia, we want you to do exactly what we say.'

Julia sighed. She knew there was no fighting them when they were in this mood, so she let her sisters set to work.

They tweaked her hair again, decorating it with two delicate diamond-studded silver combs. They powdered her face a little, adding also a touch of rouge to her lips and cheeks—and then, Pen tugged the bodice of her muslin gown just a tiny bit lower.

'No!' exclaimed Julia, looking down at herself in horror. 'I do not want to be put on display!'

'Nonsense. You will look very modest compared to the other girls there,' promised Pen. 'Georgina will have her bosom puffed up with cotton-wool padding as usual, but you don't need it and you'll look gorgeous. Now, let me put on your earrings and necklace—the pearl ones Father gave you for your eighteenth birthday. Lizzie, fetch Julia's blue silk shoes, will you? There now, Julia darling. You look wonderful and we love you very much.'

'But…why?' Julia was still mystified. 'Why all this fuss over a silly musical evening?'

Pen looked at Lizzie, then said, 'You've been away for quite some time. You'll be making a fresh start.'

Lizzie added, 'Just imagine Georgina's face when all the men crowd around you. Georgina and her mother will be livid!'

'I don't want to go,' Julia repeated. How often did she have to say it? Because if Ben was there, she really didn't think she would be able to bear it. Yes, some day soon she would have to get used to his constant presence in London. But…

Please, she silently begged her sisters. *I need time for my heart to heal first.*

Her sisters, however, clearly had no intention of changing their minds. 'Now,' said Pen briskly, 'I think our carriage should be waiting. The Sheldons live out in Kensington, so Charles has ordered it early. You'll remember that Papa has been at Richmond all day and since he intended dining at one of his clubs, he's promised to arrive at the soirée later. We'll be going with Mama and Charles, so come along, Julia! No time to lose!'

Julia sighed. No doubt Jeremy, Pen's fiancé, would be there and that was why she was in such a hurry. Without another word she allowed her sisters to drape her blue velvet cloak over her shoulders, then she followed them down the grand staircase.

Charles, who was already in the hallway and dressed as immaculately as ever, nodded approvingly when he saw Julia. 'You look very nice,' he said. He took her arm and led her out to the carriage while her sisters and mother followed, chattering away. But as Charles handed her in he took the opportunity to quietly say, 'We'll let bygones be bygones, shall we? I hope, Julia, that you have a wonderful time tonight.'

On their arrival at the Sheldons' magnificent house, they were greeted effusively by their hosts. The Sheldons expressed regret that the Earl himself was not with them, but Lady Carstairs answered promptly.

'My husband will arrive soon,' she declared.

'He better had,' whispered Pen to Julia. 'Or Mama will truly have something to say to him.' Already Pen and Lizzie were looking eagerly around the ornate hall to examine the gathered guests and Julia was surprised by their obvious curiosity, which was on the verge of appearing ill mannered. 'Are you looking for someone?' she asked at last. 'Didn't you tell me in the carriage, Pen, that Jeremy might not arrive for a while?'

'I did,' said Pen quickly. 'We are merely interested in seeing who's here already, that's all.'

At least there was no sign yet of Georgina. Julia, too, started looking around, preparing herself out of habit for the usual snubs from the ranks of eligible young men her mother would love her to marry.

But once again, just like last night, she was forced to acknowledge that something had definitely changed.

As her brother introduced her to the guests one by one, Julia noticed that the ladies nodded coolly, but the men bowed and murmured effusive greetings. Some even pressed light kisses to her hand.

'Enchanted, Lady Julia,' they said, or 'How truly delightful to meet you.' One voluble fellow said to Charles at her side, 'Where on earth have you been hiding this beauty, you rogue?'

Yes. The young men who only ever used to sigh over Pen were taking considerable interest in her. She remembered something Pen had once said, soon after she'd fallen for her Jeremy. 'It's strange, but being in love somehow makes other men notice you. It's as if you have some kind of aura about you.'

Ben had done this to her. Suddenly she felt a great and unbearable emptiness as she thought of how very wrong everything had gone between them. He was right to distance himself, of course. Right to be firm with her last night. She would have given everything up for Ben, but it was impossible.

She allowed herself to be introduced to more people whose names she forgot instantly. She talked to young men whose faces she barely registered. Jeremy had finally arrived, so he and Pen found a quiet corner where they could gaze into each other's eyes and whisper endearments. Julia's mother, with Lizzie rather reluctantly at her side, had joined a group of women who were eagerly discussing the latest fashions.

But Charles was continuing to keep a keen eye on Julia—an approving eye, as it turned out. 'Do you realise,' he said as he brought her a glass of lemonade, 'that you've become quite a talking point?'

Julia flinched. She did not want to be a 'talking point'.

Her brother was still smiling. 'You're a success, Julia. You always were quite pretty, you know, but something about you has changed. You've acquired an air of mystery. You don't appear terribly interested in any of the men who talk to you; in fact, you almost snubbed the Duke of Bristol's younger son just now.'

She was dismayed to hear that, but the Duke of Bristol's son had been so bashful that she truly hadn't been able to think of a thing to say to him. 'I'm sorry, Charles. I didn't mean to be rude to the poor man!'

Her brother patted her on the shoulder. 'Don't worry. In fact, it's rather clever of you, because you're driving all the young men wild with your lack of interest in them. Keep it up. A little aloofness on your part will land you a spectacular marriage, I promise. Who knows? You might attract a decent proposal or two before your Season even begins. Wouldn't our father be delighted? As for Mama, I think she might faint with joy.'

Julia couldn't speak.

He means well, she told herself.

Besides, it was no good arguing with him, it never was. He cared greatly for their family and she knew that if any of them were in trouble, he would defend them to the hilt. But she wanted to tear off her wildly expensive silk gown and jewels and instead put on the plain cotton dresses she'd worn in Somerset. She wanted to tug the silver combs from her carefully arranged hair, she wanted to scrub off her face powder and lip rouge and run—all the way back to Ben.

Except that he wasn't in Somerset, he was in London. He wasn't Ben, her stonemason, he was Lord Lambourne, and she'd told him she was never going to marry—but that was just an attempt to hide from him the agony in her heart. Somehow she kept a smile fixed to her face. She was polite, she talked pleasantly to the men who crowded around her and the time passed— until disaster struck.

A group of latecomers had walked in and among them was Tristram Bamford. His eyes widened in surprise when he saw her across the crowded room. Then he positively leered.

For Julia, this was the final straw. She'd had enough. She needed to get out, before this absolute horror of a man got anywhere near her. She looked rather wildly around. Charles, as it happened, had left her in order to talk about horse racing with some friends on the far side of the room and there was no sign of her mother.

Could she leave now and walk home? No, that was ridiculous—they were in Kensington, for heaven's sake! 'Such a desolate place. Why, it's positively out in the wilds,' her mother had moaned on the way here.

What could she do? Where could she hide?

Suddenly she caught sight of Pen beckoning to her furiously. The guests were starting to move around now because the Sheldons' oldest daughter, Miranda, was about to play her flute and people were either occupying the rows of chairs or—as was the case with quite a number of men—they were retreating swiftly to the card room. Julia made her way between them all to reach her sister.

'Julia,' instructed Pen, 'you must go to the orangery, quickly, before that awful music starts. Or believe me,

I shall drag you there myself! Oh, there's Mother beckoning us over. I shall go and keep her quiet. Please, just do as I say.' Pen moved off, before Julia could ask any more.

Julia was puzzled, but at least this gave her a chance to evade Tristram, so she headed for the orangery. She knew it well, for she and her mother and sisters had spent many a tedious afternoon in here sipping tea with Lady Sheldon and her daughters. Inside the glass-domed, candlelit room the delicate scent of citrus plants filled the air, while at the far end a bronze fountain trickled water into an ornamental pool. She stood there for a moment in bewilderment. Why on earth had Pen sent her here?

Suddenly she heard speedy footsteps followed by a very masculine shout of triumph. 'So that's where you've got to, you little tease!'

Julia whirled round to see Tristram Bamford bearing down on her. He slammed the door shut behind him; his strides were unsteady and his face was flushed. With a stab of fresh dismay, she realised he'd been drinking heavily and now he was coming closer, his arms outstretched to block her escape.

'I spotted you back there in the hall,' he said, 'though at first I couldn't believe it. Charles, the rogue, never told me you would be here.' He chuckled. 'Maybe he wanted to surprise me and he's succeeded. What's happened to the skinny little wallflower in the awful dresses, eh? Come here, you tantalising creature, and stop looking so cross. I know you threw champagne over me last time we met, but I like a bit of passion.

Maybe it's time to get to know one another better. What do you say?'

'Get away from me, you drunken oaf!' cried Julia. She tried to slip past him and head for the door, but Tristram caught her by her shoulders and pulled her round to face him. He stank of spirits and in his eyes was a look that chilled her, for it was a dangerous mixture of desire and anger. He was much stronger than she and he was still holding her tightly.

Desperately she pummelled at his chest. 'My brother will call you out for this!'

'But your brother's nowhere near. Is he?' He was using one burly hand to tilt up her chin while gazing hotly down at her. 'Calm down, sweetheart. And don't make too much noise, because if we're caught together in here—well, you know what people will say. So let's be nice to each other, shall we? Because I think it might be rather a good idea, since there's already been gossip about the two of us, if I persuaded you to marry me.'

She kicked him on the shin. It wasn't terribly effective, but it annoyed him badly and she saw pure rage glitter in his eyes. Then he smiled again, a deadly smile.

'Oh, dear,' he said softly, shaking his head. 'Oh, dear me. Now, that was not a good idea, Lady Julia. Was it?'

Earlier that evening, Gilly had been unable to hide his amazement when Ben told him where he was going. 'The Sheldons? I warn you, Georgina will pounce on you, my lord. There'll be no escape.'

Gilly was right as usual, because as soon as Ben was announced by the pompous butler he was approached with great delight by Lady Sheldon, with Georgina by her side.

'So kind of you, my lord,' gushed Her Ladyship, 'to show such interest in my family's musical talents!'

Georgina, who wore an extraordinary gown which displayed most of her thrust-up bosom, simpered up at him from behind her fan. 'You will not, I trust, judge my little performance on the pianoforte too harshly, my lord?'

'Of course not,' said Ben with some confidence, since he very much hoped to be as far from the piano as possible.

But Lady Sheldon had thought of that. 'You will need a comfortable chair to sit on, Lord Lambourne,' she pronounced. 'Since I imagine your poor leg causes you pain if you have to stand for too long. Georgina, dearest, why don't you sit with His Lordship over there—do you see?—and I will order champagne to be brought to you immediately.'

She was pointing to an alcove in which were a small table and two chairs.

Ben felt angry and frustrated. So far this evening he'd seen no sign of Julia or her family and now he found himself being led by Georgina into a half-curtained alcove where he half listened to the girl's babble, he drank three glasses of champagne and tried all the time to keep an eye on the room for new arrivals. When he finally saw Julia enter on her brother Charles's arm, he put his glass down abruptly.

Georgina had clearly seen them, too, for she said with a profound sigh, 'Do you know, I feel dreadfully sorry for Lady Julia Carstairs.'

Ben spoke sharply. 'Why?'

'Because, poor thing, she's totally unlike her sister Pen. Sadly, Julia has not got her sister's looks and she is of a rather awkward disposition. Many of us fear she will have great difficulty finding a husband and—' She broke off and peered in another direction. 'Oh, my goodness. I see that my mother is beckoning me to the piano!' Georgina was already on her feet. 'My sister Miranda is about to play her flute and I am to accompany her. I cannot believe how many people are eagerly awaiting our performance! So I fear, Lord Lambourne, that I must leave you for a while in order to entertain our audience. I do hope that after all your illustrious travels to the capitals of Europe, you do not find my family's offerings too pitiable!'

As soon as Georgina had gone Ben rose, too. Julia was here and it was time to find her—to speak to her in private, if possible. But unlike Georgina, who had merrily pushed her way through everyone even if it meant forcing them to move their chairs, he was trapped unless he wanted to make a public spectacle of himself. Yes, trapped, with just a bottle of champagne for company, while at any minute that awful music was about to start—

He suddenly jumped up because he'd realised that someone was underneath his chair.

Highly puzzled, he bent to investigate and saw Lizzie Carstairs gazing up at him. 'Lord Lambourne!' she hissed.

'Lizzie. What on earth are you doing down there?'

'I had to wriggle under the curtains.' She tapped the

draperies that formed a half-circle around this alcove. 'It was the only way to reach you.'

He'd assumed those curtains were purely ornamental but now, as Lizzie tugged one aside an inch or two, he glimpsed an open doorway to a corridor beyond.

'You must,' Lizzie was hissing, still on her knees, 'go to Julia now! We've sent her to the orangery and she needs to speak to you urgently. Well, perhaps she doesn't realise it yet, but trust me, she does!'

This time he asked no questions. Instead he rose and eased himself silently through that doorway while Lizzie, after whispering an excited 'Good luck!', waved him on his way. But as soon as he reached the entrance to the orangery he realised something was badly wrong. He'd noticed Tristram Bamford arriving a short while ago and Ben always avoided the man because he loathed him—but now he saw that as well as Julia, Bamford was in there, too, and the wretch had his hands on her.

Revulsion together with absolute fury rose like bile in his throat. Somehow Lizzie and Pen's plan had gone badly wrong. He strode in, noting that Bamford had his back to him so he hadn't seen him yet, but Julia had and she was deathly white. 'Ben,' she whispered. 'Ben, thank God you're here.'

Bamford turned round when he heard her, letting his hands drop to his sides. Of course, his reaction was the opposite. He exclaimed, 'Lambourne. What the *hell*?'

Ben squared up to the other man. 'You bastard, Bamford,' Ben said. 'How dare you lay one filthy finger on Lady Julia Carstairs?'

Bamford puffed out his chest. 'How is it you're taking it on yourself to interfere in what Lady Julia gets up

to? You've been out of London for quite a while and so
has she. Do I sense a whiff of scandal here?' He smirked
and glanced at Julia, then back at Ben. 'Tell me, Lambourne, you rogue. Have you taken advantage of her?'

Ben clenched his right hand into a fist, aimed it at
Bamford's chin and felled him.

It was not, he was well aware, a good idea. It wouldn't
silence the bastard for good. But damn, it was satisfy-
ing. As Bamford started to heave himself up, Ben stood
over him and waited till he was on his feet. Then he
said, 'I think you'd better go home. Your nose is bleed-
ing and some of it's on your ridiculous cravat.'

Bamford put his handkerchief to his nose. 'I'll get
you for this,' he muttered. 'You and her. Something's
been going on between you two, hasn't it?' He was
looking at Julia. 'You, my lady, have always looked so
damned innocent. But now, I'm beginning to wonder.
Her brother will definitely be interested in this—'

He broke off because Ben had grasped the lapels of
his very expensive coat. 'If I were you, I'd think hard
before saying anything about what's happened here,
You might have to explain your own actions, because
when I arrived, it looked very much as though you were
assaulting Lady Julia. You'd best remember that before
you open your big mouth, because I would rather enjoy
shutting it again for you. Do you understand?'

'If you think you can silence me with threats—'

'I certainly hope so. But there are other ways.'

With one unceremonious shove, Ben pushed him towards the ornamental pond and Bamford toppled into
the water with an ungainly splash. The fountain con-

tinued to trickle merrily away as he slowly and soggily hauled himself out.

'Well, Bamford?' said Ben, folding his arms across his chest. 'Are you still going to speak with Julia's brother? Go on, then. Off you go. He'll be in the card room, I'd guess. But I don't think he'll listen to a word you say and neither will anyone else. They'll be too busy laughing at you, because you resemble a drowned rat.'

'I'll get you for this, Lambourne,' Bamford muttered. 'Don't you worry.'

'You can try, I suppose. But I warn you, it won't be easy and if I were you I'd head for home now, before anyone sees how ridiculous you look.'

Bamford scowled and glanced briefly at Julia. Then he opened the door that led out into the gardens and disappeared into the darkness.

Silence enveloped the orangery except for the steady tinkling of the fountain. For a moment Ben stood very still, feeling as if his future lay on a knife edge. Then Julia looked up at him and said, 'You know, you really did hit him rather hard.'

She was stifling a smile and his heart soared. He said, 'I know I did. Julia, I'm sorry if my actions offended you.'

'He deserved it,' she said. 'I could have cheered. Oh, Ben.' She was coming slowly towards him. 'Ben, I have missed you so badly.'

He felt as though all the tension that had gripped his body was being steadily released. Hope began to stir in his heart, making him almost dizzy with joy. He put his arms around her and held her as if he would never let her go.

'My God, Julia,' he whispered. 'My God, I've missed you too. You don't know how much.'

To hell with waiting for her father to come to some decision. He loved this girl. He needed her to make his life in any way meaningful and from the look that was in her gorgeous eyes, she felt exactly the same.

She nestled into his embrace and laid her head against his chest as if she'd found where she wanted to be for the rest of her life and he thought, *She is everything to me. Never will I let her go again.*

Chapter Eighteen

Tristram Bamford's assault had shocked Julia. Indeed, he had terrified her, but when Ben had entered the room her heart had leaped because—oh, my—he looked so very fine in his black evening coat, with his white cravat tied so perfectly that Charles would be madly jealous. She had to smile, though, when she saw that his wayward brown hair was as tousled as ever, reminding her of the precious hours they had spent together and those kisses they had shared.

Her heart was full of emotion. She looked up at him and said, 'After last night, I thought you might not speak to me again.'

He was still holding her as he answered softly, 'I was never going to give up on you, though I guessed it might take me a while to make everything right between us. I certainly wasn't going to come here tonight, because I hate musical evenings.' He smiled, a smile that warmed her. 'But then, your sisters took a hand in the matter.'

'My *sisters*? Ben, how on earth…?'

He chuckled, that lovely, husky sound she loved so

much. 'They accosted me in the park this afternoon. Pen had recognised me from the ball last night. I gather you and your sisters have very few secrets?' Ben looked at her with one eyebrow slightly raised.

She blushed, but smiled, too. 'I love my sisters very much. I trust them, too. But oh dear, how extremely forward of them to approach you like that in the park! I gather Mama wasn't with them?'

'No, only a maid, who kept well out of the way. Anyway, they assured me that you were missing me badly.'

'Yes. Oh, yes! Ben, I felt that last night was a disaster, wasn't it? I hated seeing you with all those other girls and I didn't know how I could possibly compete. Then Lady Eleanor came for you, so I tried to act as if I didn't care.'

He was listening intently. 'I felt the same. You looked lovely, as lovely as you do tonight, and I thought I'd made such a mess of everything. I had resolved I would never give you up, but I wondered if maybe I should leave you alone for a while. Then I met your sisters in the park today and they told me that I absolutely had to come to this awful affair tonight and speak to you.'

'So Pen and Lizzie took a part in this,' she said softly. 'But how did you know, that I was in here—' she gestured around the room with one hand '—and in such trouble?'

'I did not know about Bamford,' he said grimly, 'and clearly your sisters didn't either. The man's a despicable wretch. I was looking for you, of course, from the moment I arrived, but there was no sign of you anywhere and I was collared by Georgina Sheldon. But then your sister Lizzie found me and whispered that I must come here, to the orangery. She said you needed to speak to me.'

'My sisters are mischief-makers, there's no doubt about it! Pen sent me here to the orangery and I had no idea why, but I see it all now. They wanted the two of us to meet in private. But of course they couldn't have known about Tristram. He must have been watching me. Following me.'

'I only wish,' he said, 'that I'd hit him harder. It's as well there weren't any fishes in that pond. He'd likely have poisoned the water.'

Julia almost laughed, but stopped herself. *No.* This wasn't funny. This was awful. Bamford would talk, she was sure, and Ben might be feeling that he had to offer marriage to her without really, truly wanting to, so she drew a deep breath and looked up at him.

'Ben,' she said, 'I realise you've been manipulated into a very awkward situation, for which I hope you'll forgive my sisters. They really had no business interfering, so I'll quite understand if you feel you must leave—'

He halted her by putting one finger under her chin and turning her face up to his. 'My darling Julia,' he said in that husky voice that was almost a sensual onslaught in itself. 'Do you really think that I've been *manipulated* into doing anything in my life? Do you think for one moment I would let you leave my life for good? If your sisters hadn't suggested I come here tonight, I would have watched out for you every day, thinking of your welfare, your happiness. You see, I was prepared to be patient.'

Oh. Suddenly the blood rushed to her head. What was he saying? Was he saying that he truly loved her?

She whispered, 'Do you remember what I wrote in my foolish notebook? You *did* read it, didn't you?'

He smiled. 'I'm afraid I did.' His brown eyes were full of laughter.

'I wrote,' she said softly, 'that I wished I had met someone like you earlier and I meant it. But oh, Ben! Why didn't you tell me who you were? Didn't you trust me? Did you think me a fool?'

'Never,' he said fiercely. 'Never have I thought you a fool. I'm the one who's stupid, not to explain everything from the beginning.'

Ben had his arms around her now and, thank God, she didn't move away. Instead she leaned back a little and gazed up at him. 'I suspected from the beginning you were well-born, you know,' she said.

He smiled a little. 'You kept your suspicions well hidden.'

'I did, yes.' She nodded. 'There were so many things that seemed odd, like you living at the Hall and that doctor coming out at night when you went for him. I wondered about your story of your poor father dying alone and the terrible guilt you felt. It was because of the feud between our fathers, wasn't it?'

His chest tightened. 'You know, then? About the horse your father bought from mine?'

'My brother told me when he came to take me home. Well, his version of it anyway.' Julia sighed. 'I'm afraid he is angry about it still. But it is truly unfair of him. Why should you be held responsible for your father's actions?'

Ben felt the shadows of the past clustering around them. This was it. This was the crux of the problem. He said, unable to keep the harshness from his words, 'But it was not my father's fault, Julia. He was blamed for a crime he did not commit and after that he allowed the estate to go to rack and ruin. He stopped taking care of himself. His life had lost its value to him—and I wasn't there to help.' He drew a deep breath. 'Do you remember me telling you about the man who died in the quarry?'

Julia recoiled in shock. 'Oh, no. Ben. You're not saying…'

'Yes. It was my father. Did he kill himself? There's no way of knowing for sure. His body was found at the bottom of the quarry by his valet, who'd been expecting him back hours before. He often went out to walk in the woods, so he may well have slipped and tumbled into the quarry by accident.' He added, in a voice she could barely hear, 'I should have been with my father. Defending his name. Giving him some kind of hope for the future.'

Julia shook her head. 'Ben, please don't do this to yourself. Your father must have loved you very much. Your success would have been a true comfort to him.'

'I hope that's true. But do you understand now why I felt my first priority, once I was back on my feet again, was to clear his name?'

'I do! Of course I do!' she cried. 'Have you succeeded in finding out yet what really happened?'

'I have and there's much more to the story than your brother knows. You see, there was a crook, a middle-man who stole that horse while it was being transported to your father's Richmond stables and replaced it with another that was worthless.'

'Have you proof? Can you convince my father about all this?'

'I hope so. In the meantime—' and Ben found he was smiling at last '—your sisters gave me a direct warning. They told me that I had to turn up tonight, or face the direst consequences.'

She smothered a laugh, then went to sit on one of the chintz-covered sofas in there. 'I really must apologise again for them!'

She looked so sweet that he wanted to pick her up in his arms and run off with her. Instead he went to sit next to her and took her hand. 'There's no need at all for apologies,' he said. 'Julia, I hope you can believe me when I say that I've never stopped thinking about you. Never stopped missing you. But this business with your father—I knew I had to settle it before I could do anything else.'

He stroked back a stray lock of hair from her cheek. He'd already decided he was not leaving here tonight without seeing the Earl, if indeed he arrived, which Julia's sisters had assured him would happen. He said, 'It might be sooner than you think.'

She listened. 'What,' she said quietly, 'can I do to help?'

He reached to pull her close to his heart. 'Be there for me, when all this is over. Will you promise?'

'Of course I promise! But I'm afraid my brother found out that I'd been seeing you during my stay at Lady Harris's and he was furious about it. He told me that…'

'What, Julia? What did Charles tell you?'

He sounded different now, she realised. Fierce, almost. She said, in a low voice, 'Charles told me that you must have decided to use me for your revenge. Revenge against my father, because of the trouble over the horse.' She saw his expression darken and her heart sank.

But Ben held her even closer. 'Julia,' he said, 'oh, my love, how could your brother fill your mind with such poison?'

She shook her head a little. 'He was trying to protect me, I suppose. But, Ben, I've believed in you always and I told Charles so! When he said that you must have been trying to seduce me to get your own back on our father, I told him he was wrong.' She hesitated, watching his expression. 'In fact, I told him it was the other way round—because I was the one trying to seduce *you*!'

She saw his eyes widen. 'You told him *that*?'

'Yes, I did, because it was true! You were honourable towards me, always. You tried to keep your distance, but I was the one chasing you, just like the Gorgon.'

'The Gorgon!' He laughed. 'I've been hearing that name quite often. You mean Georgina Sheldon?'

'Indeed. She told me she is determined to marry you and I loathe that girl. But I truly am worse than her, because now you've been trapped in here alone with me and, if anyone sees us, if Tristram talks, I have put you in a quite impossible situation!'

'I don't find it impossible at all,' he said. 'I find it quite wonderful. For weeks now I've lain awake at night, thinking of you. When I sleep, I dream of you. I remember the way you kissed me and what happened between us in the pavilion that last afternoon.'

'Me, too,' she whispered. 'I shall never forget it.' She laid her cheek against his chest and Ben held her even closer.

'My darling Julia,' he said. 'When I first met you, I thought you were like no one I'd ever met—you were beautiful, original and independent. But when I realised you were the Earl of Carstairs's daughter, I decided I must stop seeing you, because I guessed your father would never allow me even to speak with you, let alone dream of marrying you. Do you understand?'

'Yes,' she whispered. 'Yes, I do. But we didn't manage to stay apart for long, did we?'

Tenderly he brushed a wayward lock of hair back from her forehead. 'No. I think I would always have had to find some way to be with you again, because I've missed you very badly.'

'But what can we do?' She spoke a little shakily. 'My brother is here tonight and I'm afraid that, if he sees us like this, he will be very angry. He will tell my father that I fell in love with you in Somerset—and surely there could not be a worse way for him to learn of it.'

'I'm hopeful that your father and I can reconcile our differences soon,' said Ben. 'Because I want to ask him for your hand in marriage. Julia—will you marry me?'

Her heart was full. Who would have believed, two months ago, that the word 'marriage' could be the most wonderful one she had ever heard? How she had dreaded this ultimate commitment, but now her love for this man had melted away all her fears. 'Ben. Oh, Ben—do you mean it?'

'Of course I do.' He smiled. 'Lady Julia Carstairs, I love you very much—in fact, I adore you, so I'll ask you again. Will you be my wife?'

'Yes. Of course I will.' She could not keep the smile

from her face, and after a moment she glanced up at him almost mischievously. 'Charles might not be happy.'

'Oh, Charles.' He shrugged. 'If your brother should object, it's no problem because I'm handier with my fists than him by far, even if I have got a lame leg.'

Julia gasped. 'You mean you'd fight him?'

He laughed. 'Preferably not. My God, what a way to propose, by suggesting I could demolish your brother! I should be presenting you with flowers and romantic music and a diamond ring. But, Julia, please believe me when I say I shall do everything in my power to make you happy.'

For a moment she couldn't speak. True, there was no ring, no champagne—but there were those fragrant citrus trees and the music of the fountain to make the moment as magical as anything she could have dreamed of.

She felt like a princess in a fairy tale. No longer was she the girl lingering alone at parties, desperate to escape from the elaborate rituals of London society. She was Julia and Ben, her stonemason, loved her. Come what may, she was not letting go of this man.

She took his hands and whispered, 'You've already made me happier than I thought was possible, darling Ben.'

He pressed his lips to her fingers, causing tantalising shivers to ripple through her entire body. 'You know,' he said softly, 'if I've made mistakes—and I have, I know—it's because I never expected anything like this to happen to me. I went to Lambourne Hall to be alone while I tried to hunt for a way to clear my father's name. But then I met you—and, God help me, I fell in love.'

She smiled mischievously. 'I've told you that I fell in

love with you the moment I saw you. It was when you came to help us with the carriage.'

He pretended to look puzzled. 'I thought it was your maid who couldn't tear her eyes from me.'

'Yes, poor Betty was smitten—I remember! Afterwards, Ben, she would not stop talking about you!'

He said wickedly, 'But you were taking note of me, too, weren't you? Despite those rough clothes I was wearing.'

This time she flung her arms around his neck, wanting him so much that her blood ran hot and fast in her veins. 'You *know* I did. Didn't I tell you I would run away with you if you asked me to?'

'To live in a cottage?' he teased.

'Yes! A cottage! I truly meant it!' She added more seriously, 'Perhaps I was trying to say that I would give up everything for you if I had to.'

'But you won't have to give everything up,' he said. 'I swear it. I will never trap you into the kind of life I know you'd loathe, a life consisting of nothing but balls and parties.'

'Don't forget the musical soirées,' she said, her eyes shining with laughter as the distant sound of a warbling Sheldon daughter penetrated the peace of the orangery. 'Please, can we ensure we never have to attend another one?'

'Not a single one,' he said emphatically. 'Though I'm afraid I will have responsibilities to the estate that mean I won't always be able to live as freely as I'd wish. Do you think you can bear that, Julia?'

'Of course,' she said. 'You've changed me, in all kinds

of ways. You've made me feel free to be the person I want to be, whether I'm living in a cottage or a palace.'

'So you're quite sure you'll marry me?'

'Of course I am.' Her eyes glowed with love. 'Only can it be very soon? *Please?* And, Ben—will you kiss me again?'

Ben realised she was touching his cheek with her finger. It was only a light touch, but the caress held so much sensual promise that his blood pounded. She looked enchanting in her silk dress and her lips were full with longing. What could he do, but agree? He gathered her in his arms and her low gasp of pleasure set his blood racing all over again.

He let his lips brush hers gently at first, giving himself time to relish their velvety softness. He told himself he had the strength of mind to go no further, not here, not yet, but just as he managed to pull away, Julia took his hand in hers, lifted his fingers to her lips and kissed them one by one. When she raised her eyes to his he could see the mischief sparkling in their depths.

'I suppose, until we are formally betrothed, I should be calling you "Lord Lambourne",' she said. 'Shouldn't I?'

That did it. His restraint was demolished by her delicious smile.

'Call me Ben,' he grated out. 'My name is *Ben*.'

Then his arms were round her and he let one hand slip down her back to pull her even closer so that her small breasts were compressed against his ribs. He groaned aloud, for his loins were throbbing with need. She was Julia and she was all he could ever want.

He kissed her passionately and she opened to him,

welcoming him. He slid his tongue between her lips and her growing boldness as she responded with hers thrilled him to his core.

He felt himself losing whatever was left of his self-control, forgetting all the warnings that had been ringing through his brain—*someone might come in. Someone might see us.*

If he and Julia were discovered like this, it would be the talk of the town. He should have spoken to her father first. But whatever happened, he could not give this girl up. It was impossible—

Suddenly he heard her give a cry of alarm. He sprang to his feet to see that the door had flown open and someone was charging in—her brother. Charles slammed the door shut, shaking the leaves on the citrus trees and making all the candles quiver. He looked almost rigid with fury.

'Lambourne!' he cried. 'I *knew* you'd been trying to seduce my sister as revenge, you bastard. And, Julia, I thought you'd promised me this was all over!'

Ben had raised his hands in a gesture of peace, but Charles was squaring up to him, his fists clenched. Ben said, 'I think you've got things rather in a muddle, Carstairs. Can't we talk this over?'

'I'll do what I damned well like,' declared Charles, 'when it's a matter of defending Julia's honour. Put your fists up!'

'Ben,' cried Julia, 'please don't fight! And, Charles, you are being completely ridiculous. Ben has always behaved towards me with the utmost honour, I've told you that! And you mustn't threaten him, because surely you can see he has an injured leg?'

* * *

Julia realised instantly that she'd made a mistake, for on hearing her words Ben raised his fists as fiercely as Charles. 'Damn my leg,' he growled. 'I will not stand for these insults from you, Carstairs!'

Oh, no. They were going to fight. Julia rushed in front of Ben to protect him, but that, too, was a mistake, for Ben, her dear, beloved Ben, was clearly worried about her safety in the face of her brother's fury, so he took his eyes off Charles and pushed her to one side. At the same moment Charles let fly with a blow that landed full on Ben's jaw, forcing him to stumble to the ground.

Julia uttered a cry of distress and crouched at his side. 'Oh, my darling. Are you hurt?' She shouted up at her brother, 'You are a fool, Charles! Ben is good and kind and honourable—and haven't I already told you that it was actually *me* who tried to seduce *him*? Tonight he's asked me to marry him and I'm going to, even if we have to do it without my father's permission! Anyway, we must marry now, because you've caught us in here alone. Would you rather I was the wife of that idiot Tristram Bamford? Do you know that tonight he tried to force himself on me in here, until Ben arrived and thumped him?'

Ben was scrambling to his feet now, so she flung her arms around him and kissed him. 'Ben. I love you so very much.' She kissed him again and, in fact, was still doing so when the door to the orangery opened once more and this time her father, the Earl, came in, with Pen and Lizzie close behind. At first her sisters gasped with shock when they saw what was going on, then they looked absolutely delighted.

Ben was having trouble extricating himself from Julia's kiss. 'Papa!' Julia exclaimed. 'And Pen. And Lizzie. Oh, my goodness…'

Her voice trailed away as she realised exactly what they had all seen. But she didn't care, she truly didn't. She took Ben's hand.

The Earl gazed around at the various expressions on the faces of his offspring, then he addressed Ben. 'Lord Lambourne,' he pronounced, in the voice he used when he had something very important to say. Julia found she could hardly breathe, but still she held Ben's hand and stayed close by his side.

'I know, Lambourne,' the Earl continued, 'that you and I have unsettled business to conclude. I must confess I'd hoped to arrange somewhere more private for us to talk, but it appears that you and my daughter have been making decisions of your own. So perhaps we'd best get on with the matter now.' The Earl looked round at his family, including the still-scowling Charles. 'If the rest of you would leave us? Just for a few moments?'

'Not me, Papa,' said Julia swiftly. 'I am staying.'

The Earl hesitated, then said, 'I guessed as much. Very well.' He escorted the others to the door.

'You see, my love?' Julia whispered to Ben. 'I think there is hope for us. If not—' and she stood on tiptoe to kiss him again '—I swear, I am running away with you.'

'Rebel,' he replied. He smiled down at her. 'What *am* I letting myself in for?'

The Earl had closed the door and now he came back to face them. 'I've been checking, Lambourne,' he said, 'on everything you told me earlier this evening.'

Julia looked up at Ben with wide eyes.

'Yes, Julia,' her father continued, 'Lord Lambourne and I held a brief but enlightening discussion together and, after considering what he said, I've decided that I owe both him and his father a heartfelt apology.' He turned to Ben. 'I regret not having investigated the matter earlier myself, but…well, I hope you will forgive me? As for my daughter, I gather that you and she have formed a strong attachment.'

'We have,' said Ben. 'And I would like to assure you that your daughter is extremely precious to me.'

'I can see that,' said the Earl. Suddenly he smiled. 'Any fool can see it. Even me.' He came forward to shake Ben's hand. 'I've made mistakes, Lambourne, I see that now, and I'm sorry, so very sorry about the slur on your father's reputation. You must have felt considerable bitterness on his behalf.'

'I would be lying if I said the whole business hadn't affected me, my lord. But now that I know the truth, I realise you were tricked every bit as much as my father.' Ben looked the Earl straight in the eye. 'In some ways, I've always blamed myself for my father's unhappiness. If I'd been there for him, I might have solved Molloy's crime myself, in time to prevent the feud between the two of you.'

The Earl shook his head. 'My good fellow, you must not reproach yourself, ever. I remember that your father was extremely proud of you and your vital work for our country; in fact, I've heard nothing but good reports about you from various friends in government departments.

'As I said to you earlier, I've come to greatly regret the unpleasantness between our families. Besides, it seems—' and he glanced with wry humour at his daughter '—that Julia has already made up her mind about you. Believe me, I know from long experience that there is no shifting her opinion once her mind is made up!'

'Lord Carstairs,' said Ben, 'I realise that I've only known your daughter for a short while. But I love and respect Julia very much and I would like you to consider allowing me her hand in marriage.'

'Oh,' said the Earl, waving his hand, 'I don't need time to consider it, young man. I see quite clearly how I can make amends for the past, by allowing you to court her. Besides, it's obvious from the looks on both your faces that the matter is as good as settled, so I am extremely happy to give the pair of you my blessing.'

He stepped forward to put his hands lightly on Julia's shoulders. 'My dear, your mother will be delighted. Although I fear she'll be a little disappointed that she won't have the pleasure of your Season!'

Julia couldn't help but smile. 'Thank you, dear Papa. I always knew you were the kindest and best father in the world!'

She turned to Ben, who looked so handsome and so wonderful that she wanted to pour out all her words of love and all her hope for their future together. But not here. Not now.

There will be time, she promised herself. *All the time in the world to tell this man how much he means to me.*

So in the end, all she did was to give him a little smile and whisper, 'You see? Everything has turned out quite, quite wonderfully!'

Ben touched his jaw where Charles had hit him and

grinned a little ruefully. 'Just about,' he said. 'Although I'm not sure your brother would agree.'

The Earl was frowning. 'I gather you and my son had a disagreement in here before I arrived?'

'A slight misunderstanding,' said Ben.

'Hmm. Well, I shall have a word with Charles. He can be somewhat arrogant, so I shall be sure to take him down a peg or two.' He pointed his finger at Ben. 'But on one condition. You make sure you take good care of my precious daughter. Do you promise?'

'Of course,' said Ben quietly. 'She is precious to me, too, so with all my heart, I promise.'

The Earl was about to say more, but instead he turned towards the door—in fact, they all did, because even though it was closed they could hear the sound of more awful singing from the Sheldon sisters, accompanied this time by an out-of-tune harp.

'I think,' pronounced the Earl of Carstairs, 'that it's time I gathered up my family and we all set off home.'

Epilogue

Because Pen's much-anticipated wedding to Jeremy was to take place very soon, Lady Carstairs declared that Julia and Ben's wedding had to wait until spring. 'The month of May would be ideal!' she declared one afternoon when all the family were gathered in the sitting room. 'A wedding in the earlier months of the year would be hideously unfashionable and besides, almost all of the *ton* would be at their winter residences and unable to attend.'

'Mama,' said Julia, 'Ben and I hoped it would be sooner. I thought you might be relieved if we wanted a quiet ceremony with less preparation. After all, Pen and Jeremy's wedding is taking up a good deal of your time and rightly so!' She reached to squeeze the hand of her sister, who sat next to her on the sofa. 'Pen is your oldest daughter, so she deserves a grand affair. But Ben and I would be happy to… I don't know.' She shrugged and smiled. 'We could be married at the church in Richmond, perhaps, and hold a small party at our house there.'

Lizzie chuckled. Her mother gave a faint whimper of dismay, while Charles, who stood with his back to the fire, gave a sigh as if nothing Julia said surprised him any more. But then, much to Julia's surprise, Charles spoke up for her. 'It's Julia's wedding, Mother,' he said. 'Shouldn't she be able to say what she prefers? As it happens, I've also spoken to Ben Lambourne on the matter.'

Julia's mouth opened in amazement. 'You *have*?'

'Indeed,' said Charles. He looked faintly embarrassed by his confession, but after a moment he nodded firmly. 'I must say, I've been pleasantly surprised by the fellow. We talked about plans for the wedding and he said he'll be happy with whatever Julia and our family prefer.'

Their father, who appeared to be hiding a slight smile at this unexpected contribution from Charles, was listening in approval. 'My dear,' he said to his wife, 'I feel that keeping Julia and Ben apart for several months might be seen as a sign of unhappiness on our part, which is certainly not the case. Wouldn't you agree?'

Poor Lady Carstairs was clearly in a dilemma. 'Go on, Mama,' encouraged Lizzie. 'Do agree with Papa, please.'

'Well,' said their mother at last, 'I suppose I must. An early wedding it shall be.'

'Hooray!' said Lizzie. The three sisters looked at each other and smiled.

'In that case,' said the Earl, 'I suggest that we hold the wedding in February, here in London. In fact, I wouldn't be surprised if we have a considerable number of guests, since the countryside at that time of year can be very dull.'

'And you know, Mama,' put in Pen, 'how very good you are at arranging parties. You've had such fun overseeing my wedding celebrations and just think—once mine is over, you'll be able to start on Julia's! You will absolutely be the talk of the town!'

'That is true,' said their mother, somewhat mollified. Then she stifled a burst of laughter. 'I've had a sudden thought. Lady Sheldon has four daughters to marry off and I've heard not a whisper of a single proposal— whereas my Pen is to be married to a viscount's heir and dear Julia is marrying a baron, no less!' She smirked. 'Poor Lady Sheldon will hardly be able to face me when next we meet.'

Charles patted his mother's shoulder. 'There you are, then. I believe it's all decided.' He looked at his sister. 'Julia, I wish you every happiness in the world with Ben Lambourne. I really do.'

Julia had feared that the next few weeks would have dragged interminably, but in fact the time flew by. Pen and Jeremy's wedding in November took up much of the family's attention and was an event of great joy, while the Christmas season, too, was filled with outings and parties.

Meanwhile, the Earl had given Julia his permission to meet with Ben almost every day, supposedly with a chaperon in place. But quite often when Ben visited the house Lizzie, who was Julia's one true ally now that Pen had gone travelling to France with her husband, contrived all kinds of ways to distract Lady Carstairs from keeping a close eye on the couple. So Ben and Julia were often able to spend precious moments together in the sitting room, dreaming up plans for their future. Julia, though, found it hard to keep to society's strict rules, as did Ben.

'I hate having to be apart,' he murmured one evening as he was about to leave the family's house.

'I know,' she whispered. 'It won't be for long.'

But it seemed an eternity and she worried, too, because now that Pen was away there was no one she could really talk to about what would happen on her wedding night. Shortly after the announcement of their betrothal her mother had given her a hurried and embarrassed lecture about how babies were made and Julia listened carefully. But nothing of what her mother said tied in with how she had actually felt during those moments at the pavilion, when Ben's kisses and his intimate caresses had thrilled her.

Could she bring the same pleasure to him? Would she know what to do? Might she be a disappointment to him? Even when Pen and Jeremy returned to London, Pen was hard to reach because she was either busy shopping for furnishings for her new home or wanting to spend time alone with her husband.

Meanwhile the preparations for Julia and Ben's wedding had grown more frantic. When the day actually arrived, Julia could hardly speak for nerves while she was being dressed in her wedding gown. She even felt herself trembling a little as she walked up the aisle of the church at her father's side to where Ben stood.

But when Ben turned to her and said softly, 'You look wonderful. I love you,' she knew that everything would be all right.

After the ceremony, the house was packed with guests—including Lady Harris, who had travelled all the way from Somerset. 'Of course, I loathe London,' she told everyone happily as she drank yet another glass of expensive champagne. Then she whispered to Ben and Julia, 'But you'll know why I'm here. I had to come, to make sure that the two of you were safely together at last.'

It had been arranged that the couple would spend their wedding night at Ben's house in Clarges Street. Ben had spent weeks arranging for it to be refurbished and redecorated, and when the day of the wedding finally arrived he'd instructed all his household staff, Gilly included, to be there to greet his bride and then to disappear, which they all promptly did—although Ben did suspect that a couple of the young maids might have peeked a little as he swept Julia, still in her bridal gown, into his arms and carried her up two flights of stairs to their bedchamber.

Once there he set her tenderly down on the huge bed and asked softly, 'Is there anything at all you need?'

She smiled shyly up at him. 'Just you,' she whispered.

Until now, he had been restrained in all their meetings. For weeks he had been patient, trying to suppress all intimate thoughts of this lovely girl who had taken possession of his heart and his soul. But now, at last, the time had come.

She looked like a vision in her wedding dress—ethereal, untouchable almost. Of course he realised already what passion lay hidden beneath that shy façade and he wanted to own her, every inch of her. But he also knew he had to be patient, knew he had to take his time, even though his own body was already raging with desire.

'Should I summon a maid to help you undress?' he asked. He could hear that his voice was almost harsh, such was his effort to control himself.

She shook her head and reached to pull away her headdress, setting her hair free of its pins as she did so. She said, 'Will you undress me, Ben? Please?'

He made rather a ham-fisted job of it. Dear God, he could have laughed at himself as some buttons popped off one after another and ended up scattered around the room. As for her underwear, it was fiendish, but the effort was well worth it because of the delight he felt when she began helping him with it, in the end mischievously pushing his clumsy hands aside to roll down her silk stockings. Then—*then* she began to pull her chemise over her head.

She was naked now except for her glorious hair, which fell silkily past her shoulders. He stood very still, taking in the beauty of her coral-tipped breasts, her narrow waist and gently swelling hips. She met his gaze steadily, then she said, 'Isn't it *your* turn now?'

So he began to undress, a substantially easier business for him. When he'd finished, she did not move or avert her gaze, but he could see that she was shaken by the sight of his outright desire, so he moved closer and lifted her to lay her on the bed, tenderly kissing her and lying down beside her, to put one arm around her. 'I shall be as gentle as I can,' he warned. 'But, Julia, do you know what to expect?'

She smiled. 'I trust you, Ben,' she whispered. 'And I want you, so very much!'

So his caresses began.

Julia had already tasted something of the pleasures this man could bestow. What she had not known was that there was so much more, for as well as his fingers, teasing and coaxing, there were his lips—on her mouth, her breasts, everywhere. At first she was uncertain what to do, as well as being shaken by the low insistent ache that was blooming between her thighs and making her tremble with need.

But Ben was wonderful. He calmed her, he coaxed her, he told her she was beautiful; then, as he stroked her down *there* and slid his fingers between her silky folds, she felt the beginnings of that exquisite rush of pleasure he'd given her before. This time she wanted the same, but more, and he was surely ready to offer it, for hadn't she seen the physical evidence of his need?

It scared her a little, but it delighted her, too, and she knew this was what she wanted, yes, *this*. She gasped aloud as she felt his manhood easing itself a little way inside her. She'd had no idea what this could feel like, or what it would do to her, but as the bone-deep longing for more surged through her, she clutched at him and cried out his name.

He stopped. 'Am I hurting you?' he asked swiftly.

'No,' she whispered. 'No. Oh, Ben…' She smiled. 'It's wonderful. Please don't stop.'

He thrust deeper, but was still careful; she could tell that he was restraining himself by the tension in his face. She realised how very much he wanted her and the thought thrilled her. Yes, he was taking possession of her, filling her with his male power, but then he held still and began caressing her again, down there at the heart of all her sensation.

Suddenly, she felt a molten heat swirling through her blood, inflaming her, creating in her such tension that she cried out, 'Ben. I can't. Ben, please…'

He kissed her tenderly on her lips and her breasts, each in turn. Then he began moving inside her again, hard and hot. She found herself clutching desperately at his back and his shoulders, arching her hips to greedily take more of him, and as his strokes deepened she was gasping aloud until suddenly she could not hold back any more.

Sharp yet exquisite shafts of pleasure were beginning to roll through her. She stopped breathing. She couldn't think, couldn't speak, but somehow her world flew apart and she was shaken by wave after wave of bliss as he steadily pleasured her. Then his movements grew stronger, greedier, until she felt his hips shuddering as he cried out her name.

With a sigh he fell against her, his head on her naked breast, and she could feel his heart thudding. Tenderly she stroked his tousled hair, smiling softly to herself. This was fulfilment. This was joy. This was peace.

After a moment he lifted himself on one elbow to gaze down at her. 'My love,' he said. 'My wife. Are you happy?'

What could she say? He was her husband…he was her life. 'Darling Ben. I am very happy,' she whispered. 'Unbelievably so.'

He stroked her flushed cheek. 'I wonder,' he said

softly, 'are you going to write any more about me in that notebook of yours?'

She pretended to think about it. 'Perhaps not. After all, it might make you too conceited.'

'Minx,' he said, tickling her nose. 'I'll take that as a compliment and allow you to change the subject, because I can tell there's something else you're longing to say.'

She hesitated a moment. 'Ben. You know you said that we could go to Paris or Rome or anywhere I pleased for our honeymoon?'

'Yes, minx? Where have you thought of? Do you want to go adventuring?'

She eased herself up a little. 'You told me, didn't you, that you've made Lambourne Hall fit to live in again? Please, could we go there?'

He sat up, clearly startled. 'At this time of the year? It will be cold. We'll need log fires, There might well be snow and we could be cut off for days!'

She nestled comfortably against his shoulder and positively sighed with happiness. 'Mmm… Snow. Cut off for days. That sounds absolutely *perfect*.'

He put his arm around her. 'You really love it there, don't you?'

'I do.' She twisted a little so she could look at him. 'I know, of course, that we'll have to spend months at a time in London, but Lambourne will always be my favourite place of all. Especially…' she gave a shy smile '…in a year or so, perhaps. When there might not be just the two of us.'

'You mean when we have children?'

'Yes. Of course.' She wriggled a little so she fitted

comfortably in his arms. 'Two or three children or more, maybe. I cannot imagine a more perfect place or a more perfect father for them! They can have adventures in the woods and climb trees there, the girls as well as the boys. We could perhaps have a rowing boat on the lake for them and we can have picnics there in the summer and—'

He touched her lips gently. 'Enough, sweetheart. You've convinced me.'

Her eyes were alight with joy. 'So we really can go to Lambourne Hall and make it our true home?'

'Yes, of course we can. You've also convinced me that I've found the most wonderful bride in the world.' He kissed her and she kissed him back, sliding down the bed and pulling him with her. She was smiling a little—a secret, sensual smile. 'Ben,' she murmured, 'would you think me very greedy if I asked for some more of what we just did?'

'As a matter of fact, Lady Lambourne,' he answered softly, 'I would think it absolutely inevitable. Can't you tell? But this time, we are going to take things more slowly.' He took her hand and kissed it. 'There's no need to rush. Remember, we have all the time in the world.'

Julia gave a sigh of complete happiness. He was right. All the time in the world to share her life with the man she loved.

* * * * *

*If you enjoyed this story, why not check out
one of Lucy Ashford's other great reads?*

The Captain and His Innocent
The Master of Calverley Hall
Unbuttoning Miss Matilda
The Widow's Scandalous Affair
The Viscount's New Housekeeper
Challenging the Brooding Earl

COMING NEXT MONTH FROM

HARLEQUIN
HISTORICAL

All available in print and ebook via Reader Service and online

A DUKE FOR THE PENNILESS WIDOW (Regency)
The Irresistible Dukes • by Christine Merrill

Selina is startled by the attraction she feels for the Duke of Glenmoor, whom she blames for her husband's death! Forced to accept his marriage proposal, can Selina resist surrendering to their passion?

MISS GEORGINA'S MARRIAGE DILEMMA (Victorian)
Rebellious Young Ladies • by Eva Shepherd

Fun-loving Georgina can find joy and pleasure in anything...even her convenient marriage to frosty Adam, Duke of Ravenswood! But can her good nature and their undeniable chemistry penetrate her new husband's walls?

WEDDED TO HIS ENEMY DEBUTANTE (Regency)
by Samantha Hastings

Frederica is the *last* person Samuel, the new Duke of Pelford, wants to marry! But his beautiful nemesis is the only answer to the problems he's inherited.

THE RETURN OF HIS CARIBBEAN HEIRESS (1900s)
by Lydia San Andres

Five years after Leandro Díaz kissed heiress Lucía Troncoso, she's returned... But Leo, hardened by life, holds Lucía—and their attraction—at a distance until danger forces them closer than ever before...

SPINSTER WITH A SCANDALOUS PAST (Regency)
by Sadie King

When Louisa meets the abrasive Sir Isaac Liddell, she's shocked to discover that they have so much in common. But telling him the truth about her past might cost her *everything*!

CONVENIENT VOWS WITH A VIKING (Viking)
by Lucy Morris and Sarah Rodi

Enjoy these two spicy Viking romances! Orla strikes a deal with enslaved Jarl Hakon—she'll buy his freedom *if* the handsome warrior marries her! And Viking Fiske chooses noblewoman Kassia as his bride to save her from an unhappy fate, but her secrets threaten their newfound desire...

YOU CAN FIND MORE INFORMATION ON UPCOMING HARLEQUIN TITLES, FREE EXCERPTS AND MORE AT HARLEQUIN.COM.

HHCNM1223

Get 3 FREE REWARDS!

We'll send you 2 FREE Books plus a FREE Mystery Gift.

FREE Value Over **$20**

Both the **Harlequin® Historical** and **Harlequin® Romance** series feature compelling novels filled with emotion and simmering romance.

YES! Please send me 2 FREE novels from the Harlequin Historical or Harlequin Romance series and my FREE Mystery Gift (gift is worth about $10 retail). After receiving them, if I don't wish to receive any more books, I can return the shipping statement marked "cancel." If I don't cancel, I will receive 6 brand-new Harlequin Historical books every month and be billed just $6.19 each in the U.S. or $6.74 each in Canada, a savings of at least 11% off the cover price, or 4 brand-new Harlequin Romance Larger-Print books every month and be billed just $6.09 each in the U.S. or $6.24 each in Canada, a savings of at least 13% off the cover price. It's quite a bargain! Shipping and handling is just 50¢ per book in the U.S. and $1.25 per book in Canada.* I understand that accepting the 2 free books and gift places me under no obligation to buy anything. I can always return a shipment and cancel at any time by calling the number below. The free books and gift are mine to keep no matter what I decide.

Choose one:
☐ **Harlequin Historical** (246/349 BPA GRNX)
☐ **Harlequin Romance Larger-Print** (119/319 BPA GRNX)
☐ **Or Try Both!** (246/349 & 119/319 BPA GRRD)

Name (please print)

Address   Apt. #

City   State/Province   Zip/Postal Code

Email: Please check this box ☐ if you would like to receive newsletters and promotional emails from Harlequin Enterprises ULC and its affiliates. You can unsubscribe anytime.

Mail to the Harlequin Reader Service:
IN U.S.A.: P.O. Box 1341, Buffalo, NY 14240-8531
IN CANADA: P.O. Box 603, Fort Erie, Ontario L2A 5X3

Want to try 2 free books from another series? Call 1-800-873-8635 or visit www.ReaderService.com.

Get 3 FREE REWARDS!

We'll send you 2 FREE Books plus a FREE Mystery Gift.

FREE Value Over **$20**

Both the **Romance** and **Suspense** collections feature compelling novels written by many of today's bestselling authors.

YES! Please send me 2 FREE novels from the Essential Romance or Essential Suspense Collection and my FREE gift (gift is worth about $10 retail). After receiving them, if I don't wish to receive any more books, I can return the shipping statement marked "cancel." If I don't cancel, I will receive 4 brand-new novels every month and be billed just $7.49 each in the U.S. or $7.74 each in Canada. That's a savings of at least 17% off the cover price. It's quite a bargain! Shipping and handling is just 50¢ per book in the U.S. and $1.25 per book in Canada.* I understand that accepting the 2 free books and gift places me under no obligation to buy anything. I can always return a shipment and cancel at any time by calling the number below. The free books and gift are mine to keep no matter what I decide.

Choose one:
☐ **Essential Romance** (194/394 BPA GRNM)
☐ **Essential Suspense** (191/391 BPA GRNM)
☐ **Or Try Both!** (194/394 & 191/391 BPA GRQZ)

Name (please print)

Address   Apt. #

City   State/Province   Zip/Postal Code

Email: Please check this box ☐ if you would like to receive newsletters and promotional emails from Harlequin Enterprises ULC and its affiliates. You can unsubscribe anytime.

Mail to the Harlequin Reader Service:
IN U.S.A.: P.O. Box 1341, Buffalo, NY 14240-8531
IN CANADA: P.O. Box 603, Fort Erie, Ontario L2A 5X3

Want to try 2 free books from another series! Call 1-800-873-8635 or visit www.ReaderService.com.